From Fear to Freedom

A Story of Addiction, Misdiagnosis, Survival, Hope and Healing

---

Don Killian

From Fear to Freedom
Copyright © 2015 by Donald L. Killian

All rights reserved.
No part of this book may be reproduced or transmitted in any form or by any means without written permission from the author.

This book is a true representation of events that actually occurred in the author's life. Most names of characters and places are fictitious.

ISBN-13: 978-1511589956
ISBN-10: 1511589957

Edited by Phoebe Killian Keifman

This book is dedicated to:

Aryana, Ellen, Holly, Kris, Marcy, Pauline, Sabine

*"I was shown, but I refused to see.
I was told, but I refused to hear.
Then I, too, was wounded.
I felt the pure anguish.
Now I understand.
Now I believe.
I know."*

- Lee Lucas

Preface

This book represents one of the "stops" on the path of my life. The journey to get to this point could not have been planned or even predicted by anyone in the human realm. Looking back, it is still hard to fathom the road that has been traveled to get to this place in my life.

Throughout my schooling from grade school through college, I had no desire whatsoever to write. I cannot think of one writing assignment during my entire educational experience that gave me any sort of pleasure. I was more interested in mathematics and science and excelled in those studies. Mathematics is very straightforward. There is always a specific, correct solution to every problem. It is very cut and dry. A number is a number regardless of one's perspective. No need for interpretation or emotion. I liked that.

Similarly, there are aspects of the sciences that are unchanging, especially in physics and chemistry. I did well in them because they also possessed the qualities of predictability and duplicability. The acceleration of gravity is the acceleration of gravity, no matter how many times it is subjected to the scientific method. The speed of light is the speed of light. Sodium chloride and water always result from the reaction of sodium hydroxide and hydrochloric acid. Chemical reactions can be duplicated over and over with great predictability.

For some reason, I decided to major in biology in college. I learned many things in that discipline, but the most important truth I came away with from the countless hours of study and reflection is extremely fundamental. All living organisms are in a constant state of change or flux. (I was a slow learner.) There are probably no two moments in a person's life when we are exactly the same – chemically, physiologically, anatomically, or any other "ally" (possibly including spiritually which is a whole other discussion).

There are many aspects of each individual's life experience that affect the body's chemistry, physiology and anatomy. At any moment in time, there are probably thousands of these "aspects" that a person experiences. In a very real sense, how we each react to these, *in toto*, over time, becomes our life story. Each life story is necessarily vastly different.

This book tells much of my life story or how I have reacted to life around me and inside me. Unfortunately (or fortunately), I am unable to tell it with mere equations and application of scientific laws. I must use words. Words are always subject to interpretation based on the reader's perspective which is largely based on the reader's life experiences.

My story is one of early life tragedy and the resulting addiction to alcohol with its mental and emotional distresses. As is far too common, those distresses were medically misdiagnosed, and my life became one of additional chemical dependency on psychotropic drugs. If the story had ended there, it would, indeed, have been (and would still be) a profound human tragedy. Happily, the story did not end there. I survived that period in my life and am now happy, joyous and free – very free. I am well – very well.

My story is only one example of a great truth which somehow our culture has overlooked. Perhaps, it is more correct to say it has been led astray. The truth is simply that we are each the expert with respect to our own life story. No other human being can look inside our head and see what has transpired in our life or see the thoughts of our mind. No guru can do it. No psychic can do it. No pastor or priest can do it. No psychiatrist or therapist can do it. Only we have that ability and privilege. Certainly, we can share those thoughts with others if we so desire. Therein lies the solution to resolving most life distresses.

Of course, every person who reads this book will perceive it differently. Each one will come away with a different opinion and point of view. No two perceptions will be the same – just as no two individuals react to the same life experience in the same way.

The intent of the words written in this book is simply to give hope to anyone who can relate to any of the difficulties and suffering I have experienced. My circumstances were dire – very dire. I survived those circumstances and found my way to wellness and a life filled with incredible wonder and amazement. My life is better than it has ever been. I may be the most positive person I know which is a complete turnaround from the doom and gloom man who lived in this body only three years ago. The release from the prison of alcoholism and psychotropic drug dependency has affected me profoundly.

If my words can provide hope for even one person to continue through the suffering of anything (especially suffering caused by withdrawal from psychotropic drugs) and make it to this shore of tranquility, joy and freedom, then I have succeeded.

Don Killian
January 1, 2015
Harrisburg, Pennsylvania

Acknowledgments

There are many individuals whom I must recognize with respect to the writing of this book. Several are mentioned in the text of the book with either their real name or a fictitious name. One of them, in particular, I must mention here. Her name is Kayla. It is my hope, Kayla, that one day you will read this book. Without you, I would have been gone from this earth fifteen years ago. From the deepest part of my heart, I thank you for coming here on a rescue mission.

Of course, there are many others who must be acknowledged. There are thousands of individuals whom I have met on my journey who are struggling through the torment of benzodiazepine withdrawal. Each and every one has been part of the inspiration for me to continue with them on the journey as best I can and to write this portion of my story.

There are some very special "co-sufferers" whom I must mention by name who have each had a profound effect on me and have helped me (probably unknowingly) to become a better human being. They are:

Alison, Ally, Andrew, Angela, Antoinette, Barry, Baylissa, Candace, Cindy, Collin, Danny, Donnie, Emily, Erika, Got, Ian, Jan, Jarrod, Dr. Jenn, Jennifer, Jessica, Joanne, Joel, Juan, Karen, Kathy, Kiesha, Laura, Linda, Lisa, Luis, Madeleine, Madonna, Maggie, Marc, Marie, Matt, Melanie, Missy, Nancy, Nicole, Nina, Mr. Puffin, Ramona, Rebecca, Renee, Robb, Robert, Ruth, Serena, Sleepy, Sommer, Sue, Tiffany and Traci

A special thank you also goes to my editor: Phoebe Killian Keifman. You are an incredibly wonderful and talented woman, and I am proud to call you my niece. Thank you for untangling and deciphering my jumbled, often obtuse wording so it makes sense.

Part One

Chapter One

Saturday, January 16, 2010

"The bottle."

"The bottle?"

"Yes. The bottle. Upstairs in the sock drawer."

"But what...?"

"Just get it. You have no choice. We have no choice."

"There must be some other..."

"Do it! You heard what she said."

"Maybe she meant..."

"No. You know what she meant. It's over. Move!"

"Okay."

As he got up from the sofa, he felt like he had just lost the final battle. Or maybe this was the start of something new and supremely better. Maybe it had to be this way so that he could get to the next place – a much nicer place. Yes. It was supposed to be this way. Of course, this was all part of the plan. He had been wrong all along.

He shuffled toward the stairs in a daze. Nothing seemed real to him as though he was in some sort of altered state. He looked at his feet as they approached the first step. Were these his feet? He felt like he wasn't there – almost like he was watching himself from somewhere else. He touched the handrail as his foot contacted the first step. He felt the handrail. He felt the step. He didn't sense any connection to them at all or to anything or anyone anywhere – not even to himself. He had felt this way for months. Soon it would be a memory. Yes. This had to be done.

Would he even have memories after this? What if.... Terror gripped every part of his body. Panic attack. He was dizzy – very dizzy. He steadied himself against the hallway wall. Feeling less dizzy, he feebly trudged to the doorway and peered into the bedroom. There was the chest with his sock drawer. He had the strange feeling that it was looking at him as he stood there – beckoning him to come closer. As he contemplated what he was about to do, dread washed over him and consumed him. He turned his head away and closed his eyes. He was confused. He was utterly and completely confused. He had this feeling that he should just surrender, but he had no idea what that even meant or how he would do it or to whom he should surrender. So, he stood there in the doorway paralyzed with fear and confusion.

"Don't do it, Lee. Don't do it. Just hold on."

"Don't listen to that drivel. You have to do this. There is no escape. You have tried so hard for so long, and it's just not working for you. It's no use. Come on. It's easy."

"Well, yeah, it has been a long time. It only gets worse and worse. Unbearable really."

"That's right. Get the bottle. That's all you have to do."

"I can fight this and sink deeper and deeper, or I can just..." Lee shuddered at the stark reality of the thought he could not finish.

"Those pretty, pure white pills. Two milligrams each. There's plenty in the bottle to end the misery. Just a handful, and this nightmare will be over. You can do it."

"Hold on, Lee. Hold on. There must be a way."

"Maybe doctor..."

"Get real man. He's the one who prescribed those little suckers that have you ready to jump out of your skin. Take them all and get it over with."

Lee cringed at the thought of Ruth coming home and finding his lifeless body who knows where. What a horror that would be for her and everyone else. How would she get over it? Could he do something so cruel to someone else? He groveled in the pit of hopeless despair. Why couldn't the walls just cave in and take him far away? Somewhere distant from this mental anguish and away from the swirling, confusing voices battling inside his head.

"Call Jane. She will tell you what to do. She knows what's wrong."

A voice of hope and reason? Lee wasn't so sure of that, but it was an option, and options were non-existent at the moment as they had been for three torturous months.

But what could Jane tell him that would change anything? She's the one who just emailed him with the news that the pills were sapping the mental and emotional life from him and would continue to do so until he stopped taking them. Sure, that sounded like hope, but he had also read that withdrawal from them could last as long as two years. He could not bear the thought of feeling this way for two more years – or two more days. It was simply out of the question – completely undoable. He would rather... He would rather...die. Yes, die.

Besides, Lee had no idea how to stop the pills. He had read there was a risk of seizures if it wasn't done properly. The pills were killing him. He felt it. He knew it. If he quit taking them, it would no doubt cause him indescribable misery before he would find rest in death. It would be much easier to end it now and hope that peace was on the other side.

Lee turned and made his way back into the hallway and hobbled to the stairway again. He shakily descended to the living room where he sat on the edge of the sofa as though he must hurry and do something...but what? He ran the options through his mind for the millionth time. He couldn't keep taking the pills. He couldn't quit taking the pills. He couldn't live in his current state of total mental anguish. The anxiety, the panic, the depression were slowly devouring him till he could no longer think or muster the slightest bit of hope. Life was completely black and had been that way for three months despite all the different drugs he was prescribed. Now he knew it was the drugs that were causing his torment, but he was permanently wed to them. There could be no divorce...unless...

Lee looked over toward the stairs that he had just ascended and descended. He ran the scenario through his head. The thought that this could be the last time he would ever go up those stairs stunned him. How many times had he gone up and down those stairs in twenty-three years? His mind thought back to when Lynn was a little girl and how he would go up and tuck her in bed each night. He thought about how he would sit on the steps and talk to Michael while he was in the bathroom to keep him from being afraid. He thought about the dent in the drywall where he had smacked his elbow when he slipped on the steps carrying Michael when he was an infant.

The thought that the next time he came down those steps he would be in a body bag or wrapped in a sheet was gruesome. All the hopes and dreams of life he had carried during the thousands of other times he came down those steps would be over. How could this be right? Something deep inside Lee spoke, "You can't do this. You just cannot do this."

It was not one of those incessant, pestering voices from inside his head. It came from somewhere within his very being – a vastly mysterious place. Whatever or whoever it was, it had complete authority. He could not end his life at his own hands.

What was he going to do? The voice (or whatever it was) told him what he could not do, but it gave him no clue about what he should do about his unbearable pain. Lee stumbled out to the kitchen and found the address book in the dry sink. With shaking hands, he paged through it and found Jane's name and phone number.

What would he say to her? How do you start a conversation with someone when you are trying to tell them you are contemplating suicide? What words do you use?

He reached up over the dry sink, took the phone from the wall and walked into the living room. He sat on the edge of the sofa again rocking back and forth. He was exhausted. He hadn't slept in days and had lost thirty pounds since this ordeal began because he could not eat. But he had to rock as he sat there. He could not keep still.

"I don't know what to say. I don't know what to say. I don't know what to say."

His hope started fading again. His mind began wandering back to the grotesqueness of his body being carried down the steps. He shuddered. He looked at the phone and, with trembling hands, began to dial Jane's number. He held it to his ear and listened to it ring. He wasn't even certain that he could speak if she did answer.

"Hello," came a man's voice. It was Jane's husband, Jayson.

"Hi. Uh...this is Lee...is...uh...Jane there?"

Lee had known Jayson and Jane for a few years. They both knew Lee had struggled with drinking for quite a while and also that it was the drinking that got him on these pills that now had him at their mercy. Lee was certain that Jayson knew the gravity of his situation, so he didn't expect Jayson to attempt any small talk. Conversation was beyond Lee anyway.

"Yeah, Lee. Hold on."

Lee got up from the sofa and paced back and forth between the kitchen and the living room. He still had no idea what he would say. He wasn't even thinking about that. The voices inside his head were starting to speak. He was feeling a growing terror that he might go back upstairs and do the unthinkable. Where was that "whatever it was" from deep inside that forbade him from taking his life? Lee could feel a panic attack on its way. He was getting lightheaded. He could feel his heart racing.

"Hello." It was Jane.

"Uh. Hi Jane...uh...uh...I'm...uh." Lee could not find the words. "I'm...uh...thinking about...killing myself."

There was silence for a moment. Then in a calm, matter-of-fact voice Jane asked, "Have you called your doctor?"

Lee didn't know if it was her peaceful voice or something else, but he felt a twinge of relief – maybe even hope. Her voice was nothing like the anxious voice inside his head that had suggested exactly the same thing only a few minutes ago.

"No."

"Is Ruth there with you?"

"No. She's at work."

"Just call your doctor. He will know what to do."

"I don't know if I can. I mean, I'm not..."

"His office will have someone on call. Call and tell him just what you told me."

"Okay."

That was it. Lee hung up and stood with the phone in his hand. Maybe Dr. James would know what to do. Surely contemplating suicide would get someone's attention. Someone would do something to make

Lee feel better now. If there was a way to get to the experts in something like this, this would surely be the way to find them. Wouldn't it? The drugs and counseling up to this point hadn't helped at all. Maybe they made things worse. Lee didn't know. Yes, if he could get to those expert in mental problems (or whatever this was), he would soon be well. He would get his life back. He wouldn't feel like dying. Dr. James would know what to do.

Lee opened the address book once again and found the phone number of Dr. James' office. The same dilemma returned. What should Lee say and how should he say it? He wasn't feeling suicidal at the moment. He had a tiny spark of hope. He felt more like he was trying to shout out in hopes that someone might hear him, "I'm hurting. I'm hurting really bad. Please help me!" Surely, he was soon going to get real help.

Lee found the number and dialed it trembling once again. One ring. Two rings. Three. Four. A voice. "You have reached the office of Dr. James. Please leave your name and phone number. If this is an emergency, please hang up and dial 911."

He was dumbfounded for an instant. This was not an emergency at the moment unless he didn't get to talk with Dr. James. Then it would become an emergency. He tried to reason what he should do, but the fog in his brain was too thick. Nothing was coming to him so he just blurted out his name and number into the receiver and quickly hung up.

Lee wasn't sure what he just did, so he had no idea if he did the right thing. He went back to the sofa and started rocking. He leaned forward and put his head in his hands. He couldn't think. He could feel the terror begin to grip him again. He grabbed the arm of the sofa tightly as if some force was going to take hold of him and drive him upstairs to his self-inflicted doom. What if he called the wrong place? What if no one called back? What if he did it wrong? What if he couldn't hold on? His hope dwindled. He was certain that no one would hear his call. He was afraid.

As he wallowed in his depression and dread, the phone rang. It startled Lee. He got up and answered it. In a nearly silent voice he spoke into the receiver, "Hello."

"Hello. This is Dr. James. Is this Lee?"

"Yeah. I'm thinking of committing suicide." No reason to mince words. He was desperate.

"Is Ruth there?"

"No. She's at work."

"Can you call her?"

"I don't think I can," Lee replied in a vacant, far away voice. He felt like he was in another world and could do no more to help himself. He had spent all of his mental and emotional energy making these two calls.

Dr. James knew that Lee had been in a severe state of depression and anxiety in the past few months. "Can you get to the emergency room?"

"Uh...I don't think so. No."

"Do you have Ruth's cellphone number? I can call her."

"Uh...I don't know if I can...uh..." Lee was spiraling rapidly. "Here...here it is." Lee could barely whisper the number into the receiver.

"Okay, Lee. Just stay there. I'll call Ruth. You just stay there."

Lee hung up without replying. He was numb with fear and drowning in hopelessness. He went into the living room and perched on the sofa again – head in hands once more. He wanted desperately to get up and pace, but he was afraid his feet would take him back upstairs and end this nightmare for good. He was sure of it. He held on to the arm of the sofa again. He sat there for what seemed like hours playing the "what if" game inside his tortured brain.

Lee heard the front door open and glanced at Ruth as she entered the room. He felt as pathetically weak as an infant. Even more, he felt completely worthless. He would have been embarrassed, but he no longer cared what anyone thought of him.

Ruth gave Lee a bewildered look. She knew something was very wrong. She measured her words and chose her tone carefully. "What's wrong?"

"You didn't talk to Dr. James?" he asked in a forlorn voice as he looked down at the floor.

"No. What's the matter?" She tried to be as calm as possible because she knew Lee had been very fragile in the past few weeks.

"I…uh…I called him. I said I was going to kill myself."

"What did he say?" She wanted to know more but tried not to agitate Lee any more than he already was.

Lee looked up at her with tears in his eyes and began to sob. In a muffled voice he said, "To call you. He was going to call you."

"Oh, he must have left a message."

Lee continued, "And to…" He stopped and began sobbing again.

Ruth got her cellphone and listened to Dr. James' message. "He says to go to the emergency room downtown or out to Community. Which one?"

Lee had no idea. None. He didn't care. He did not respond.

"Let's try Community. The parking will be better." There. Ruth had made the decision.

Lee sat on the sofa with no idea what he should do. What does a suicidal person take with him or her to an emergency room? Where would he be going anyway and for how long? These were questions that could be answered after he got there. Ruth would take care of all those things. Lee did feel a slight bit of hope knowing that he was going to a place where they would certainly know how to help him.

Ruth took his coat out of the living room closet and handed it to him. "I guess we better get over there."

Lee got his wallet and keys from the dry sink and put on his shoes and coat. He wandered to the door in zombie fashion and went out to the car while Ruth locked the front door and followed him.

In a few moments they were on their way to get Lee some help. He noticed that it was a beautiful sunny day but not because he felt any enjoyment from it. On the contrary, he was thinking that it was a day that should make him feel good like everyone else. That knowledge made him feel even sadder because he knew he was incapable of feeling anything other than mental anguish. He tried to recall the last time he felt happy or something other than miserable. He couldn't do it. Maybe he never felt happy in his life. Maybe it was all fake happiness. He let that thought pass.

It was replaced by an equally troubling thought. Would he have actually killed himself if he hadn't called Jane? Was he really suicidal earlier? Or was his mind just faking the suicide with the intent of getting the attention of others and letting them know he was in extreme emotional pain? Was he only crying out for help, or was he mentally ill? Was he going insane? Terror gripped him once more. Why couldn't his mind just turn off all the bizarre thoughts and let him alone? Why all the mental gymnastics?

Twenty minutes later they pulled into the hospital parking lot. There was a great deal of construction activity and materials which took up much of the closer parking space so they parked at quite a distance from the hospital. As they got out of the car and began walking, Lee had that ever present boaty feeling that gave him the sensation that he would fall over at any moment to one side or the other. It was a strange combination of dizziness and imbalance mixed with intense anxiety and near panic. It was extremely disturbing and had been with Lee for years. He had pretty much accepted it as part of who he was – something that would be with him for the rest of his days.

As they approached the emergency room, Lee noticed that there was a great deal of mud from the melting of snow that had fallen earlier in the winter. It was a very warm day for the middle of January. He began obsessing once again about how he could not conjure up any enjoyment from such a seemingly pleasant day. Nonetheless, the solution to this dilemma would hopefully be apparent on the other side of the emergency room door. Someone inside would see to it that Lee got to where he needed to go.

Ruth opened the glass door and stepped inside with Lee following behind. Before them was a counter with three hospital employees sitting behind it whose job it was to take information from the customers or patients. Lee wasn't sure which word was more appropriate. It seemed more like a bank than a hospital to him. Ruth approached the middle teller.

"What can I do for you?" the teller asked in a pleasant voice.

Ruth answered while Lee stood behind her. "My husband. He's

having some problems."

"What sort of problems?" came the next inquiry.

"Emotional problems."

"Oh, I see. Please have a seat here."

Ruth and Lee sat and began giving all the necessary insurance information to the teller as well as answers to more specific questions about his emotional problems. Lee found it embarrassing to mention his suicidal thoughts to the young lady who clearly had no cares in the world compared to him.

After the first round of information gathering, they were instructed to have a seat in the middle area of the room. Someone would assist them shortly. As they sat there, Lee looked around at the others sitting nearby. Clearly, many of them were afflicted with the typical ER assortment of broken bones, bleeding wounds, and respiratory ailments. Lee could not see anyone who looked as afraid and depressed as he felt. They would all have their maladies diagnosed and treated and be on the way to recovery soon. Lee was not so hopeful about his own prognosis. He didn't even know what was wrong with himself other than something called a dual diagnosis which he was duly labeled a month earlier at a different hospital. The specialist at the time had said it meant Lee had not only an addiction problem but also one or more mental disorders. It was a double whammy that sounded like a life sentence of misery and psychiatric drugs. Lee's heart and hope plummeted one more time.

"Mr. Lucas," came a cheerful voice.

Ruth and Lee stood and followed the smiling lady down the hallway as she tried to make small talk with Lee. Lee always had to work at idle conversation, and he wasn't in the mood to try now. He followed the woman in silence.

She led them to a nice cheery room with a bed and television. She took Lee's blood pressure and pulse and asked a few more questions before telling Lee that he could lie on the bed and relax. Someone else would be with him in a while.

Sitting in silence, Lee and Ruth glanced at the television now and then. Lee wondered what Ruth was thinking. He imagined she was sorry that she ever met him. Twenty-nine years of marriage had brought her to this chair sitting beside a man who was no longer of sound mind – and maybe never was. If he had been, he could no longer remember such a time. The past was a complete blur. He felt sorry for Ruth. If he knew how to do it, he would shake this whatever-it-was loose like a chain and take her hand and leave this place. Lee had tried so very hard for so very long to beat this thing and had nothing left. The more he resisted it, the tighter the chains seemed to envelop him. He sat there on the bed engrossed with his self-condemning thoughts.

"Mr. Lucas." He was momentarily rescued from his thoughts by a young man dressed in white who was all business. "It says here that you have had problems with addiction. Could you fill me in on that a little?"

"Yeah. I drank for a lot of years and quit back in October. I started having anxiety and panic attacks when I quit. I was taking clonazepam too, so I up-dosed that when the anxiety got bad. It didn't help. I need to get off of it."

The young man wrote something on the pad he had with him and asked, "Do you have any of that with you?"

Lee reached into his pocket and pulled out a brown bottle of two-milligram tablets of clonazepam. "I brought it along in case it gets late and I need a dose."

The man snatched it from Lee's hand and sneered at him as though Lee was a drug addict and said, "You won't be needing these anymore."

Lee responded in near terror, "But what if I have a seizure?"

"You won't have a seizure." And with that the young man was gone.

Lee sat there feeling bewildered and very uneasy. The guy had glared at him like he was some junkie who just wandered in off the streets. It was very reminiscent of the young man who gave him the dual diagnosis a month earlier at another hospital. It could have been the same person as far as Lee knew. Maybe Lee had only imagined the derisive look. His brain did have a tendency to magnify things since he quit drinking. He surely hoped the guy was right about the seizures.

A few minutes later another pleasant lady came into the room. She was apparently a social worker of some kind and informed Ruth and Lee that there might be a bed available later in the day at Oogden Institute of Psychiatry in the city. They wouldn't know for another hour or so. Otherwise Lee would have to go to another city.

They continued to wait in relative silence. "Institute of Psychiatry" sounded pretty impressive to Lee. He wasn't exactly sure what such a place might be like, but his mind conjured up visions of a well-kept facility with private rooms. Above all, such a place would most certainly have a quiet atmosphere in which kind, wise staff members would gently help him back to health. There would be consultations with lab-coated doctors who would study his charts and who would prescribe the best treatment possible based on the observations of the staff and the results of whatever types of tests may be necessary. Lee was feeling a bit more confident as he viewed the picture his brain was painting.

Lee's reverie was interrupted by a voice, "Good news. They have a bed for you at Oogden. Do you know where that is?" The pleasant lady was back and quite happy about her proclamation.

Ruth and Lee looked blankly at each other. Lee could not respond so Ruth replied, "No, I'm not sure."

"North Thirteenth Street across from the Witmer Complex and a block from Parting Street."

"Let me think a minute," Ruth responded. After taking a moment to locate it in her mind, she replied, "Okay, yes, I know where that is."

Lee ran the location through his cloudy brain. He tried to focus. He had taken the Thirteenth Street bus for many years to and from work. He got on and off the bus thousands of times at the stop right before Parting Street. Suddenly the light went on in his searching brain. No, that couldn't be Oogden. It wasn't possible, was it? His friend, Gary, had been a patient in that building at least once that Lee knew of, and it was not a pleasant stay at all according to Gary's description.

Worry began to morph quickly into panic in Lee's mind. The familiar numbness of the last three months began to make itself known in Lee's body. Surely this was not the same place. He tried to rationalize this dire news before he went into a full panic attack. It was a big building so Gary was probably in some area different from where Lee would be. Yes, that must be it. Lee would be in another area. Lee began to calm enough to stave off a panic attack, at least for the moment.

"Good," came the lady's reply. "When you get there, you can park in the parking lot in the front and walk around to the north side of the building. Push the buzzer at the entrance and tell them your name. They will be expecting you. Okay?"

"The side of the building?" Ruth asked.

"Yes, the north side, and push the buzzer."

"Okay. Do we need anything else?" Ruth questioned.

"No. That's it. You're good to go."

Alright. Thank you," Ruth answered and walked out into the hallway and toward the door they had entered hours earlier. Lee followed close behind Ruth like the helpless soul that he was.

As they walked back outside, Lee noticed that the warm, sunny, spring-like day had changed to a cold, dark, wintry night. It matched the black, fearful depression inside Lee. Try as he might, he could not get out of the shadows that had been covering him for three months now. In a few minutes, they were back in the car.

"So, where do you want to eat before we go to the hospital?" Ruth asked.

Yeah. Hospital. It didn't sound nearly as professional and hopeful to Lee as institute of psychiatry. He just sat there.

"Lee, where?" Ruth became impatient.

"What? Oh, uh, I don't care. Doesn't matter."

"Wendy's is okay? Advance Avenue?" Ruth continued.

"Yeah."

Ruth started the car, and they pulled out of the parking lot. There was silence in the car but lots of noise in Lee's head. Institute of psychiatry. Fancy words for a mental hospital. A psych ward. Psych hospital. Mental institution. Insane asylum. Nut house. Why wouldn't the noise stop? Lee felt like he was going insane.

In ten minutes they were at the Wendy's drive-through, and Ruth ordered. Lee thought about all the happy times this same scenario had been played out over the years he had been married to Ruth. He thought of the times they brought Lynn and Michael to Wendy's when they were little. Michael always had fries and a Frosty and dipped the fries in the ice cream. Fun times. Good memories. Happiness. Where did they go?

The attendant handed the bags of food out to Ruth, and they drove across the street and sat in the car in the parking lot while they ate. Any other time, Lee would have been delighted to feast on a chicken sandwich, fries, and a soda no matter where he was. He sat there and ate his meal without speaking a word. There was a lot of conversation inside his head - too much. He sat there shaking inside as he was being tortured by the incessant thoughts and horrid feelings.

Surely, they could do something for him at Oogden – Institute of Psychiatry, mental institution, or whatever it was. He couldn't sink any lower, could he? Up was the only direction he could go from here, wasn't it? Lee had been to many Alcoholics Anonymous meetings in the past couple years. They were always talking about everybody having a different "bottom." It took many months for him to understand what that even meant. This day had to be his bottom. It just had to be. He had been moments away from committing suicide only a few hours earlier. The only way his bottom could be lower is if he had actually killed himself. He wasn't sure about that, but he prayed he was right. He prayed that he would at least begin his ascent from the depths of his miserable existence at Oogden.

Chapter Two

Lee and Ruth were silent as they sat in the car in the parking lot at Oogden. It was somewhere around 10:15, and there were very few other vehicles in the parking lot. It was not well-lit which only added to the eerie atmosphere inside Lee's head. He was wondering what Ruth was thinking. He pitied her. It was Saturday evening, and Ruth would normally be at home either reading on the sofa or going to bed. This was normally her favorite evening of the week to relax from a long week. Instead, she not only had to waste her entire Saturday tending to Lee but also now had to spend more time getting Lee checked into the Oogden Institute of Psychiatry. While it might be called an institute of psychiatry, there was no denying it. This was a psych ward. When she got home, Ruth would still be beside herself with grave concern for her unfit, pathetically weak husband. Lee was spent as he let these thoughts wander through his head. He was too numb to feel the guilt or the grief. He was just "there." Just plain numb to the pain.

Lee looked over toward the north side of the building. There was a street going by the north side, but it was more like an alley. It seemed obvious to Lee that they wanted their mentally and emotionally distraught clientele to enter the building in the most unassuming manner possible. He wondered if that was for the protection of those entering or because they simply didn't want the outside world to know what they did in this building. The thought of slinking in the shadows to get to the side door did nothing to bolster Lee's self-esteem and only served to ratchet up his sense of worthlessness one more notch.

Ruth broke the silence, "Well, you ready?"

"I guess," Lee muttered. He almost wanted to call it off and go back home, but his ailing brain with all its condemning voices and thoughts would have to go along with him. If he could leave them here, he would gladly renege on this venture and return home. That was not an option.

Lee resigned himself to the fact that he must face reality and follow through with this plan. He reached for the door handle.

As they walked slowly toward the alley, Lee could feel winter in the cold, crisp air. He recalled that same feeling from hundreds of other times he was outside on winter evenings. It was always invigorating and gave him energy. Not so tonight. It was only one more reminder of how ill he was, and it depressed him to a new level of low. His bottom seemed to be getting deeper by the minute.

When they got to the door at the side of the building, Ruth pushed the buzzer by the doorway. No answer. She pushed it again, and the door cautiously opened outward.

"Mr. Lucas?" came a woman's voice.

Ruth answered as Lee stood behind her, "Yes, Mr. Lucas is my husband." She made a motion toward Lee.

"Come in."

Ruth and Lee entered as the lady walked over to a desk in the corner of a small room. It reminded Lee of some sort of remodeled room; perhaps it was a mailroom in its former life. He had a former life too. Maybe he would be remodeled in this place.

"Please have a seat," the lady suggested as she pointed to two chairs in front of her desk.

She pulled out a folder and several forms, sat down behind the desk, and began asking questions. As usual, Ruth did the talking while Lee tried to focus on the woman's words. He was able to pull his insurance card from his wallet with some difficulty when the time came.

As Lee sat there trying to get his brain to concentrate, he noticed someone coming into the room from the other side. The man was tall and wore what Lee would come to recognize as the garb of psychiatrists in this particular institute – a white lab coat. He appeared to be in his fifties and smiled as he looked down at Lee or on Lee. Lee was not sure which one – maybe both.

The lady spoke, "This is Dr. Ingerson. He is the shift doctor tonight."

"Good evening Mr..." He stopped.

"Mr. Lucas, Lee Lucas," the lady said.

"Yes, Mr. Lucas," he parroted. "How are you this evening, Mr. Lucas?" Dr.Ingerson asked.

Lee was not sure if that was supposed to be humorous or not. He was checking into a mental institution in the middle of the night. Was the good doctor expecting something like the standard "I'm fine, and you" or "I want to die. Please help me"? Lee was clueless. So he just sat there and looked blankly at Dr. Ingerson, and the doctor, with that iron-on smile, looked quizzically at Lee. Lee had answered the question without speaking a word.

"I see," said Dr. Ingerson. "So could you tell me a little bit about what has brought you here this evening?"

That was a question that Lee could answer, so he launched into the whole story of the past several months. He spoke of falling into a state of severe depression and relentless anxiety since he had quit drinking three months earlier. He spoke of panic attacks, weight loss, sleepless nights, useless counselling, dual diagnosis, suicidal ideation, and psychiatric drugs. Lee was on a roll. He was finally telling someone about the misery of the past three months. Dr.Ingerson was listening and nodding his head with every sentence Lee was offering. This was the man who could help him – the man who would help him. Lee finally felt he was in the right place after all.

After Lee had finished, Dr.Ingerson responded, "I am going to name three objects, Mr. Lucas. I will ask you later to repeat them to me. Book, penny, chair. You mentioned that you are on some medications now. Could you tell me what they are?"

"Clonazepam. That's the one I need to get off of. Mirtazapine. That's so I can eat and sleep."

"Anything else?"

"Uh, yeah. A PPI for reflux. Eye drops. Travatan."

"Travatan. That's the eye drops?" Dr.Ingerson asked.

"Yes, those are eye drops. I take them at night."

"I see. Clonazepam?"

"Right," Lee answered.

"Do you know what dose you take?"

"Four milligrams. One morning. One afternoon. Two at bedtime."

"And the mirtazapine?"

Lee nodded. "I take fifteen milligrams at night. The PPI is thirty milligrams in the morning." Lee was very familiar with his drugs.

"Do you know where you are right now, Mr. Lucas?"

Lee was taken by surprise and a bit alarmed at the question, but he answered. "Oogden Institute of Psychiatry."

"That's right, OIP. And what state are you in?"

The first thing that came to Lee's mind was "a state of depression," but he was pretty sure that's not what Dr. Ingerson was after.

"Pennsylvania."

"Can you name the three objects that I mentioned earlier?"

Lee sat there for several seconds and tried to extract those names from somewhere very far away because he could not remember any of them. "Uh, desk, penny, apple?"

"Book, penny, chair," Dr. Ingerson corrected Lee.

Lee suddenly felt defeated. He couldn't even remember the names of three objects for five minutes. He feared that maybe he was going insane. He did not yet know this was a test that would be repeated many times over the next three weeks.

"Well, Mr. Lucas, you will be feeling much better when your stay with us is over," spoke the doctor once again through that smile and in a voice that seemed to genuinely convey sincerity.

Lee truly hoped that the good doctor was right and that he would walk out of OIP feeling like a new man. Even feeling like any man would be an improvement because Lee had felt like a child for what seemed like an eternity. Lee tried hard to believe those words, but it was hard to fathom any kind of feeling other than misery. Still, Lee feebly hoped.

"Do you have any questions before you are shown to your room?"

If Lee's brain had been functioning with any kind of clarity, he would have had many questions. But, he knew he could not call on his brain for any type of assistance so he just mumbled, "No," and shook his head as he studied the tiles on the floor. He just wanted them to do something, anything, that might make him feel even slightly normal.

"Okay. We will take good care of you here." With those parting words Dr.Ingerson left the room as quietly as he had arrived.

Within a few minutes a smiling nurse came through the same door the doctor had just exited. "Hello, Mr. Lucas? My name is Melissa. I will be taking you up to your room. Do you have any questions before we go upstairs?"

Lee hadn't thought of any questions in the last few moments so he muttered one more "No."

Turning to Ruth, Melissa continued, "You are Mrs. Lucas?"

Ruth answered, "Yes."

"It's very nice to meet you. Will you be coming upstairs with your husband while we get him situated?"

Ruth nodded.

"Very good. Just follow me, and we will get you both up to the floor."

Melissa turned and proceeded through a side door which led to a long hallway. Lee and Ruth followed silently. There was no small talk or any type of chit chat. This walk somehow seemed to be a more serious procession than the walk he had taken only a few hours earlier at the emergency room at Community Hospital.

In moments, they were getting on an elevator that took them to the seventh floor of Oogden Institute of Psychiatry.

As they stepped off the elevator, Lee noticed that the staff area was straight ahead. There were not many people working. This was the night shift. Melissa went to the desk and spoke to another lady apparently announcing the arrival of their newest guest. The woman glanced in Lee's direction and nodded her head as she was having a short conversation with Melissa. Lee knew he should feel embarrassed or self-conscious, but he felt nothing. He stood there completely expressionless.

When the conversation between Melissa and the lady behind the desk ended, Melissa motioned for Ruth and Lee to join her at the desk. She introduced them to the woman. "This is Nurse Jones. She will be showing you around the floor this evening. They will be taking good care of you here."

She turned and walked to the elevators, pressed the button, and was gone.

Nurse Jones appeared to be tired either from this particular evening's events or from many night shift evenings she had worked over the years. Lee didn't know or particularly care. She didn't seem to possess that medical staff smile that he had grown accustomed to during this day. Maybe she was as exhausted as he was. Lee thought that was highly unlikely.

"Mr. and Mrs. Lucas," Nurse Jones spoke. "You can come onto the floor through the door to your right after I unlock it for you."

Lee looked to his right and saw a wall made entirely of glass except for the door positioned in the middle of the wall. Through the glass he could see a hallway with a few rooms on the opposite side. He wondered about the door. Was it locked to keep unwanted intruders away from the guests? (Lee didn't know if the people staying here were more properly called patients, clients, inmates, or residents. He thought "guests" covered them all.) Was it locked to keep the guests from escaping? Lee noticed that he was playing word games in his head which, when added to the locked door question, bothered him – but only slightly. He was pretty sure there would be much larger things about which to be disturbed before this night was over.

Ruth and Lee walked to the door and heard a clicking sound that indicated the door was now unlocked and ready to be opened. Lee stood behind Ruth who pulled the handle toward her as the door opened. Nurse Jones met them in a moment and motioned for them to follow her.

The first stop was just on the other side of the nurses' station. Nurse Jones opened a wooden door and asked if Lee had anything that he would like to keep in this room until he was discharged from OIP. Lee wandered inside for a moment and peered at a rather large number of items – many of which appeared to have been stored there for quite some time. Lee wondered how long he would be in this place, hopefully not as long as many of these belongings.

For a moment Lee looked at the grey coat and blue scarf he had been carrying and vaguely recalled all the times he wore them on cold, dark winter mornings when he would get in his car to go to work. There was a sadness about the memories of his former normal life. He didn't dwell on it. It was just one of the countless reflections that constantly passed through his brain. He gave the coat and scarf to Nurse Jones who tagged it with Lee's name. Somehow it reminded Lee of a death certificate and burial.

"Anything else?" Nurse Jones inquired.

"No."

This was the cue for Nurse Jones to launch into the speech that she must have made many times during her tenure at OIP. "This is the suicide watch floor, so you must not be in possession of anything that could be used to commit suicide. In three days you will be re-evaluated and may be taken off suicide watch."

Lee stood and stared at Nurse Jones as she finished her routine. To her, this was a mere statement of fact and nothing more. To Lee, it was a statement about his pitiful life and seeing to it that it did not end in this place. He hoped they would do more for him than just keep him from killing himself. The tone of the message made Lee uneasy, but he was not sure why.

"I will have to ask you to remove your belt as well as the strings in your shoes."

Lee could understand the belt, but the leather laces in his Dockers were each a foot long at the most. Maybe if he tied them together they would be long enough to hang himself. It was possible. He removed the belt and strings as instructed and noticed that his jeans were extremely loose without the belt. In the last three months he had lost more than thirty pounds. He had very little appetite, and he could barely swallow from the fierce anxiety that would not leave him – not even for a meal.

"Would you like to take them with you, Mrs. Lucas?" she asked, in a tone that seemed more like a command than a question. There was definitely an atmosphere of control in this place.

Ruth nodded as Lee handed the belt and leather laces to her.

"The wedding band must go too, Mr. Lucas."

Lee removed the silver ring from his finger and looked at it for a moment. He hadn't taken it off his finger in years. He felt like the last bits of his identity were being stripped from him. He handed Ruth the only symbol he had left of his connection to anyone else. Lee felt naked and defeated.

"Let me show you the rest of the floor," Nurse Jones commanded as she began walking down the hallway toward a set of swinging double doors.

Ruth and Lee followed. Lee had to shuffle along. The ever-present unbalanced feeling made walking hard enough, but now he couldn't lift his feet without his shoes falling off.

The doors opened into an alcove that spilled into a very large room. The room was divided into two basic areas. There were about two dozen chairs of different sizes, shapes, and colors lined around the outer walls of the left portion of the room. There were large partially-drawn curtains on the wall covering a large patio-like window and door. Lee noticed some sort of deck or patio on the other side of the door that overlooked a parking lot. Lee assumed that was the parking lot where his car was currently parked. He wondered if he would be well the next time he got in it.

As he continued to look around the room, he noticed a television attached to the wall on the far side of that half of the room. He supposed that this was some sort of community room. In the corner of the room near the television was another door that opened to another hallway he would soon be walking down. Adjacent to the door was a closed wooden door. He would learn on Sunday that it was the medication room from which all drugs were dispensed.

Lee turned his attention to the area on his right. This was a smaller area with two long tables around which were a couple dozen folding chairs. Along the far wall were shelves holding various games, puzzles, craft materials, and books. There was also something that appeared to be a boom box on top of the shelves. In the corner was a large refrigerator. The only things in this area that made any impression on Lee were the puzzles and books. Something inside him yearned to do puzzles and read. These were things he enjoyed doing in his former life. Now his brain would allow him to neither do nor enjoy them. It was a bad impression.

Lee's thoughts were interrupted by Nurse Jones' voice, "This is the community area where you will have group meetings and group therapy sessions and eat your meals. This is also where all medications will be dispensed."

Nurse Jones continued across the large area toward the door on the other side without another word. Ruth and Lee followed.

She opened the door, and all three walked through. To the immediate right Lee noticed what appeared to be a much smaller community room with chairs and a television. Maybe it was for those who preferred to be away from the large group or who were having small group therapy meetings. Nurse Jones didn't stop or make a single remark about that room.

They proceeded down the hallway until they got to the third room on the right. "This is your room, number 702." Lee peered inside but did not enter. The room was dark except for a dim light located beside a bed by the window. There was someone in the bed. Apparently Lee had a roommate. There was a second bed immediately inside the doorway and to the right – apparently Lee's bed.

"You can come back later after I show you the rest of the floor." The tour resumed. They encountered another set of double doors which required a momentary stop while Nurse Jones unlocked them. Lee vaguely wondered why these doors were locked, but he really didn't care.

On the other side of the doors on the right was a small room with a washer and dryer. "This is the laundry room. You must get the key from the staff area if you need to use it."

A short distance from the laundry room and on the left were two shower rooms. "When you need to use the shower, you must get a key from the staff. They will also provide towels." End of tour.

In a minute they were all back at their starting point right outside the staff area. Lee stood between Ruth and Nurse Jones and could not remember anything about the last ten minutes. He knew they had walked down the hallway and through some doors. He remembered there had been a big room somewhere in the tour, but he couldn't recall anything about it. The only thing that really registered in his memory was that he would have a roommate. That thought troubled Lee. This was a mental institution so there was no telling what sort of person he might encounter in that room. As Lee was trying to process these thoughts, Nurse Jones interrupted the conversation inside his head.

"Mrs. Lucas, do you have any questions before I show your husband to his room?"

Apparently, it was time for Ruth to leave.

Ruth simply asked, "Yes, what are the visiting hours here?"

"Visiting hours are seven to eight in the evening," came the reply.

"One hour?"

"Yes."

"Can I bring other clothes in for him to wear during the week?"

"You may bring clothes and other things. They will need to be checked at the nurses' station before you come in the door."

Lee thought about that for a while. He was told downstairs when he checked in that he would be under suicide watch for at least three days. They would certainly take precautions to keep him from harming himself which included checking things brought in from the outside. He wondered what the problem was with all the other…what was the right word? Patients? Residents? Inmates? He wasn't sure, so he settled on "residents" this time having forgotten that he had earlier referred to them as "guests." "Residents" sounded normal although he wasn't feeling anything remotely similar to normal, and that brought his thoughts full circle to the other residents. He hadn't yet seen any of the other residents. Everyone was in bed he supposed. He had heard screaming, moaning, and crying from time to time on the tour, so not everyone was sleeping, and not everyone was happy. Maybe no one was happy. Lee wasn't.

Nurse Jones interrupted his thoughts once more, "If you don't have any more questions for now, you may take a few minutes to say goodbye. Tap on the window to the nurses' station when you are ready, and I will unlock the door for you to leave."

Lee felt piercing terror and deep sadness at the same time. This was it. He would be alone here with strangers in a mental institution. Ruth had taken care of him for the last three months. She had to leave now. He envisioned her going home alone and walking into an empty house. Chloe and Hannah would be there, but what comfort were two cats when the person you've spent nearly thirty years with has just checked into an institution? The protector instinct inside Lee knew he should be leaving with her, but it was clear that he was too fragile and weak to do so. Guilt began to overwhelm Lee yet again.

Lee and Ruth looked at each other. Lee wanted to hold her and comfort her. It was what he did in times like these for so many years, but he couldn't do it. That part of him was gone, maybe forever. Nothing he had done or thought in these past three months could marshal even the slightest bit of courage. On the contrary, the more he had tried and the longer he had prayed, the faster and deeper he spiraled into a pit of weakness, fear, and despair. The hardest part to accept, the part he could not accept, was that he did not know why this was happening to him. What did he do to cause himself such agony? He had always thought that he would never crack mentally. He had prided himself on weathering many emotional hardships and coming out of them stronger and wiser. He had always believed the words of Nietzsche: "What does not kill me makes me stronger." Maybe this would kill him.

Lee's thoughts were interrupted by Ruth's quiet voice. "Well, I guess I'll see you tomorrow night." Lee knew she was relying on a strength not created within or conjured up by her humanness. It was a strength from a far higher place – a strength that had been given to her years ago in a situation very similar to this one. She had told Lee about it many times.

They turned to each other, and Lee put his arms around her. It wasn't the hug of a strong man consoling his mate but rather the hug of a child holding onto his mother for comfort and never wanting to let go. But he did reluctantly drop his arms, and she walked over to the window and gently tapped. Lee heard the click of the lock on the door signaling that Ruth could now leave. He walked beside her to the door and watched her push the door open and go out. He watched her walk to the elevators and push the button. In a moment the door to the middle elevator opened, and she entered and stood looking at Lee. Lee and Ruth waved to each other as the elevator doors closed slowly. Tears dribbled down Lee's cheeks. He stared at the middle elevator as if he could will it back open and see Ruth again. He had felt this infinite kind of sadness only once before in his life. The memory was still vivid as he played it inside his head.

May 1985

It was twenty-five years ago, but the warning signs leading up to it had begun three years earlier after Ruth had given birth to their daughter, Lynn. Soon after Lynn was born, Ruth began having problems that were completely foreign to Lee. Ruth worked part time on the evening shift as a registered nurse at a nearby hospital. On her days off, Lee would often come home and find Ruth sitting at the kitchen table staring into space and thinking what appeared to be very deep thoughts. On such days, he would usually tell her that he would sit and talk with her as soon as he finished his workout downstairs in the basement. Exercise had always been a huge part of Lee's daily routine. It kept him both physically and mentally strong. It relieved the stress of the day.

Lee would often dread coming upstairs on those days when Ruth was staring into space. He knew that he would spend the next hour or two trying to resolve her problem that he did not understand. Ruth would often talk about the people at work and how they were thinking all kinds of very bad things about her and talking behind her back. She was certain of it. She focused primarily on her supervisor, Megan. She was sure that Megan didn't like her and thought she was incompetent. Ruth was isolating herself from everyone else in her mind. Lee would sit for hours listening and trying to reason with Ruth telling her over and over that no one at her work was targeting her. They had their own work to do. She was a very likeable person. There would be no reason for such conduct. Lee chalked it up to the same kind of paranoia that most people feel at times.

As time went on, Lee would come home from work and find Ruth crying over the same thoughts. Things were spiraling downhill quickly, and they continued to do so until it affected her work. Eventually she was dismissed from the hospital. Ruth was distraught, and Lee was confused. In a few weeks, papers came from Ruth's supervisor explaining the reasons for Ruth's dismissal and recommending that she get help. For some time there was no improvement in Ruth's state of mind. She obsessed continually about her dismissal. She finally got to the point where her brain could find no rest, so she made an appointment at a nearby mental health clinic. That appointment was never kept, and, in time, the extreme obsession and paranoid thinking subsided although it never disappeared completely.

Things went well for the next two years until Ruth had another baby, their son Michael. Shortly after Michael's birth, Ruth's strange thinking patterns returned and accelerated rapidly into bizarre behavior. She told Lee that she knew he was not going to work where he said he worked but was going somewhere else. That was news to Lee. She was also certain that her brother, Steve, was secretly building them a house on a parcel of land he owned in the area. That was news to Steve.

One Friday afternoon six months after Michael was born, Lee got a disturbing call at work from his mother-in-law. A friend had stopped by their house to visit and found the front door hanging open and no one home. There was no sign of Ruth, Lynn, or Michael, and the car was gone. Lee was immediately frantic with worry and rushed home. When he arrived, he was informed by a neighbor that his daughter and son were at an elderly neighbor's home across the street. Ruth had had enough mental forethought to keep them safe, but where was she?

Lee spent the rest of the evening taking care of a baby and a toddler and worrying about where their mother might be. She finally returned home long after dark as though nothing out of the ordinary had happened. She said she had dinner with an old friend who lived about an hour away. She also mentioned that she stopped by the hospital where she worked more than two years ago and got her job back. She would be starting in the morning.

Lee was beside himself with fear and confusion. He knew that, if she did visit the hospital, nothing good came from it. Ruth certainly was in no condition to work there. She was obviously delusional, and Lee had no idea why. Did she really go to the hospital? What was he going to do if she got up in the morning and tried to go to work? How would he take care of Lynn and Michael in the morning if things went awry? He could feel his own anxiety building quickly.

Lee was relieved that Lynn and Michael were upstairs in bed and couldn't hear Ruth's increasingly loud voice. Ruth abruptly decided that it was time to go to bed so she could get up early and go to work. They both went to bed. Lee's mind was in overdrive as he lay there trying to decide what he would do in the morning. Ruth was restless - very restless. She bolted out of bed, got the telephone, and announced that she needed to make calls to several friends and apologize for things done in the past. She was loud, agitated and out of control. Lee wondered if this was what was called mania. He had heard the word but never really gave it much thought. He didn't need to do so until now.

He got up and grabbed the phone from Ruth. He didn't need two children waking up and crying. He already had his hands full. Ruth looked right through him with piercing eyes and, in a loud voice warned, "Give me the phone or I'll scream. I don't care if the kids wake up."

Desperate, Lee handed her the phone.

Ruth spent the next hour calling various people. He was sure they were as perplexed as he was. When she had had enough, Ruth hung up the phone and announced that she needed to get some sleep before work. She got in bed, turned out the light on her nightstand, and there was silence. Lee once again lay there and wondered what the morning would bring.

Ruth was up at 4:30 a.m. and in the shower preparing to go to a job that Lee was certain she did not have. If he got any sleep last night, he didn't know it. He knew he couldn't just let her leave the house. He decided to call Ruth's mother to see if she could come over. 4:30 was awfully early. She would think this was an emergency. Lee thought for a second. This was an emergency.

He went out to the kitchen and called Pat. She answered right away, and Lee explained the situation. She said she would be right over. Lee could still hear the shower running. Good. Ruth would not suspect that he was trying to interfere with her plan.

Pat and Jerry arrived about twenty minutes later. Ruth was excited and delighted to tell them that she would be going to the hospital in a little while to resume her employment. It never occurred to her to ask them what they were doing visiting at 5:30 in the morning. Pat looked at Lee with a "what do I say?" expression. Lee could only shrug. He had no idea what to say to Ruth. Pat would have to think of something on her own.

Pat started the conversation slowly with some questions about the day before, being careful not to turn Ruth's good-natured excitement into suspicious agitation. As the minutes passed, the discussion went into other areas. Ruth was getting distracted which would hopefully put aside her plans to go to the hospital. After several minutes, Lee thought it would be good to call in more forces to divert Ruth's attention.

Lee called Joe and Lynn, a married couple who were close friends. He gave them a brief explanation of the situation. Could they please come over and help out?

Joe and Lynn arrived about an hour later while Pat was still speaking with Ruth. Pat's questions had begun to create confusion in Ruth. Lynn sat down on a chair near Ruth and joined the conversation. Time passed beyond 7:00 a.m. which was the time Ruth thought she was to report to work.

A few minutes later, the front door opened and Ruth's brother, Steve, walked into the living room. After Pat had called him and told him about Ruth's plan, he had stationed himself up the road so that he could intercept Ruth if she left. Since it was past 7:00, he decided the plan had been interrupted and it was safe to see what was happening at the Lucas'. He hated to see his sister in such an unstable state of mind.

The rest of the morning and afternoon was spent trying to convince Ruth that she might benefit from talking with a counselor at the mental health center. She adamantly refused time after time and was becoming more bewildered and agitated. Her mind kept trying to process the same thoughts over and over until she had become so tormented that she could no longer tolerate the unceasing thoughts. Finally, in late afternoon she simply said, "I can't do this anymore." She was ready to get some help.

For over two years, Lee had a front row seat to Ruth's increasingly strange behavior. She had finally cracked. Lee could not understand what was happening. Why was Ruth acting this way? She looked fine on the outside. No matter how hard he tried, he could not reason this problem out or convince her to behave normally. He was scared for Ruth and for Michael and Lynn. Surely the experts at the center would know what to do and would help her.

Late Saturday afternoon Lee drove Ruth to the mental health center and met with a counselor named Barry. He sat with Ruth and Lee and calmly asked Ruth about how she had been feeling and what types of thoughts she had been having. She had been so agitated from her world of obsessive, bizarre thoughts for so long that she seemed to have no mental or emotional energy left. Lee found himself answering most of Barry's questions and explaining Ruth's strange thoughts and behavior of the past several months and especially those of the past twenty-four hours. Ruth nodded in agreement every now and then seeming to have surrendered completely to whatever it was that had been tormenting her for years.

After Barry's questions had been answered to his satisfaction, he said that Ruth's thoughts and behavior seemed to be symptoms of schizophrenia. He said that paranoia, hostility, thoughts of unreality, and agitation were very common indicators of that condition. He reassured Ruth and Lee that she could be helped greatly at the center. His voice was calm and had an air of confidence.

He asked, "Would you like to stay here so that we can help you?"
Ruth looked down blankly and repeated, "I can't do this anymore."

With those words, Ruth had resigned herself completely to the fact that she needed help even if she had to stay in a mental institution for some time. Ruth was taking Barry at his word.

In a few moments, Ruth and Lee stepped off an elevator and, for the first time in either of their lives, onto the floor of a psychiatric ward. They were met by a staff nurse who spoke quietly with them as she showed them around the floor. Lee tried to be unassuming as he looked around. He did his best not to stare. It certainly was an atmosphere he had never experienced in his thirty-one years of life. As they continued on their tour, Ruth did not speak. She was resigned to whatever was going to happen to her here.

The tour ended at the same elevators they had gotten off a few minutes earlier. This was clearly the cue for Lee to leave. He said, "Well, I guess this is it. I'll see you tomorrow, okay?" He looked at Ruth who responded with only a nod. She was obviously still being tortured by her thoughts. They hugged briefly. In the past several months Lee could sense Ruth drifting from him more and more. He missed her tremendously, but now he wouldn't even be able to be in the physical presence of his wife. He felt completely alone.

Lee pushed the button for the elevator. Ruth stood beside him quietly while he waited. In a moment the bell rang signaling the arrival of the elevator. The doors opened, and Lee entered never taking his eyes off Ruth. She looked forlorn and pathetic standing there expressionless and alone. Lee felt forlorn and pathetic as the elevator doors slowly closed hiding Ruth from his sight. He had never felt such a profound and bottomless grief in his life. Tears flowed from his eyes and down his cheeks. Something had slowly taken his wife from him over the past two years. Now she was physically absent too, and Lee had no one and nothing to blame. Lee could only sob.

January 16, 2010

"Mr. Lucas."

Lee was still caught in the reverie of twenty-five years ago when Ruth was the one watching him enter the elevator. It seemed surreal. How could it be possible? But it must have happened. He had felt this depth of sorrow only once before in his life. It was a hazy image in his current mental state, but the feelings were identical. It had certainly happened. Ruth was well now and had been for many years. If she could be released from the abyss of mental anguish, he could be too. There was hope for Lee.

Nurse Jones repeated, "Mr.Lucas. We need to show you to your room now. Do you remember the number?"

"What? Uh….it's seven…uh…seven something," Lee was suddenly awakened from his daydream and was confused. He wondered if he would have remembered the room number anyway.

"Room 702. Follow me."

Lee tried to convince himself that he was pleased that he had at least known he was on the seventh floor. He was keenly aware that he was playing a mind game with himself, and that troubled him. He tried to ignore that thought, but it made him dwell on it even more.

Lee shuffled along behind Nurse Jones as they headed for room 702.

Chapter Three

Lee sat on his bed in a daze and tried to decide what the appropriate thing would be for him to do. What does one do in a mental institution? He had only been in such a place once before – as a visitor. This time he was not a visitor. He was a resident. This place seemed to be much different from the facility Ruth was in twenty-five years ago. Residents were clearly separated from the public as evidenced by the locked door he came through earlier in the evening. There were no windows or doors separating the public area from the resident area where Ruth had stayed. Visitation was allowed all day until well into the evening at that facility. What was the point of having only one visiting hour here? Lee could only speculate that the intent was to keep residents from getting too agitated. He wondered about the rest of the residents. It was late in the evening so everyone else was in bed he supposed. Were there violent people here? Was he safe? He was in no condition to try to defend himself either physically or mentally. He wondered if everyone here was under suicide watch.

He returned to his first question. What should he do? Should he get under the covers and lie there? He knew there would be no sleep tonight. He looked over at his roommate. Should he say something to him? He seemed to be awake. Making decisions in the last three months had become increasingly impossible.

He sat there and took in his surroundings. He had a night table beside the head of his bed. There was a dresser with a mirror at the wall to his left beside the doorway. In the corner on the left he noticed a brown wooden sliding door. It looked very much like an old closet door. It was partially open, and through the dim light he could see what appeared to be a vanity and sink. He was too tired and scared to get up and see what else was in that room. He assumed it was the restroom. At the foot of his bed and over along the wall was a cabinet of some sort probably for clothing.

He looked over to the other side of the room where there was a window and heater directly underneath. He noticed his roommate looking over toward him. Great. Lee didn't want to make an enemy his first night here. He didn't want to acknowledge the existence of his roommate or even be in his presence, but he was afraid he had no choice.

He looked over to the stranger and gave a little wave, nodded, and uttered a minimal greeting, "Hey."

The stranger replied, offering little more than Lee had offered, "Hey, how's it goin'?"

Oh great, a question. "Okay," Lee lied. What a stupid answer. If he was okay, he wouldn't be in this room right now.

His roommate apparently wasn't buying it and continued, "What are you in here for?"

Another question. Okay. Lee really didn't care, so why not just cut to the quick? "Suicide watch."

"Me too," came the quick reply.

Lee thought about that for a moment. Common ground. Maybe this guy was okay. Maybe he would understand.

In the next ten minutes, Lee learned that his new friend's name was Paul. He was much younger than Lee, maybe late twenties or early thirties. He had been a resident at Oogden more than once. Somehow Paul had recently been homeless and ended up here. He had been here for five days and would have to be released in two more days unless he could convince the doctors that he needed to stay longer. Lee wasn't sure if the fog was allowing his brain to decipher Paul's words correctly or not. Why would anyone want to stay here if they could function outside? Maybe it was a simple matter of having shelter and food.

Paul listened to Lee describe his story of suicidal behavior, depression, panic attacks, hopelessness, and on and on. He was especially interested in the four milligrams of clonazepam that Lee was taking.

"Four milligrams. That's a lot. I keep telling them if I could get some benzos, I would be a lot better. They won't give them to me. I wouldn't even need four milligrams."

Somehow that didn't sound right to Lee. Why would anyone want to be on benzodiazepines? Jane and Jayson had told Lee that the clonazepam was what had been making him severely depressed. Jane even sent him information about it on the computer. He hoped they would get him safely off the clonazepam here and he could go back home then. Maybe Paul craved benzodiazepines and the staff knew it. Maybe that's why they wanted to release him against his wishes. He didn't seem like he was suffering from any mental sort of problem like Lee was. Lee just listened without responding.

"Okay guys. Visit's over. Lights out and in bed." It was the voice of one of the staff. Lee would learn tomorrow that lights had to be out at 10:00 p.m. every night. Paul and Lee had a reprieve this evening only because Lee was new to Oogden.

Whoever had made that announcement left the door hanging wide open allowing the light to shine directly into the room and onto Lee's bed. Lee walked slowly over to the door and closed it enough so that it was slightly ajar. He then went over to the dresser that was now his and momentarily looked at his darkened reflection in the mirror. He gazed directly into the eyes of his image and whispered, "What are we doing here?" Somehow it did not seem like he was talking to himself but rather to another person. Lee did not feel real, but the man in the mirror seemed like he was present and might give Lee an answer. He stared at his reflection for a few seconds and turned to sit on his bed. That guy had no answer either, or, if he did, he was going to let Lee figure it out by himself.

As Lee sat there once more, he began undressing. He easily kicked his laceless shoes onto the floor as he unbuttoned his flannel shirt. He removed the shirt and slid his beltless pants down to the floor. He bent over and removed his socks. That was it. What should he do with his clothes? He was incapable of making the decision about which drawer to put his clothes in, so he decided he would just ball them up on the floor right beside the bed. He didn't think anyone here would care if he wandered around in wrinkled clothes tomorrow. If he would put them in a drawer, he would probably forget where they were by morning and think someone stole them during the night. Yes, best to keep them within sight and reaching distance.

    Lee stood and glanced again at the mirror and saw a frail-looking, very gaunt man. His beard looked white as snow, and he appeared to be easily in his eighties. Lee felt sorry for him. Three months ago that same man was thirty pounds heavier and the picture of physical health. Now his eyes appeared to be sunken, and he had no expression. Lee wanted to stare at him, but he was repulsed by the image and the fact that deep within his mind he knew he was looking at himself. It was too much to bear. He had to look away in a type of frustrated horror. Lee wanted to cry. He wanted to sob, but he was just too… He couldn't find the right word. It was a combination of sadness, fear, frustration, confusion, hopelessness, and dozens of other nameless emotions that would not even allow him to shed tears. There really was no word for it. He wondered why he could cry when he was with Ruth earlier but not now. Maybe it was because he knew someone else cared when he was with her. He felt completely alone now. He knew no one here really cared. How could they?

    He turned again to the bed, pulled down the covers, and with difficulty slid in between the sheets. He reached over to the wall for the switch that turned the light above the bed off. He was exhausted from the trauma of the day, and his joints and muscles ached. He lay there feeling as though he was thinking about everything in the universe but actually thinking of nothing in particular. He didn't know what to think about specifically, so his mind simply raced. His thoughts were one huge jumble of confusion. He wished he could turn the switch off in his brain as easily as he had just extinguished the lights.

    He stared at the ceiling and thought about counting the tiles, but there was not enough light. He looked over at the window and wondered why he was in this room in this place when he should be on the other side of the window and miles away from here living the life he thought he must have lived at one time. Not that he really wanted to be out there in this condition. After all, he was out there only twelve or so hours ago and decided he should be in here. That made no sense to Lee. He didn't want to be out there. He didn't want to be in here, but he wanted to be – to exist. He had not given in to the voices earlier in the day to end his earthly existence. Something would not let him.

As Lee was dwelling on his existence, he noticed the door to his left open slowly, and he heard someone step inside for a moment. He saw a shadow for a few seconds which vanished as abruptly as it had appeared. The door remained wide open allowing the bright lights from the hallway to shine into the room, onto his bed, and into his eyes. He wondered if another resident had opened the door. Surely, if the visitor had been a staff member, he or she would have closed the door at least enough to prevent the light from shining into the room. It must be about… Lee looked around and saw no clock. He had no idea what time it was. He knew for certain that it was late. He got up and closed the door again.

He lay there for a while and thought about the fact that he had taken no medications since his morning dose of clonazepam. He didn't even take his eye drops. He began to obsess over these thoughts, and a blanket of dread quickly fell over him. What if he had a seizure in the night or couldn't fall asleep? Without the clonazepam he could have a seizure. The mirtazapine was for sleep. Now he was certain he would not sleep. No eye drops. Would he be blind in the morning? He could feel his heart and mind starting to race even faster. He tried to calm himself with self-talk and by gently patting his leg. "It's going to be okay. It's going to be okay," he whispered inaudibly.

The light from the hallway slowly crept over the bed again and further into the room this time. He heard someone coming into the room. He closed his eyes and pretended to be asleep. He could hear faint footsteps going toward the window across the room. He opened one eye slightly to see what was happening. He saw a nurse shining a flashlight on Paul. She paused for a long moment, maybe to see if Paul was breathing. She turned toward Lee's bed. He closed his eyes. Through his eyelids he could see a glow from the flashlight being shone on him. He was now being examined for signs of life. He made sure he wasn't holding his breath so that the nurse would determine that he was alive. In a few seconds, she was satisfied and left the room leaving the door hanging wide open once again.

Lee lay there and surrendered to the notion that the door was going to open every ten or fifteen minutes and remain that way unless he got up to close it. He was too tired for such games. He turned onto his right side with his back to the open door. He could hear Paul breathing heavily on the other side of the room. He was jealous. His mind was still racing. He could not sleep.

After another four visits from the nurse with the flashlight, Lee felt himself approaching that twilight between consciousness and sleep. He was suddenly awakened by moaning and wailing from somewhere outside the room. It echoed loudly in the hallway. It continued uninterrupted for a very long time. Lee kept waiting to hear the voice of a nurse comfort whoever was so distraught. He never heard any such voice, no gentle words of comfort from anyone, no words at all. It was as if there was no one else listening to the poor soul uttering his or her deep despair except for Lee. There had to be a staff member nearby. Where was his frequent visitor? Surely she heard the agonizing sounds.

After long periods of time, the noise would stop momentarily and then resume with the same depth of suffering. It was as though the person in misery had to stop to catch a breath.

The visits went on throughout the entire night as well as some form of noise. Loud screaming and shouting from somewhere else in the hall often accompanied the moaning and crying. Lee was too exhausted to try to imagine who was responsible for that and what it meant. He concluded that he was, indeed, in a mental institution.

Lee tried to comfort himself with the thought that his body was getting rest even if his brain was getting no sleep. For what must have been hours, he listened to the noises and he feigned sleep when he was approached by the flashlight. At some point in the morning, he heard normal voices and footsteps in the hallway. It sounded like a new day was beginning and that the dayshift staff had arrived to relieve the nightshift.

Through the window Lee could see that light was returning to the outside world. It was the start of another day. After the strange night without sleep, Lee would have normally welcomed the day, but he knew he was not well and would not likely be well any time soon. As he thought about living another day, this day, a nurse entered the room and announced that breakfast would be served down the hallway in half an hour. Lee just lay there with no physical, mental, or emotional response to the news. He couldn't even recall the last time he felt like eating. The only thing of value about food was that it helped him survive and live one more day. Lee didn't know if that was something to be valued or just a statement of fact. He was alive, thanks or no thanks to food.

Paul was out of bed, dressed, and ready to go. Lee watched him rush out the door as though nothing was bothering him. He was obviously hungry. Lee got up and sat on the side of his bed. He looked down at his clothes balled up in a pile on the floor. It seemed like he had just put them there a few minutes ago.

Lee bent down, retrieved the ball of clothing from the floor, and placed it beside him on the bed. He slid his feet and legs into the jeans as quickly as he could, not wanting a nurse or anyone to see his nearly naked, emaciated frame. He pulled them up to his hips and noticed, as he stood, that they wanted to slide back down. He reached over to the bed and grabbed his flannel shirt. He slowly put it on and buttoned it. It was very large on him since he had lost weight, but somehow it gave him a strange sense of comfort like he was hiding inside a tent instead of wearing a shirt. He sat back down on the bed and picked up the socks beside him. He realized they were the only articles of clothing that still fit. Apparently, his feet hadn't lost any weight. He stood again and slid one foot at a time into his laceless shoes.

He stood for a moment and peered into the mirror on the dresser. He recalled how he would look at himself in the bathroom mirror at home when he would get up in the morning before work. On most mornings, he would look himself in the eyes and say with disgust, "I hate you," to his reflection. Of course, that had to do with the drinking spree the night before after he had promised himself that same morning that he would not pick up a drink.

His feelings about the guy he saw in the mirror this morning were different. He had no feelings really other than pity and confusion. This guy was not disgusting and did not evoke any sort of anger or rage. This guy was pathetic. He seemed like a stranger to Lee although Lee was still oddly aware that he was looking at himself. It was as though he was trying to mentally detach himself from himself in hopes that he was not whom he saw in the mirror. In that way, maybe Lee could be someone else, someone who didn't feel so hopeless or look so pathetic. Lee noticed that the disheveled hair of the man in the mirror had a rooster-like quality. He didn't care.

Lee wasn't really sure where to go for breakfast so he shuffled out into the bright lights of the hallway and followed others who were all walking in the same direction. They went through a door and into a large room which Lee assumed was the community room he was in last night. On the other side of the room was an alcove where other residents were standing apparently waiting for their breakfast. In their midst were two tall carts with several breakfast trays in each cart. Two staff members were pulling trays from the carts and calling out names. Lee's tray was one of the last to be pulled because he was one of the newcomers to the floor and had not ordered his meals for the week yet. This would be a generic breakfast. When he heard, "Lucas," he walked over to the cart and was given his tray by a staff member.

Lee wandered over to the eating area, set his tray on a table, pulled out a folding chair, and sat down. He knew no one at the table and, even if he was capable of starting a conversation, he had no idea what he would talk about. He knew nothing about life other than the constant misery he felt.

He decided to focus on the task at hand – eating breakfast. It occurred to him that he was about to eat the first meal he had ever eaten in a mental institution – scrambled eggs and two small sausage links, a plastic container of some kind of fruit juice, a small carton of white milk, and a banana. First he had to get the little white plastic eating utensils out of the clear plastic wrapper. This proved to be very difficult because his hands were shaking and he seemed to have lost much of his strength over the last several weeks. Something inside him also seemed to be forcing him to try to rescue the utensils as fast as possible from the wrapper which only made the task more arduous and his efforts more frustrating.

After Lee freed the utensils from the wrapper and placed them on the tray, he lifted the lid from the eggs and sausage. He had always loved scrambled eggs and sausage for breakfast. As he looked at them, something inside him wanted to devour them just as he had done hundreds of times in his life. He wasn't hungry though. He wanted to be hungry, but he wasn't hungry. He prodded his memory and tried to get that desire for eggs and sausage back, but he could not do it. He finally decided that he would just force himself to eat this meal and ignore the fact that it would provide no pleasure. Pleasure was something that he hadn't experienced in a very long time. Lee could not remember the last time he enjoyed anything, not even food.

As he sat there forcing down his flavorless meal, he noticed very little conversation. There were inquiries by some of his fellow residents about whether or not he and a few others at the table wanted their milk and banana or anything else that might be edible. There was also some discontent voiced by one of the larger residents claiming he was supposed to have a double portion of eggs, meat, and milk.

Lee wondered what all these people were doing in this place. He wondered what it was about each of them that landed them in Oogden. Some appeared to be in the same mental condition he was in, and others clearly had other problems. Maybe he would learn more about them during the time he was going to reside here.

Somehow Lee had managed to eat his entire meal without forfeiting any of it to one of the other more voracious residents. He picked up his tray and took it over to one of the carts and slid it into one of the slots. He was relieved that breakfast was over and he would not have to force himself to eat again until lunch. He noticed that others were walking over into the community room so he thought he should do likewise. He sat in a chair along the wall across from the windows and waited for whatever was next. He had neither anticipation nor expectation. He was waiting with a mind completely absorbed in its own anguish.

With little interest, Lee glanced at the others who were also in the room. They were quite a motley bunch. No one was smiling. No one appeared to be even slightly happy. That seemed to be a common denominator for everyone. Why would one be happy in a psych hospital unless one was delusional? There did appear to be one individual who fit that description or something similar. His name was Sam. He was a big guy who had sat near Lee at breakfast. His hygiene left a great deal to be desired which was not particularly important to Lee. Sam seemed to have a continuous conversation with someone Lee could not see. The strange thing about Sam was that he was very relaxed and content. None of the other residents could make that claim. Perhaps Sam was the only one who didn't know he was in a mental institution and that his behavior was not normal. At the moment Lee had no idea what the word normal even meant or if there was such a thing. He certainly couldn't remember if he was ever normal. If he had been, it must have been in a previous lifetime.

Lee also noticed that many of the others were very lethargic and appeared to be extremely drugged. There was very little conversation, and the lone topic had to do with a drug named quetiapine. Lee was familiar with the name. He had taken fifty milligrams of that drug one night before bed not too many weeks earlier to get some sleep. It did nothing for him. He was awake the entire night. That was obviously not the case for many of these people. They seemed dopey, tired, and completely unaware. One of the young women had even brought her pillow and was still in pajamas. She apparently didn't have the energy to change clothes or to get up in time to make it to breakfast.

As Lee sat there in a kind of resignation that this was his lot in life, he noticed a young man enter the room and make his way to the front. He clearly was not a resident. He waited for a few minutes for each of the residents to take a seat. Everyone seemed to know the drill pretty well and sat down quietly. When there was silence, the young man introduced himself as John and gave the instructions for the group meeting and some other information.

For the benefit of the newcomers, he briefly explained what the morning group meetings entailed. First, someone from the group would read the various rules of conduct for the meeting. Only one person could speak at a time, and no crosstalk was permitted. There should be no profanity or confrontational language. Most importantly to Lee, everyone had to state his or her name and say something about their morning or previous day and also state what they hoped to accomplish in the upcoming day. Lee was relieved to learn that the rookies of the group (of which he was one) would get a reprieve from that rule, but only once. Lee was safe for now.

After the reading of the rules, the person sitting immediately to the left of John gave her name and began to share her hopes for the day. When she finished, the man to her left continued until, one by one, everyone in the room (except the newbies) had a turn. Lee was unable to focus on any of the words that were spoken. None of it meant anything to him anyway. What could anyone accomplish in a mental ward especially with brains that were so clouded with drugs? He sensed that it made no sense, but he really didn't know if that was a valid thought or just an artifact of his current inability to think clearly.

John's voice interrupted Lee's musing. He made a few announcements. The first was related directly to Lee and the other newbies. Because this was Sunday morning, the regular staff psychiatrists were not on duty. The newcomers would be seen by Dr. Richards this morning for a medication consultation. Tomorrow morning they would be seen by an assigned psychiatrist.

The second announcement applied to those in the entire group whose assigned psychiatrist was Dr. Briggs. It seemed that Dr. Briggs had decided to take a vacation until further notice. His patients would be divided between two other psychiatrists, Dr. Stoker and Dr. Rona. Lee was a bit troubled by this. He had heard one of the nurses mention that he would be seen by Dr. Briggs, but now Dr. Briggs was somewhere a lot nicer than this place, probably the Bahamas where it was warm and sunny in January. Lee tried to put it out of his mind but couldn't keep from viewing this as a bad omen.

The final announcement was that the medication room would now be opening and that everyone needed to be close by to get their prescribed meds. John then left the room. Lee noticed some of the residents beginning to form a line in front of the wooden door at the front of the room. He vaguely recalled seeing that door last evening on his tour with Nurse Jones. As he sat there watching, the top half of a wooden door opened inward, and a young lady stood there and viewed the growing crowd in front of her. This was the medication room, and she was ready to pass meds to the waiting residents. Lee thought it had an eerie resemblance to inmates in a prison chow hall slowly proceeding one-by-one past the servers who put life-sustaining food on each plate. It had a very strange appearance – almost surreal. Maybe more like automatons than prisoners – or both prisoners and automatons. Lee wondered if the drugs were life-sustaining. He thought it to be neither good nor bad – purely an observation.

Lee wondered if there would be any meds for him yet since he had just arrived last night. He waited until the line had dwindled to two people, got up from his chair, and ambled in his laceless shoes toward the end of the line. He stood behind the young lady who was still in her pajamas. She seemed as though she could barely stand. Lee wondered what such a young person with her life ahead of her could be doing in this place. Why was she here? He felt sorry for her but not in the same way he felt sorry for himself. He had lived fifty-six years and was pretty certain his life would soon be over. He doubted he would see fifty-seven years on this earth. His father died at fifty-seven. Lee would probably not outlive him. He didn't really care anymore. This young woman surely could not be more than twenty or twenty-one. She was just a child. Through his own anguish, Lee wept for her from somewhere deep inside. His tears were coming from the same place that strange voice resided – the voice that had kept him from taking his own life only yesterday.

Lee watched her step up to the wooden door and mumble what must have been her last name and a date – probably her date of birth. The young lady on the other side of the door looked down at a notebook, found the name, and turned to retrieve the proper meds, or at least that's what Lee assumed. In a few minutes, she returned with two small paper cups, one of which appeared to contain four or five variously colored pills and the other containing water. She handed them to the young lady who tilted her head backward, dumped all the pills into her mouth at one time, and chased them with the water in the other cup. She gave the cups back without a word and shuffled away with her pillow.

Lee stepped up to the door and waited for the young lady on the other side to return from disposing of the cups she had just been given. When she returned, she looked at Lee and waited for the magic name and date. Lee was looking blankly into the med room for no particular reason. He looked up and met her waiting eyes. "Oh, uh, Lucas. Nine. Twenty-two. Fifty-three." Lee had to process it for a moment to make sure he got the numbers right. Yeah. September 22, 1953.

Again, she peered into her notebook and turned away to find Lee's meds. Apparently, Lee got his name and date of birth correct. She was back in a few minutes with two cups. Lee held the cup with the pills and placed the other cup on the ledge of the bottom part of the door that remained closed. He looked into the cup and noticed two familiar friends. The little purple capsule with the three gold rings. His PPI. And his other friend, a green, one-milligram tablet of clonazepam. Lee was especially relieved to see the green one. Even though he had missed his two-milligram dose last night, he did not have a seizure. The young guy who confiscated Lee's bottle of clonazepam at the emergency room yesterday had been right, at least for now. Lee put both pills in his right hand, put his hand to his mouth, threw his head back, and gulped them down with the water from the cup in his left hand. He put both cups back on the ledge. That was that.

Lee turned and stood by himself for a moment wondering what he should do. No one had given him any further instructions concerning where to go or what to do. He looked around and noticed a few people sitting in the community room staring up at the television on the wall. He had no desire to watch television, and, even if he did, his brain was too cloudy to make any sense out of what he would see. He couldn't follow any plots of even the simplest shows or understand the very same sports he had played and watched most of his life. He decided he would go back to his room. He didn't really want to, but then again he had no desire to do anything. It had been this way for three months, and that was one of the reasons he was now a resident at Oogden, that and the fact that he wanted to die.

As he slowly walked toward the door of the hallway that led to his room, he remembered that he was supposed to see a psychiatrist today, Dr. Richards. Maybe the doctor would be able to help Lee back into the land of the living or at least into the land of the people who wanted to live. Lee had a plan. He would go back to his room and lie on his bed until he could see Dr. Richards. That way the staff could find him easily.

Lee tried to make his way through the haze inside his head to remember his room number. He recalled it was on the right side of the hallway somewhere after the small community room or group meeting room he had seen the night before. He knew it started with a seven, but then, this was the seventh floor and all the room numbers began with seven. He thought if he ambled slowly enough and appeared to be confused, which he was, he would fit right in as someone who was mentally impaired, which he also was. Perhaps, if someone objected to him peering inside their room, they would see that he was even worse off than they were. There was every likelihood that such an assumption was true.

After managing to push the door to the hallway open, Lee noticed the small community room immediately to his right. He was pleased that he had correctly remembered that little bit of information and even more so that it was not something he had conjured up in his imagination. He looked down the hallway and noticed that there were only three rooms on the right side before this part of the hallway ended at a large set of double doors. If he remembered correctly from last night's tour, they were locked. Lee was slightly relieved that he would only have to stare into two rooms at the most. He began walking and tried to nonchalantly glance into the first room as he approached. His visual acuity had gotten very poor in the past three months so he found himself stopping at the threshold of the room and gawking inside. He squinted for a few moments. No one was in the room, for which he was grateful. He looked to the right where his bed would be and noticed that there were objects on the dresser by the bed. It wasn't his room. He had nothing to put on his dresser yet. He turned and continued down the hallway.

As he approached the next room, he looked at the number by the door. 702. That seemed to spark a memory. With less apprehension, he looked into the room and saw someone across the room lying on the bed. It was Paul. Lee was relieved. He made a right turn directly toward his bed and sat down. Safe at last. He hoped that over time the act of finding his room would be easier and less adventurous. 702. He must remember that.

Lee sat there for a few moments and pondered what he should do. What does one do in a mental institution while waiting to see a psychiatrist? What does one do in a mental institution any time? He didn't want to do anything. That was one of the countless reasons he was in this place. Even if he had some sort of desire, he was incapable of even the simplest actions. His cognition had left him weeks ago, and he was just one big mass of fear, anxiety, and depression.

Lee really wanted to get some sleep, but he knew that was impossible. The insomnia had been brutal for many weeks. Even when he could manage a few minutes of slumber, he would wake up in some kind of terror attack with his heart pounding and insides burning. He was almost better off not falling asleep. No. He was better off staying awake. That whole set of thoughts terrified him. He had to sleep to stay alive, but he couldn't sleep. It was as if he was being severely punished and zapped with terror if he even dared to take a nap. He felt like he was stuck between the proverbial rock and a hard place. There was no way out of the sleep dilemma just as there was no way out of this whole mess. Maybe there would be no way out of Oogden now that he was in. Maybe he would be here or in other institutions the rest of his life.

"They gonna let you see a doctor today?" Lee was temporarily rescued from his self-inflicted hopelessness by Paul's inquiry.

"Yeah. Dr. Richards."

"I saw her when I got here my first time. She's just on weekends and gives you something till your regular doctor comes in on Monday," came Paul's reply.

It seemed like a statement of fact to Lee so he said nothing else. He wanted to say something to possibly get something out of Paul that might help him. He was desperate after the scare he had just inflicted upon himself. He wanted reassurance of some kind from Paul that the people in this place would help him. The mere fact that Paul had been in this facility multiple times and didn't even want to leave now essentially answered Lee's unspoken question. He didn't speak.

In a few minutes, Paul got up and walked out the door. Lee knew that Paul was just biding time until Monday when he would try to convince his doctor that he needed to stay at Oogden. Lee wasn't sure what to make of Paul. Did Paul really have some sort of mental condition or was he just addicted to prescription drugs and needed a place to stay? Lee knew he should care, but he didn't. He had overwhelming problems of his own and couldn't try to resolve someone else's woes or even think about them. Lee heaped more guilt on his already tortured brain.

He reclined on the bed and stared at the ceiling. His plan for the day resurfaced in his mind. He was going to wait here in his room on his bed all day, if necessary, until he was able to see Dr. Richards. He didn't have to do anything. The bed was a safe place. He looked up and counted the tiles on the ceiling. Nine and a half across and twelve up and down. He tried to do the math, and after several tries settled on one hundred fourteen tiles. His brain would not let it go, so he ran the multiplication through his head again and again. Still he was not satisfied. He counted the tiles one by one two times through to make sure he was right. There were indeed one hundred fourteen tiles, but Lee found no pleasure in being right. Instead, he was troubled by the reality that his brain could not rest even for a moment. It was a mix of obsession-compulsion, intrusive thoughts, strange existential thinking, catastrophic thoughts, and any other type of thinking that required his brain to run without pausing for the tiniest of moments. It was as if part of his brain was trying to destroy him while the rest of his brain was forced to feel the torture but was powerless to do anything about it.

Lee decided to change the channel inside his head and focus on his plan again. He would be seeing Dr. Richards soon. His thoughts momentarily went back to thirteen years ago when he had his first hopeful encounter with psychiatry and the mental health field. He was desperate then, and the effectiveness of that first encounter and all the ensuing encounters was bleak at best. Actually, his experience with the mental health system thirteen years ago was a fiasco that nearly resulted in his demise, again, at his own hands. Surely, great strides had been made in mental health care in the last thirteen years. At least that was Lee's hope.

It seemed strange to Lee that he could recall quite vividly what had happened to him during his eighteen months of mental torment beginning in the summer of 1997 and ending at the close of 1998, but he could remember at this moment almost nothing else from his life either before 1997 or after 1998 except for the anguish of the last three months. For some reason, his brain could only remember and focus on the greatest miseries of his life.

Lee gave himself permission to journey back to a former time and place of desperation with the hope that he could glean some hope from that experience – a hope that he desperately needed now. Lee stared at the ceiling and returned to late summer in 1995 when the stage had been set for the beginning of the misery of the last thirteen years.

Chapter Four

September 1995

The announcement came as no surprise to Lee as he sat at his desk going over some calculations in a document that he was reviewing. He had anticipated this meeting with apprehension and a feeling of dread for a few weeks.

"That's at two o'clock in Sydner's office," came Arlo's words framed more as a command than an option. "Mike will be there too."

That last statement had some calming effect. Mike Landro was Lee's immediate supervisor. He was an excellent boss – more like a coworker than a supervisor. He was very technically astute and someone Lee could converse with using scientific jargon and concepts knowing that Mike either understood completely or understood enough to ask the right questions. Lee knew that his ideas weren't easy to follow sometimes. Mike was also very fair, and he assigned work that had a purpose. Mike abhorred "busy work" just as did Lee.

Mike worked directly for Arlo Rowan. Arlo was a man "stuck in the middle." He did not wield the power that those above him had at their disposal, but he also was not a true technical staffer. He occupied "no man's land" – that place between the meaningless demands of the often arrogant, self-serving managers above him and the intellectual, frequently arrogant technical thinkers below him. Lee would not trade places with Arlo for the highest salary in the world. No amount of money would be worth the stress, anxiety, and other problems that came with the job. The demands often required deception which Lee would never be able to rationalize in his own mind. It always reminded him of the Bible verse he learned long ago, "What shall it profit a man if he gain the world and lose his soul?" No thanks.

Lee was pleased to be in his current position except when he had to be in the presence of Mr. Jack Sydner. Political correctness radiated from the man. If the work of Lee or others happened to support the politics of an issue, Sydner praised it. If such work provided no political advantage, it was ignored regardless of the work's scientific merit.

Lee once again felt very anxious about the two o'clock meeting. Nothing good had ever happened in Sydner's office when Lee was involved. He suspected that this meeting would be no exception. The current administration was under extreme political pressure on many sides. It was no secret that the governor only had one more year remaining in his second and final term. The time had arrived for the other political party to paint an ugly picture of the flaws of this administration and the mistakes and injustices that it had perpetrated. Its environmental policies would not be spared criticism and embarrassment even if such criticisms were based on pure fantasy. Perception seemed to matter more than truth or substance.

Lee viewed all of this as political "target practice." He knew that the work he had done in the past year would be the subject of the meeting with Sydner. Somehow Sydner would attempt to use it in some self-serving political fashion under the guise of defending the current administration. Lee did not feel that it was yet time for his research to go forward without substantial peer review. He would have a few hours to prepare himself mentally before the certain confrontation occurred and before his project was put on the firing line.

Lee set aside the report that he had been reviewing and retrieved his lunch – a sandwich and some yogurt. Contemplating the impending meeting, he did not even taste the food that he was eating. He got up from his desk and decided to take a walk during the rest of the lunch hour. Perhaps the sunny day and brisk September air would help to soothe the anxiety that had begun when Arlo announced the time, place and subject of the meeting.

As Lee walked through the park, a gentle breeze touched the leaves of the trees causing them to flutter and rustle softly. Lee felt himself relaxing. He thought that it might be nice to be a tree – nowhere to go, no demands, no disappointments, no weariness. He thought to himself that, if trees could think, they probably would like to be human with places to go, things to do, others to visit, and feelings to feel. Maybe being a tree would be extremely boring. It seemed like some sort of paradox to Lee. Perhaps trees were satisfied with their place in creation.

Lee was awakened from his daydream by an approaching man. The stranger was intently bouncing a yellow tennis ball and seemed very nervous. Lee had seen him on the streets many times. He wondered if the man had been bouncing the same ball over the years or if it had to be replaced from wear. The stranger passed by Lee without casting a glance at him. Lee felt strangely sympathetic toward the man. What kind of life did he have on the streets? It could not be very pleasant. What kind of decisions or circumstances had led him to the streets? It couldn't have been anything good. Lee's problems seemed miniscule at the moment. The meeting at two o'clock paled in comparison to the difficulties this poor fellow must surely have to endure.

Lee returned from his walk and proceeded to his cubicle. He pulled out his file with all the work he had done on this project over the past year. He wanted to be completely familiar with every aspect of the work so that he could explain its technical basis and field the questions that would certainly be asked. He also needed to be ready with reasons for why his research should not be used for developing any sort of guidance or policy yet. He knew Mike would back him up on that, but Arlo was "between a rock and a hard place" and would not be able to ward off the demands of Sydner.

Lee checked the equations for what seemed like the hundredth time. He reviewed the text that he would be presenting at the meeting. He scratched some notes on a sheet of paper so that he could explain the technical aspects in layman's terms. Lee was confident that he had prepared as well as he could. He looked at his watch – only five more minutes. With file and scribbled notes in hand, Lee rose and proceeded to Mike's office. Perhaps, arriving at Sydner's office together would give Lee a little more confidence at the outset of the meeting. Mike grabbed a writing tablet and pen and asked, "Ready for this?"

Although Lee knew the question was rhetorical, he responded anyway. "Is it possible to be ready for this? Nothing good ever happens in that office. It's not going to be pretty. I do have my work ready to discuss, but I think that will be a side issue at the most. He's going to talk about other things. Science is just a formality with him – a tool to be used for whatever is on his agenda. Anyway, we better get over there and face the music." There was a tone of resignation in Lee's voice.

The two men began the journey toward Sydner's office. As they passed by others on the way, Lee wished he could trade places with any one of them. He knew his day was about to plummet.

"Have a seat, guys." Sydner addressed them in a feigned pleasant tone of welcome.

The office seemed obscenely large for one person. The front of the office was virtually all glass. This undoubtedly was to give the illusion that the occupant of the office had an "open door policy." In reality, an appointment with Sydner was virtually impossible to get – not that Lee ever had such a desire. The back wall of the office was also one huge window. Being on the fourteenth floor, it provided a stunning view of the Capitol and river. The side walls held a variety of pictures and numerous plaques honoring the years of public service that Mr. Jack Sydner had given to the citizens of the state. Lee felt ill.

There was a large executive desk in the middle of the room and a relatively large conference table by the door. Lee had been to a few staff meetings at that table when none of the supervisors in his work area were available to attend. Those meetings were extremely unpleasant just as he knew this one would also be.

"Thanks. Hi, Arlo," came Mike's response as he and Lee took their places beside Arlo who had arrived earlier and was already seated at the table. Lee said nothing in the way of pleasantries. Mike's greeting had been sufficient.

Arlo began by explaining the reasons for the gathering. Sydner cut in rather quickly and went into an unnecessarily lengthy discussion about this administration, politics and perception. Lee sat there and looked out the window. After some time, Sydner relinquished the floor long enough for Arlo to ask Lee to explain his work. Sydner interrupted one more time asking that the explanation be kept simple. He joked something about Lee and Mike having more brains in their pinkies than he had in his head. It was the typical patronizing approach that Lee had heard many times from this man.

Lee provided a very short, straightforward explanation of his work. At the end, Mike immediately took the floor stressing that the work needed substantial peer review and that there would be many technical and non-technical implementation issues concerning Lee's findings. Sydner ignored Mike's concerns and said he wanted the findings implemented as soon as possible. Mike pressed the matter further. Arlo was silent.

Sydner got up from the table, closed the door, and threw a tirade of cursing and degradation at Mike and Lee. He told them that there were no issues with the report and that Landro and Lucas were not running the show. Lee just stared at the man and envisioned him crashing through the back window and free falling. After about ten minutes of the verbal assault, the meeting was more or less over. The whole thing had the feel of military basic training, but this office was clearly not the proper place for such unprofessional treatment.

Mike and Lee got up from the table and left the office while Arlo stayed probably to get his "orders." Lee knew that the secretaries and rest of the staff had seen the show and were probably relieved that today had not been their turn. Lee felt emotionally beaten and bruised. It was worse than he had even anticipated. In his mind, he kept picturing Sydner freefalling fourteen stories with arms flailing. The vision didn't bother Lee in the least.

In the next three months, the findings of Lee's work were distributed for the world to see. In six more months, the Republican business and industry political hacks had his technical research destroyed. Sydner refused to let Lee defend his results. Lee's reputation as an able and trusted scientist, as well as his work, were virtually destroyed overnight. Lee seethed with anger and bitterness.

October 1995

"You know, Dad, now that I'm thirteen, I can go out with my friends and do things on the weekends."

Lee listened to the words as Lynn and he were taking a leisurely walk through the neighborhood. The air was cool and crisp on this night in late October. Lee could see the vapor trails of their breath as they both spoke. Lee liked this season of the year. It was refreshing. As they walked, Lee was a bit uneasy. Lynn had wanted to talk to her dad about something. On such occasions, Lee knew from the past that the conversation would be in the area of demands by his daughter. In the last few years, Lynn had become very strong-willed – "ten going on twenty." The small, smiling girl who trusted her father implicitly was gone. Lee saw her vanishing into the distance day by day. This evening he had suggested that they walk as they talked. He could always think better on his feet, and he sensed the challenge before they even left the house.

Trying to respond nonchalantly about her proclamation of freedom, Lee replied, "Oh yeah? What kinds of things?"

"Mostly going over to the skating rink Friday and Saturday nights. A lot of kids from school go over."

Ruth and he had often taken Lynn and Michael over to the rink and stayed with them while they skated. Lee would sometimes observe the teens in the rink and outside the rink as they waited for rides. He heard the foul language of many of these kids and watched several of them smoking and making no effort to hide it from anyone. In his mind, this was open-faced rebellion to authority. Lee did not have a good feeling about his daughter being with her friends at the rink without some sort of adult supervision.

"Mom or you could drop me off to meet my friends there and pick me up later," Lynn continued.

"I don't know, Lynn. Some of those kids aren't exactly 'cream of the crop' – swearing, smoking and who knows what else."

"I'll be fine."

Lee knew an older boy from church who hung out there virtually every weekend. He was pretty rough looking and scraggly, but Lynn seemed to think he was cute. Lee had seen him a number of times smoking outside the rink. Lee was not feeling any better about his daughter's insistence.

"We'll see what we can do, Lynn."

"I think three weekends a month would be good," Lynn proceeded with her scheme.

The discussion circled around her plans for the weekends as if her dad were not even walking with her. For the first time in their thirteen-year relationship, Lee realized that his daughter was no longer listening to a word he said. A very real feeling of anxiety and dread fell over him. Suddenly, the sunny, blue sky that he and his family had lived under for so long was being threatened. Lee could sense the dark, foreboding clouds on the horizon.

June 1996

"Good morning, Lee Lucas," Lee spoke into the phone's receiver.

"Lee, Lynn is missing." Ruth's voice was shaking. "She was babysitting over at Alvin and Wendy's. Wendy came home early, and Lynn told her just to drop her off at the strip mall across the road instead of bringing her home. She said it was okay with us. I drove over, and she's not there. I have no idea where she is." Lee could detect the mounting agitation in Ruth's voice.

"Okay, I'll be home on the next bus. About forty-five minutes. Try to calm down. We'll find her." Although his tone was composed, Lee felt like he had swallowed a lead weight.

As he sat on the bus, Lee's emotions were a mixed bag of fear for his daughter and anger that she had lied to Wendy.

Getting off the bus, he walked the short distance to his car thinking the worst. When he walked through the front door, Ruth and Michael met him with tense, troubled expressions. Lynn obviously had not come home yet.

"I've looked all over the neighborhood for her and called up to Brian's. I don't know where she is. I called Wendy again. She said there were two guys in a car in the parking lot that Lynn was talking to."

"I'll go over and look around again. I'll be back. If she comes home, don't let her go anywhere."

Lee grabbed the keys to his car and disappeared out the front door. He cruised through the development quickly to see if he could get a glimpse of Lynn. No. Nowhere to be found. He looked outside the strip mall and inside some of the shops. No Lynn. He called Ruth from a pay phone. No Lynn at home either. He decided to go back to the house.

He walked back through the front door as he had just done an hour earlier to the same worried faces. He sat down on the couch, and the three of them pondered the current crisis. While they were contemplating their next move, he spied Lynn walking up the sidewalk in front of the house. Knowing that Lynn had lied, Lee instructed, "Here she comes. Just let me talk first. We'll get the scoop."

"Hey guys," came Lynn's voice as she entered the living room where they were seated. All eyes were on her, but she was not meeting anyone's gaze. "What are you doing home, Dad?"

"Mom didn't know where you were and called me. Here I am."

"Wendy came home early so I went up to Brian's to hang out for a while," Lynn replied without meeting her father's eyes.

"You could have called."

"I know. I'm sorry."

"Okay. You get one chance to tell us the truth, and I mean the truth. One chance. Do you understand what I'm saying?"

Lynn knew she had been caught in a lie. Lee repeated, "The truth."

She sheepishly looked down at the floor not knowing how much her father knew. "I was up at Brian's and. . ."

"Wendy dropped you off in the parking lot across the street, and you were talking to two guys. The truth!" Lee was getting impatient, angry, and loud.

"It was just Corey and Charlie. They drove me around awhile and dropped me off. I walked home."

"I know Charlie. Who's this Corey, and how old is he?"

"He's Charlie's friend. Eighteen, I think."

"Eighteen?"

"I think so." Lynn began to cry.

"Go to your room. Mom and I have to talk about this. I'm not real happy right now."

The dam broke in Ruth, and she started in on Lynn before she even got halfway across the living room. The scene was ugly – one of anger, stress, worry, and betrayal all mixed into one distorted mess. Lee felt horrible. So, now Lynn was lying openly to them. He hadn't thought that his stomach could feel more knotted than it did just a couple hours earlier. He was wrong.

April 1997

Lee stirred in a half-awake, half-asleep startle. "I must have been dreaming," he thought deliriously. In seconds, he was sleeping again.

There it was again. A doorbell? He looked at the clock on the nightstand – 1:41. No. Who would be visiting at this time of night? He laid there for another minute or so and began to doze off once more. This time the same sound sent a shot of apprehension through all the nerves in his body. It was definitely the doorbell. Stumbling through the bedroom in the darkness and trying to put on a pair of sweat pants simultaneously, visions of pranksters or a drunk or someone with ill intent dashed through his mind.

Lee made his way down the six steps in complete darkness and into the living room. He shuffled slowly over to the window and cautiously peeped between two of the vertical blinds. He hoped that the street light would provide enough light for him to see anyone who might be at the front door. Although his eyes had not yet adjusted completely to the surroundings, he noticed the lights of a car in the driveway – a police car. He peered over to the front porch. There appeared to be one very tall person and one or two shorter ones standing by his or her side. The doorbell rang again as Lee clicked the switch for the outside lights.

Opening the door, he was face to face with a very tall township police officer. At the officer's side were Lynn and her friend, Jennifer.

"Mr. Lucas?"

"Yes."

"I'm sorry to disturb you, but I found your daughter and her friend with Mr. Royal down in the park. They weren't causing any mischief, but they were violating curfew. If you could just sign this acknowledging that they have been returned, I'll be on my way to return Mr. Royal to his home."

Lee's shaking hand turned on the living room light and scribbled his signature on the form. His eyes glanced over at the police car. There was someone in the front seat – Brian Royal apparently, one of Lynn's friends

"Thank you, officer. I'm sorry about this," Lee mumbled with embarrassment as he returned the signed form to the officer.

"It's okay. They weren't hurting anything, but there is a curfew," the officer replied as he turned to walk to his car.

The two girls stepped into the living room, and Lee closed the door behind them. In his anger and disappointment, Lee's only words were "Nothing good happens at 1:30 in the morning. You two could have been killed or raped. I don't want to talk about it now. I'm too tired, and I'm too mad. We'll have words tomorrow."

In silence, Lynn and Jennifer went back down to the family room. Lee turned out the lights and went back to bed. He knew that the girls must have sneaked out one of the windows of the family room. He would have heard them go out the front door. He spent the next hour awake in bed. He was hurt and angry. He thought about the words he should speak in the morning. His feelings were overpowering him. There was a strange sensation running through his body – almost like a low-voltage electrical current. He tossed and turned this way and that but to no avail. Was it caused by being startled out of a deep sleep or the anger and disappointment in his heart? Maybe it was the fear that Lynn was slipping away from him and Ruth. Whatever it was, Lee could sense that it was having a very bad effect on him, and he didn't know what to do about it. Ruth was working tonight and would be home at 6:30. How would he tell her about tonight's incident without her going ballistic? As all these thoughts scrambled back and forth in his head, he fell asleep for a few hours.

Lee's eyes opened again at 6:00. He immediately recalled the incident that had occurred just a few hours earlier. He had hoped that it was a dream, but it was not. He felt that twitching electrical surge through his body. Being wide awake, he went downstairs to make some coffee. When Ruth came home, he was sitting at the kitchen table. "What's wrong?" were her first words.

"Nothing. I just felt like getting up early." He wondered why he even spoke the words. Ruth knew him like the alphabet.

"What happened last night? Something must have happened."

Lee was a terrible liar, and in minutes the story was out. Ruth went down to the family room and woke Lynn up. The three of them sat at the kitchen table and discussed what had happened. Having reasoned with Lynn and thinking that they had filled her with sufficient fear and guilt, Lynn assured them that it would never happen again. Lee was still uneasy. Somehow he knew she could not keep her word even if she wanted to walk the straight and narrow path. Lee sensed there would be a next time, but he had no clue what it would be.

April 1997

"Lee! Lee! What's wrong? What's wrong?" Ruth shouted in terror.

Lee was wondering that himself. He was filled with more terror than Ruth's voice revealed. He had just bolted out of the bed and onto the floor seemingly without moving. He was clutching his chest. His heart was racing at an astounding rate as though it might explode. He was utterly terrified. What was happening to him?

"Lee! What's wrong?"

"There's something moving around in my chest!" he blurted out as he gasped for air. He wasn't in pain, and he had no clue what was happening to his body. As he stood there panting, he tried to take slow, deep breaths to calm himself. His heart rate began to diminish as did his level of panic. In a few minutes, he sat down on the side of the bed and regained his composure.

"There's something wrong inside my chest. I gotta go see the doctor and take care of this," Lee said as he got back under the covers. He glanced over at the clock. 11:21. He had only been sleeping for twenty minutes. That seemed strange. He lay there for a few minutes and worried about what was happening to him. Something very serious was definitely going on. Eventually, he fell asleep.

The following morning was Saturday. Lee tried to sleep while Ruth got up and went downstairs to make some coffee and start the day. Thoughts of the episode during the night began to go through Lee's mind. He tried to logically explain the cause of that "attack" to himself. Nothing definite was coming to him which worried him more. He did recall numerous times when he had dozed off on the sofa or in his chair only to wake up in a "mini-attack" or startle. It felt the same, but last night's was much more intense. Perhaps they were related somehow. Lee concluded that whatever was moving around in his chest was the genesis of this trouble. He would have his chest checked out by the doctor before things got out of hand.

Feeling a bit more assured, Lee got out of bed, put on his sweat pants and tee shirt, and plodded down the steps to greet Ruth and get some coffee. Coffee always made the day seem better. As they sat at the table sipping coffee, they planned the errands of the day. There was plenty of yard work to do. Today was mulching day although there were many other jobs to be done in the yard – trimming, mowing, edging and weed pulling. They also had to pick Michael up early in the afternoon. He had gone to an overnight birthday party.

After a few cups of coffee, Lee put on his jeans and work boots and went out to spread mulch. By noon, he had the huge pile of mulch that had been on the driveway spread nicely around the shrubbery. It was an extremely humid day, and he was exhausted. He felt a strange sensation in his chest, and his thoughts returned to last night. "You're definitely going to see Mr. M.D. soon, old boy." Somehow saying it aloud made Lee feel better.

Having dispensed with the physical labor of the day, Lee went inside and quenched his thirst with water from a one-liter plastic bottle that he kept in the refrigerator. That bottle had been the subject of many discussions between Ruth and Lee. He never felt that it was necessary to wash the bottle – no matter how many times he used it or how grimy it would become. For some reason, Ruth prefered this bottle to be sparkling clean.

Lee guzzled the water from the bottle and set it on the counter. From the morning's activities, it did look pretty nasty – even to Lee. He smiled to himself and rinsed it off. That would please Ruth although she did have this thing about using soap too. "Maybe she won't notice," he whispered to himself in case she was nearby.

He looked at his sunglasses sitting on the dry sink. The lenses were streaked with dry salt from the sweat of his labors in the yard. If Ruth was particular about the cleanliness of his plastic bottle, then she was compulsive about his sunglasses. Lee laughed quietly, "Just do it." He put the glasses under the warm water streaming from the faucet and actually squirted a little hand soap from the dispenser on each of the lenses. After rinsing them, he retrieved a paper towel from the roll on the wall and dried each lens carefully. "There. That should keep me out of trouble."

"You ready to go get Michael?" came Ruth's voice from upstairs.

"Yeah, let me grab a shower first."

Within fifteen minutes Ruth and he were in the car and ready to get Michael. Lee hooked his seatbelt and began backing out of the driveway. Ruth was talking about getting some flowers to plant around the mailbox post later in the day. It sounded like a good idea to Lee. Planting flowers was relaxing and much easier than spreading mulch.

As Lee pulled up to the stop sign at the end of the street, he signaled for a left turn. As he made the left turn, the pressure in his chest returned. It felt like his breath was being taken away. A strange feeling started in his abdomen and rapidly moved up into his stomach and chest. He was suddenly filled with intense panic. He was getting dizzy. He started gasping for air. What if he passed out behind the wheel or even died? The panic increased.

"Lee, what's happening to you?" Ruth screamed.

Lee could only say "Something's wrong." All he could think of was that he was having a heart attack and that he needed to pull the car off the road. Still gasping, he brought the car to a halt by a chain link fence and leaped out without a word. He ran to the fence, put his hands on its top and began taking deep breaths. The strange sensation inside him dissipated within several seconds, and the dizziness retreated. He felt fairly normal again. The intense fear subsided.

Ruth had emerged from the car and was by his side. She didn't know what to say except, "Are you alright?" Lee didn't know the answer to her question. They both stood there for a few minutes and calmed themselves. Returning to the car, they said very little and continued on their trip. Lee couldn't keep from thinking about these attacks or whatever they were. Having them in bed was one thing, but behind the wheel of a car was altogether different. Lee's level of anxiety was growing, and he knew it. He sensed that serious, impending trouble would soon be at his doorstep.

June 1997

For a Saturday morning, the traffic was pretty heavy on the interstate. Lee had always enjoyed driving on this highway for some reason. He glanced over at Michael who was looking out the passenger window. Lee imagined he was thinking the thoughts that twelve-year-old boys think. He didn't appear to have a care in the world. They were on their way to pick up Lynn who was staying at a friend's house. Lee had been there several times in the past year or so. Today he decided to take a different route – one that he had never taken. He was pretty certain that this would be a bit faster and also more scenic once he was off the interstate.

He had his right hand on the top of the steering wheel and was very relaxed as he contemplated the remainder of the day. He had spent three hours earlier in the morning swinging a mattock, digging, and hauling soil in a wheel barrow. He was physically exhausted in a calm sort of way. He was pleased that he had the rest of the day to himself to do whatever he wanted. Maybe he would have a nice dinner out with the family or just stay at home, order pizza, and have a few drinks. He had more than a few drinks last night which he regretted, but he would be more careful this evening and have a bit more control. Alcohol seemed to relax him like nothing else could.

As the car cruised along in traffic, Lee noticed a strange feeling in his chest. His first reaction was to try to rationalize it. Surely, it was not that feeling he got in his chest when he had those bizarre attacks in bed and driving once before.

With that mere suggestion, Lee immediately felt the "whatever it was" start down in his lower abdomen and work its way up into his stomach, his chest, and finally his brain. He started gasping for air and clutching his chest. He tried to breathe evenly and get control, but he couldn't. Michael was still looking out the window without noticing what was going on with his father. Lee was getting extremely dizzy and was becoming terrified that he might pass out on the busy highway. The more terrified he became, the dizzier he got. He began to feel numb with fear. He spoke, "Something's wrong. Something with my chest or something."

Michael looked at Lee in fear as he watched his father gasp for air and clutch the steering wheel tightly. Lee steered the car into the right lane and tried to compose himself enough so that he could explain to Michael what was happening. All he could say was, "We need to pull over at the first place we see."

Lee drove further in pure terror that he might lose consciousness and wreck. He pulled into a large rest area along the interstate. Lee and Michael both got out and walked slowly toward the restrooms. The "thing" was still moving around in Lee's chest. He had never had a heart attack, but he was sure this must be what he was experiencing. Lee was horrified that he might die right there at the rest stop in front of Michael. Sadly, he made the worst of his fears known to Michael who just walked beside Lee without speaking.

Lee noticed a pay phone in the pavilion of the rest area. He called Ruth and tried to explain his dilemma in the best way he could. He was afraid and confused. She was going to come pick him up because he could not muster enough courage to drive back home. He had been so consumed with the fear of dying that he had no sense of how long he had been driving or how far he had gone. He did know that he was at the first rest area on the other side of the river. Ruth didn't really know how far that was, but she would be there as soon as possible.

Lee and Michael spent the next two hours pacing around the rest area. Michael had to listen to Lee talk about his heart and dying and any other morbid thing that would come to Lee's mind and proceed out of his mouth. This was really not the way Lee wanted to bond with his son.

After a great deal of difficulty finding the rest area, Ruth finally arrived with her parents and Lynn in her parents' car.

Lee gave the car keys to Ruth. Michael got into the backseat of his grandparents' car with Lynn, and they headed for home. Lee got in the back seat of his car and lay on his back not wanting to awaken that "thing" in his chest which had calmed for the time being. As they were traveling to the hospital emergency room, Lee tried to explain the last three hours to Ruth but had no real hard facts to divulge except that he was afraid and something was severely amiss with him, but he didn't know what.

Ruth mentioned that Lynn was extremely upset and was thrashing around in the backseat of the car on the way to the rest area because she thought Lee was dying. Lee understood because that is what he also feared. Ruth also told Lee that Lynn was screaming ,"Why is this happening to Dad? He would never hurt anyone. Why is this happening?"

Even in his present state of fear, Lee was both sad and surprised. In recent months, since Lynn had become a teenager, her relationship with her father was rapidly deteriorating. Lynn had a mind of her own and often expressed her activities to Lee and Ruth more as a statement of fact rather than seeking permission. Usually, the activity she planned was not okay, and Lee was always the one to voice his displeasure by forbidding Lynn to do whatever she had her mind set on. It was gnawing away at their once very close relationship. Apparently, Lynn still remembered how they once loved each other. At any other time, Lee would have been heartened with this bit of care and concern, but this knowledge was tempered by the fear that was threatening to consume him.

Even so, there was something inside him that felt compassion for Lynn. The thought of her screaming and flailing moved Lee, especially since he was the reason for it. He wanted to hold her and calm her as he often did when she was younger. He wanted to tell her he would be alright. He realized though that, even if she were here in the car, he couldn't do it. The expression of such compassion was just not in him. His mind was focused completely on himself. He wasn't sure if he would ever be alright again.

Twenty minutes later Ruth and Lee were pulling into the parking lot outside the West Shore Hospital. As they walked toward the emergency room, Lee tried to keep himself as calm as he could and his gait as smooth as possible so that he would not awaken the monster lurking inside his body. He knew the beast was still hiding because it had reared its ugly head many times in the past six months always after Lee had hoped he had seen it for the last time. Maybe he was now on the verge of finally dragging it out into the open so it could be identified and eradicated. This was a hospital, and he would be seeing doctors who surely had dealt with this type of problem before. Lee felt calmer as he rested in that thought.

It was not a busy day at the emergency room to Lee's relief. After going through the check-in formalities fairly quickly, Lee and Ruth were escorted to a small room with the standard examination table, chair, stool, and various other items one would find in any examination room. Lee and Ruth stared at the walls occasionally remarking about what sorts of tests Lee might need to undergo.

After about ten minutes, a doctor entered the room and began asking Lee questions. She was surprisingly unaffected as Lee described the various attacks he had endured in recent months. He particularly emphasized the strange feelings in his chest, the racing heart, and the almost immediate lightheadedness that always accompanied those sensations. When Lee had finished relating his harrowing experiences to the doctor, she got up from her stool, excused herself, and left the room.

While she was gone, a cheerful, smiling nurse came into the room carrying a small cup with some sort of liquid in it. "Dr. Williams would like you to drink this cocktail."

Lee thought for a moment about the drinks he had planned to have this evening. Of course, this was not that kind of cocktail. He assumed it was something he had to drink in preparation for the tests he would now need to take so Dr. Williams could determine what was wrong with him. Lee reached for the cup.

Within thirty seconds of swallowing the contents of the cup, Lee felt completely relaxed and wondered why he had even come to the emergency room. This was a feeling very much like the buzz after a second or third drink of liquor, wine, or beer. The feeling was incredible. Lee was ready to go home. There was clearly nothing wrong with him.

In a few minutes Dr. Williams entered the room and handed Lee a few small boxes of free samples of Prilosec. Lee had no idea what that medicine was so Dr. Williams launched into her diagnosis of Lee's problem, even though, at this point, Lee felt wonderful and was more curious about what was in that cocktail than anything else. The doctor explained that she thought Lee's trouble was a condition known as reflux which could be caused by a number of different things. The Prilosec would keep Lee from having heartburn from the reflux according to Dr. Williams. Lee had been having a great deal of heartburn in the past few months. He wondered how the doctor knew that.

She didn't mention anything about a heart attack, an EKG, or anything else related to his heart or any other part of his body. Her final recommendation for Lee was to make an appointment with his family doctor and have a more extensive checkup.

Right now Lee felt fine and was looking forward to dinner and, of course, some nice drinks when he got home. He still wondered what was in that cocktail.

June 1997 (two days later)

It was late Monday morning, and Lee found himself sitting in the waiting room of West Side Medical Practice. He was flipping through a sports magazine and marveling at how Ruth had managed to get him an appointment so soon after his Saturday debacle. Ruth was one of those people who didn't wait to do whatever had to be done. Lee was a bit of a procrastinator about such things. He would have waited until next week's vacation was over before calling for an appointment. He even tried to tell Ruth it could wait, but Ruth insisted, so here he was. Ruth could not get an appointment with Dr. James whom Lee usually saw. Lee would be seeing Dr. Harper today. Lee had seen him once before and was not impressed with his demeanor. He was too aggressive and direct which made Lee feel uncomfortable.

Nevertheless, Lee thought he should make the best of this opportunity to speak with the doctor about things he had been noticing lately. There were quite a few actually. Of course, there were those nasty attacks he had experienced in his sleep and while driving. A feeling like something or someone was taking control of his body. A numbness and tingling starting in his lower abdomen and rising up through his body. Racing heart. Gasping for air. Dizziness.

There were other things too. He had been having this strange burning sensation in his chest that would go up into his throat and make his tongue and mouth burn. He had tried antacids thinking that it might be heartburn, but they gave no relief. He did notice that, when he drank any sort of alcohol, the burning subsided and disappeared almost immediately. He simply thought that was a strange coincidence. Maybe the booze just relaxed him so much that he didn't notice the burning. And there was the sleep. No matter if he fell asleep during the day or at night, he would always wake up after about twenty minutes in what he called a mini-terror. He would be breathing heavily with a racing heart and feeling the burning in his chest. He would feel afraid. In a couple minutes, the feeling would subside and he would be sleeping again.

There was also another very strange symptom that troubled Lee. Whenever he would walk anywhere, he felt a bizarre type of lightheadedness or dizziness which made him feel unbalanced to the point that he might fall over. It also gave him a weird sensation that he was floating. This was a feeling he had been experiencing for some time, but it was getting worse as the months passed. In fact, a few years back he had been worried that it was caused by a brain tumor, so he had an MRI. It was negative. He even had some sort of test for nystagmus which was also inconclusive. He was given a medication for vertigo which brought no relief. In fact, it enhanced the dizziness. Eventually, he was told that it was probably an inner ear problem and he would just have to live with it.

As Lee was ordering these things in his mind to tell Dr. Harper, he was interrupted by the voice of the nurse calling his name. He responded by rising, smiling, uttering the standard greeting and following the cheerful nurse to Dr. Harper's office.

After the formalities of height, weight, blood pressure, pulse, current medications, and "What brings you here today?" the nurse informed Lee that the doctor would be with him soon and left the room.

For ten minutes Lee looked at all the different medical paraphernalia in the room before hearing a quiet knock on the door. Dr. Harper entered the room, shook Lee's hand, perched on his stool, and proceeded with the rest of the formalities after which Lee expounded upon the issues he had mentally rehearsed in the waiting room.

Dr. Harper sat patiently, listened, and jotted notes as Lee described his lengthy list of episodes, symptoms and concerns. When Lee had finished, he was certain that Dr. Harper would be just as confused as Lee was, but Dr. Harper showed no sign of shock or even a modicum of surprise.

"Do you drink?" was the first question posed to Lee.

Lee had to roll that back and forth in his head before answering. What was the point of such a question? This subject had never been posed to him by anyone in Lee's life prior to this moment. In that regard, it was completely uncharted territory for Lee. He hadn't even thought about it that often other than having the knowledge that, yes, he did drink. Didn't nearly everyone? It was an exception these days if someone did not drink. Did Dr. Harper think that Lee's symptoms were the result of a condition caused by alcohol abuse? Maybe damage to his heart, liver, kidneys, or brain?

Surely, he did not drink beyond what would be within the bounds of typical alcohol consumption. He only drank on the weekend, and even then it was maybe up to a half dozen drinks or so on any given day. It was true that he drank more than others in the family, but then he was much larger in physical stature than anyone else in the family. He found that alcohol relaxed him in a way that nothing else could. Besides, he liked the taste of alcohol. He did have to admit to himself that he always drank way past the "buzz" of the first twenty minutes or so. He was sure that he was not the only one who drank in such a way. He had known many others who "drank to the full."

Still, Lee felt a little uneasy divulging too much information about his drinking habits to Dr. Harper. Lee responded in the safest way he could without telling an outright lie. "A little bit on weekends. Maybe two or three drinks sometimes." There were two or three drinks included in six or more drinks. Right? That was the truth.

"It's not a problem for you then?" came the quick reply from Dr. Harper.

"No," Lee responded uncertain whether or not his answer was true.

The next question completely confused Lee. "Have you ever taken any type of antianxiety or antidepressant medication?" Did Dr. Harper think this was all in Lee's head? Did he think Lee was crazy?

All that managed to come from Lee's mouth was simply, "No."

"All the things you have described to me are symptoms of anxiety. I will write you a prescription for an anxiety medication which you can take as needed and also one for an antidepressant which has been found effective for treating anxiety. I can give you some samples of the antidepressant which you can take before filling the prescription. Make sure you get started on the antidepressant right away because it will take a few weeks to kick in."

Lee wanted to protest, but he didn't know what kind of argument to make about his diagnosis or the medications. He sat there speechless. He had a very dark feeling about taking an antidepressant. Although he had often heard others describe antidepressants as "happy pills," he knew better. Maybe they helped some people, but he knew plenty of others who took them, and they were certainly a long way from being happy.

Lee just couldn't let this happen to him without voicing some sort of objection. "But what about the…" was all he could utter before Dr. Harper cut him off in a tone that was clearly a betrayal of the patience Lee thought doctors should have.

"Anxiety. It's anxiety." No bedside manner in that voice. This had turned into an "I'm the doctor. You're the patient" visit.

Lee sat there and simply nodded. He would sort out the antidepressant issue later.

Dr. Harper got up from his stool, went over to the cabinet, opened one of the cabinet doors, looked through several dozen samples, and pulled out three small colorful boxes. He handed them to Lee. Lee looked at the name on the boxes. Paroxetine. It was a name that was foreign to Lee. Dr. Harper also offered two slips of paper to Lee. These were the prescriptions.

Dr. Harper walked to the door and opened it. Apparently Lee's appointment was over.

As Lee walked to his car, he looked at the writing on the two slips of paper he had just been given. He knew one of the prescriptions was for paroxetine, but his interest was directed more toward the second one. Although Lee did not know what all the numbers and letters on the paper meant, he was able to decipher the name of the drug. Alprazolam. He knew it was a tranquillizer of some sort because someone in the family had once taken it for panic attacks. He would ask her about it. He glanced at the colorful boxes of paroxetine. He had a very uneasy feeling about them and didn't even want to read any of the information inside or on the outside of the box. He was reluctant to take any of those pills.

He got in the car and put the papers and boxes on the passenger seat beside him. As he sat there, he was beginning to feel "that feeling" again – the same one he had only a couple days ago that resulted in a two-hour stay at the rest area. He decided he had better get to the drugstore and fill the prescription for alprazolam because it appeared as though an "as needed" moment was fast approaching.

Lee started the car unaware that he was about to embark on a fifteen-year journey that would include addiction, confusion, hopelessness, pain, terror, and abysmally deep depression. The greatest woes of his life were about to begin.

Chapter Five

January 17, 2010

"Do I really want to revisit all of that?" Lee heard himself say out loud to no one. He was still looking at the tiles of the ceiling in his room. Room 702 of Oogden Institute of Psychiatry to be exact. Lee felt a hint of satisfaction in remembering the room number. He looked around the room to see if anyone heard him talking to himself – not that it would be an unusual occurrence in a mental institution.

He wondered how long he had been lying there remembering the early days of his mental and emotional instability and his concomitant initiation into the world of psychiatric care. "Care" really was not the proper word. "Treatment" was probably more correct. Yes, psychiatric treatment.

Paul had not returned from wherever he had gone, and no one had yet announced to Lee that it was time to see Dr. Richards. So, Lee assumed that he had only been on his virtual journey into his past for a few minutes. It seemed strange to him that he could flip through several months of his past in only a few moments with great accuracy, but he could recall almost nothing that happened to him in the past three months with any precision except for flashes of memory here and there. It was impossible to connect the information from all the flashes into a cohesive set of memories. He could clearly remember that this recent bout of misery started on the first day of his current period of sobriety, October 20, 2009. It began with panic attacks as he was driving to visit his sisters and had not ended since that day. It had been a non-stop nightmare of anxiety, fear, depression, and insomnia.

He got up from his bed and walked across the room to the window for no reason. He felt like he needed to do something. He stared out the window at nothing and sensed that familiar feeling of purposelessness and hopelessness. He needed to find his way out of this mess. It was like looking for a door in a room that had no door. He knew there was no door, but he still kept searching for one. He turned and went back to his bed and lay down.

He thought back to the past that he had visited only a few minutes ago. He had been in a similar predicament at that time – a hopeless place. He knew he had found the seemingly nonexistent door back then and that it had stayed open for eleven years until it closed on him again. Maybe he could find it once more by continuing the journey from which he had just returned. It was a frightening proposition for Lee. Perhaps he could succeed, find the door, and escape. But, alternatively, he feared that he might actually determine that he was insane and had only fooled himself these last eleven years into thinking he was mentally sound. That prospect was terrifying and would seal his fate – or so he thought.

Lee lay there and ran the countless permutations of what a trip back to that part of his past might do to his psyche that was already teetering on the precipice of total destruction. He had nothing else to do right now and already suspected that he was hopelessly insane. In fact, he was nearly certain of it. He knew returning to his past would bring him to a period of eighteen months that were very similar to the three months he had just lived. They were filled with the same kind of seemingly impenetrable mental torment in which he was now drowning. Yet, he did survive that torment and recovered, or at least he thought he had recovered.

"Okay, Lee. Let's do it. Let's go back and finish it. Can't get any worse, right?"

With that, Lee gave himself permission to travel back to the rest of those eighteen months of misery in search of an answer to his current quandary. He had no idea what that answer might be or if there even was an answer. What if the answer was a confirmation of his permanent mental and emotional incapacity? If there was something that might offer even a tiny bit of hope, he hoped he would recognize it.

June 1997

It was a beautiful June morning for a round of golf. As Lee stood at the foot of the slope up to the first tee box, he felt a bit uneasy. It was only a week ago that he had that episode at the rest area with Michael. The following week was not wonderful, but it was not terrible either. He had filled the prescription for the alprazolam and had only taken one of those little white pills two times when he felt "that feeling" coming on. He had to admit that whatever was in those tablets stopped whatever-it-was in its tracks. It seemed miraculous, but the extreme calmness that they granted only lasted a few hours. Though there were many times through the week when Lee felt the "edge" of whatever-it-was, he had managed to get past it without taking a pill. He had only succumbed twice. Lee had always been averse to taking pills. He preferred to deal with pain and problems head on.

Lee was about to play a round of golf with his father-in-law and two friends of the family. In his mind, this was the ultimate in pleasure – a relaxing round of golf on a nice day with friends. It could not get better than this. As the last member of the foursome ahead of them teed off, they slowly walked up the incline to the tee area. Anticipating the beginning of the round, Lee had momentarily let the uneasiness fade from his thoughts. He stood and watched the two golf carts as they meandered up the first fairway. What a great day for golf. He turned and walked to the back of the tee area to take a few practice swings. He slowly pulled the club back into his backswing, began shifting his weight forward, and, as he started the downswing, there it was, that feeling in his chest. On its heels followed immediate terror and panic. Lee's body went numb. He froze. He felt like he would pass out. He wanted to gasp for air but was cognizant of the others in his group and didn't want to scare them or, more truthfully, didn't want to embarrass himself.

Somehow he walked as nonchalantly as he could to the very edge of the back of the tee area and reached into his pocket for the bottle of pills. He managed to open it, retrieve one pill, and put the cap back on without incident. He looked over at the members of the group. They were talking among themselves and didn't notice what Lee was doing. He popped the little white tablet into his mouth and swallowed quickly. He prayed that it would work its magic. He stood for a moment and pretended he was looking at the golfers out on the fairway. He felt himself calming and relaxing within seconds. Wow, alprazolam was great!

Lee teed off last and felt fine. In fact, he could not recall the last time he had been so relaxed and worry free. He was very glad he brought that little brown bottle with him. He didn't understand how a little pill could change pure terror and fear into such a state of tranquility.

The next four hours were wonderful. Lee did not golf all that well, but he really didn't care. He was having a great time laughing and enjoying the warm, sunny day. When the round was over, they drove the carts over to their cars, changed shoes, loaded their golf bags, and began the short drive back to the vacation cottage on the lake.

As Lee considered all the activities he would be doing with Ruth, the kids and the in-laws during this week of vacation, he noticed that "edgy" feeling returning. It wasn't the same sensation of panic he had experienced earlier but rather a nagging feeling that he could not put out of his mind.

Lee had always been a problem solver so he put his brain to work. He knew he had alprazolam at his disposal, but he also knew that he could not just eat it like candy. He would use it for moments when he felt like he was out of control, moments like the one on the first tee. Hopefully, those would fade the longer he used the alprazolam. He could also take one at bedtime to prevent that mini-attack he always got shortly after he would fall asleep. Maybe that would also help him sleep through the night. He had been having more and more trouble with that lately.

If he had any trouble with the edginess in the evening, he could always have a few drinks to calm himself. Lee felt a little better having this newly conceived plan. If it had any kinks in it, he would adjust it and eventually optimize it to meet his needs. One thing he knew. He would definitely need a few drinks when they returned to the cottage. It was okay because it was part of his treatment plan.

After they arrived at the cottage, they shared their golfing stories with Ruth and Pat over a few beers. With that first gulp of beer, Lee knew the plan he had just concocted was working splendidly. Ruth and Pat shared the happenings of their day. Life was good. This was a great vacation. Lee finished his first beer quickly and retrieved another from the refrigerator. He walked outside where Lynn and Michael were sitting on lawn chairs hanging out. Lee pulled up a chair and sat down with his beer. The three of them sat quietly gazing at the lake. Lee was finding it harder and harder to relate to Lynn. They did not connect at all anymore really. Lee suspected that the episode at the rest area last weekend had further damaged his struggling relationship with Lynn. He didn't know how to fix it. He didn't know what to say. So he sat there sipping his beer in silence.

In a few minutes, Ruth and Pat came outside. Since there were only three chairs, Lynn and Michael got up so the women could sit down. Lynn reseated herself on her mother's lap, and Michael sat on his dad's lap. Lee's relationship with his son was quite different from the coldness that had developed with his daughter. Michael had a much different personality compared to Lynn. Michael loved being a kid. He had once said that he never wanted to grow up. It was sort of a Peter Pan complex in Lee's mind. On the other hand, Lynn couldn't wait to grow up and do adult things. That troubled Lee and made him sad. He didn't want her to grow up. He wanted her to be his "Ol Sweetie Pie" forever. That little girl seemed to be gone though.

Pat decided that she should take a picture of the four Lucas's sitting there, so they put on their best smiles for the camera and posed for posterity. Lee wondered what they would all remember in years to come when they looked at that picture. Would they remember the great tensions that existed within the family, or would they only recall the good times of the vacation and pretend they had all been happy in that picture? He pushed that thought from his mind.

Ruth shared the plan for the evening which was to go to a restaurant in the area for fish sandwiches. That sounded good to Lee. He hadn't eaten since breakfast and was hungry from the round of golf. Until then, he would have a few more beers as he sat in his chair enjoying the view of the lake.

Lee felt strange as he got into the bed that night. He replayed the events of the day in his head as was his custom. He thought about the round of golf, the beers, Lynn, fish sandwiches, and the cottage they were staying in at the lake. There was nothing of particular note in the memories one way or the other, but something was causing a sense of discomfort in Lee. He couldn't put his finger on it. It didn't seem to have a source, or at least not one that Lee could identify. He reached across the bed for the bottle of little white pills on the night stand.

"What's wrong?" Ruth asked.

"I don't know. I don't feel quite right. Kind of jumpy inside or something. Maybe it's an 'as needed' moment. Think I should?" Lee always asked Ruth about medical things since she was a nurse.

"I don't know. Do you feel anxious? Can you sleep?"

"I don't know if I can sleep or not. Maybe I should read a while." Lee again reached over to the night stand and replaced the bottle while grabbing a book he had brought along. He lay on his side and leafed through the pages till he found the place he had last stopped. Within minutes he was drowsy and dozed off with the light still on. In what felt like seconds, he awoke in a mini-terror. He was silent and still. He stared at the wall and tried to reason out what had just happened. His heart was racing as it always did when he had such an attack. He knew it was not a problem with his heart, which gave him slight comfort, but what was it? In a few minutes his heart rate slowed, and he was thinking more clearly. It was obviously an "as needed" moment. He closed his book, returned it to the night stand, and retrieved the pill bottle. He took a little white alprazolam from the bottle, popped it in his mouth, swallowed, and reached for the lamp switch. He was asleep within moments.

The next morning Lee felt very...he wasn't sure what the right word was. He had never felt this way in his life. He was afraid somehow, but he didn't know why or of what. What was causing the fear? Where were all the weird feelings he had been having coming from? Why couldn't he decipher his way out of what seemed to be a deepening hole being dug by something inside him? It was something like the feelings he had when his mother died when he was eight years old. He had a reason for that though – grief and sadness. There was no reason for this feeling that he could think of. He had a growing fear, bordering on dread, that he was losing his mind. Was he going insane? What else could it be?

Lee decided to get dressed and go out to the kitchen for some coffee. Coffee always seemed to lift his spirits and get him motivated for the day. When he got to the kitchen, he discovered that a pot had already been made. He poured a cup and went outside to sit. Ruth was sitting there already sipping coffee. "How did you sleep?" came her first words of the day to Lee.

He sat there and thought about the question trying to process it so that he could give an honest answer. He wasn't really sure. He was too troubled by his growing thoughts that he was going insane to focus on the question. He chose the most neutral answer he could think of, "Okay, I guess."

"You don't know?"

"Well, I was asleep so I don't really know." Lee knew the answer made no sense, but he was too wrapped up in his thoughts to care.

Ruth did not respond. She knew from experience that Lee was engrossed in some otherworldly place at the moment and might as well have just grunted a response.

"I don't feel right. Something is wrong," Lee added after a few moments of silence.

"What do you mean?"

"I don't know…I don't know. I feel like I'm going crazy."

Ruth looked at Lee with searching, concerned eyes. "Did you take another pill?"

"Not this morning. Last night," Lee responded wondering if Ruth thought he should take one this morning or not. He had no idea anymore what an "as needed" moment was. "As needed" for what? For these kinds of feelings? He was totally confused.

Ruth sat there silently and did not respond. She apparently had no answer either. Lee wondered if Ruth thought he was losing his mind too. Was it becoming obvious?

That evening Lee sat at the end of one of the docks staring at the sky and the lights reflecting on the lake water. He honestly felt like he was losing his mind. His brain kept trying to process what was happening to him and find a reason for it, but it was impossible. There was simply no solution. He had been a scientist and mathematician for years. He could always find the answer to the problem, but this was a different kind of problem. It reminded him of the null set. No solution. Cannot be computed. Lee was terrified.

As Lee sat there being brutalized by something unknown and unseen, Lynn came down the dock and sat beside him. Even though they had been at odds over the past several months, this seemed like a gesture from a daughter who knew her father was hurting and in need.

Lee struggled for the right words to say to his daughter. He desperately wanted to mend their relationship and reestablish the father-daughter bond that had once been so strong. All he could say was, "Lynn, there's something wrong. I feel like I'm going crazy. I don't know what to do."

Lynn sat there without saying a word. What is a fourteen-year-old daughter supposed to say in response to such a statement? She sat there silently for a few more moments, got up, and walked back to the cottage. Lee felt he had failed. She had given him a chance to begin the healing process, but he was too consumed with his failing mental state to know how to start. He wanted to be the strong, self-assured father she needed, but he had no fatherly words. Lee and Lynn would not connect again in a good way for another year and a half.

The remainder of the week was more of the same. Lee never learned how to swim, so he spent much of his time sitting on the shore of the lake with Ruth and Pat watching everyone else have fun in the water. He was actually somewhat amused when Jerry waterskied across the lake. He wondered how a man twenty years his senior could do this with such apparent exhilaration. Jerry was a man who seemed to have no cares in the world. He had a zest for life. Lee wondered if he himself had ever been so carefree. If he had such moments, they were buried somewhere in his past in a place his mind could no longer access.

Moment by moment for the rest of the week Lee was consumed with the certainty that he was nearing the precipice of complete insanity. What if he tumbled over the edge? What lay at the bottom of the cliff? Was there any way to get back out? He could think of nothing else. He had continued to take his little white pill every night before bed, but it didn't seem to be helping at all. He also had several beers each evening which did take the edge off for a little while, but the dread always returned within a few hours. It was the dread that was sapping the life from him. He was so absorbed in his worry about feelings of fear that he could find no pleasure in anything. He was becoming weary, and hope was dwindling.

Friday morning it was time to say goodbye to the cottage, the lake, and the friends who owned the cottage. Lee was somewhat relieved. Maybe his return home to familiar surroundings would help him to escape these dark feelings. He was doubtful though because this fear, worry and dread were coming from inside him. He was afraid it would be with him and follow him relentlessly no matter where he went.

After a few hours into the drive back home, they pulled into a rest area along the interstate to stretch their legs, get some snacks and drinks, and refuel the car. Lee had spent the entire trip in the back seat staring out the window trying to figure out what was wrong with his brain. Every attempt resulted in the same conclusion. He was, for some unknown reason, losing his mind. There seemed to be no other explanation.

Before they had departed from the cottage, Lee put both his bottle of alprazolam and a free sample pack of paroxetine in his pocket. Maybe it was time to consider the paroxetine. What could go wrong? He would be sitting in the back seat the rest of the way home. There would be nothing stressful. The trip had been very quiet so far. He would be sitting beside Ruth. After all, she was a nurse. It would be okay to give this a try. Maybe it was the answer to his dilemma. The solution to his problem might be in his pocket.

He watched as Pat finished paying the lady at the cash register for some snacks for Michael and Lynn. He reached into his pocket and pulled out the colorful cardboard packet of pills. He opened it and pushed one of the small red pills through the aluminum blister on the back. He put the pack back in his pocket, popped the tablet into his mouth, walked over to the water fountain, and took a few swallows of water. This was it. He was cautiously hopeful.

On the way back to the car, he mentioned to Ruth that he had taken one of the antidepressants. Ruth had always known that Lee was averse to taking nearly any medications. He typically wouldn't even take an aspirin unless he was in extreme pain, but these were clearly not typical times. He had already taken alprazolam for a week which was an admission that he was in some kind of distress and an indication that he was desperate for relief. Taking an antidepressant was completely beyond the convictions of the man she had married. She never could have imagined the time would come that Lee would succumb to doing something so drastic. She was worried. He was being tortured. She felt sorry for him.

"You did?" was all she thought she should say.

"Yeah. We will see," Lee responded in a doubtful voice that he tried to make as hopeful as he could, more for himself than for Ruth.

As they cruised down the interstate, Lee resumed staring out the window and thinking about his sanity. He wondered how long it would take for the paroxetine to work or if it would do anything at all. Dr. Harper had said something about it being a low dose that Lee would probably have to increase over a few days until it would then be considered effective. Lee wasn't sure what that meant. He recalled Dr. Harper also saying something about antidepressants taking several weeks to "kick in" completely. Lee supposed that "kick in" meant "become effective." He didn't really want to wait weeks to feel sane again. Well, at least he had taken the first dose. Maybe he was on his way.

Fifteen minutes later Lee realized his wait was over. It started as that strange feeling in his lower abdomen and rapidly progressed up through the rest of his torso and into his head. In an instant he was in pure terror. But it didn't stop there as it had in all the other attacks he had experienced over the past several months. It felt like something must have exploded inside his chest and traveled to every other part of his body within seconds. He felt like he was vibrating inside and outside. He felt like he could not sit still. He was extremely restless. The restlessness seemed to be at the very core of his being. He didn't just want to jump out of his skin. He wanted to explode into millions of pieces so that this horrendous sensation would be gone. It was unbearable.

Lee tried to appear calm on the outside and not move, but he must have given himself away. "What's wrong?" Ruth whispered as her eyes widened. Apparently he hadn't done a good job of appearing at ease.

Lee could only shake his head. He had no idea what was happening. He was terrified. He wanted to scream but didn't want to startle everyone else. He sat there beside Ruth and began rocking back and forth. He couldn't sit still. His eyes glanced over at the door beside him. He thought about opening the door and jumping out so he could end this torture. Ruth put her hand on his thigh and tried to calm him. All he could do was look at her in terror.

For the next several hours Lee sat in a nearly catatonic state and tried to focus entirely on nothing. He hoped that if he could put his mind in some sort of suspended animation that he might be able to make it home without jumping out of the car. Lee was very familiar with pushing through physical pain and exhaustion, but he had never experienced anything like this type of pure mental anguish. He sat in his seat between Ruth and the car door and rocked back and forth quietly with only one thing on his mind – survival.

Six hours later the car was pulling into their driveway. Lee felt like he was in another world. He recognized the house but felt no attachment to it as though he had never been in this place. He could remember nothing since he had entered into his self-imposed survival mode. He had no idea if anyone had spoken to him during the remainder of the trip or if they had made anymore rest stops. He was unaware of anything except the fact that he was extremely....extremely...something. Was he ill? Was he having a nervous breakdown? Was this some sort of reaction to that little red pill? He had no idea, but he knew he had to move. He couldn't stay in the car any longer.

He reached for the door handle and noticed his hand shaking. Every part of his body had a very fidgety sensation inside. It was an inner feeling of being tickled or having ants crawling around. It was relentless and felt like torture. He had to move. He opened the door and immediately began walking down the driveway and away from the house. He couldn't stop to help unpack the car or say thank you, good-bye or anything. He had to walk. He had no choice. He knew it was rude. He didn't care.

He didn't even look back to see if anyone noticed his departure. He simply had to get away from… he wasn't sure what. If he walked far enough, he might be able to make this torture end. Or maybe if he walked fast enough, these horrid sensations would leave. With that thought came the whole "I'm going crazy" narrative again. That's what this was. Insanity. He had finally gone over the edge. This was it. This was what craziness was like.

Lee was now walking as fast as he could without running. In ten minutes he found himself at the end of the sidewalk. He turned around and headed back toward the house. His mind was racing and probing any nook and cranny that might give him some sort of answer for what was happening to him. But it always followed the same mental path that led him back to the same conclusion. There is no solution. But there had to be a solution. There was always a solution. His brain kept rummaging through anything that might yield a clue.

Lee walked for two hours and was mentally and physically exhausted. The agitation was dying off for now. He could not go on. His pace had slowed and so had his mind – not because he found the answer to the unanswerable question but rather because he was fatigued. He walked across the lawn to his house and entered the living room through the front door.

Ruth was somewhere downstairs probably doing the laundry from the vacation they had just returned from. Lee wasn't sure if she would be angry with him for not saying good-bye to Pat and Jerry or if she would be concerned for him and let his rudeness pass without comment.

Lee sat on the sofa and noticed that he still had some residual vibration inside. He felt like his body was idling like a car at a stop sign. He got up and started pacing between the living room and kitchen even though he was physically drained.

"Are you okay?" came Ruth's voice behind him.

"No," was all he could reply. He didn't know how to elaborate on his answer.

"How do you feel?"

Lee thought about that question for a moment. How would one describe these kinds of sensations? They were too bizarre to be described, and, even if he could, Ruth would think he was crazy. Maybe he was. He really didn't know. "Uh. Weird." It was the best he could do without going into the indescribable and unbelievable specifics.

"Weird? How?" Ruth wasn't giving up.

The rest of the evening Lee paced between the kitchen and living room trying to explain his feelings while Ruth sat and listened. Occasionally he would succumb to tiredness and sit down for a few seconds. Ruth listened attentively without remarking much. Neither of them could determine if this episode was related to the antidepressant or just some sort of anomaly. Maybe the condition for which he was taking the paroxetine was resisting the effects of the paroxetine and the condition would yield shortly – kind of like an infection resisting an antibiotic. They both agreed that Lee should continue taking the paroxetine. Surely it would smooth him out if given enough time. Tomorrow would be better.

The next morning was Saturday, and Lee was very tired. He had only slept about two hours during the night. He had even taken an alprazolam before bed. Ruth was still in bed so Lee made a pot of coffee and sat in the living room wondering why he couldn't sleep last night. Was it the effects of the paroxetine, or was he really going insane? These thoughts dogged him continually. He could think of nothing else. He had just gotten out of bed and was already mentally weary.

As he went into the kitchen and poured a cup of coffee, he heard Ruth coming down the stairs. "How are you this morning?" came the question. No more simple answers would suffice. The question had become much more difficult to answer.

"I don't know. Tired I guess. I didn't sleep much."

"Did you take an alprazolam?"

"I did, but I still hardly slept. I don't know."

"Once the paroxetine gets into your system, like Dr. Harper said, maybe things will get better."

Lee had been thinking about that little red pill. He was almost certain that was what caused the indescribably horrible feelings yesterday. He didn't ever want to experience that again. "I don't know. I think it caused that mess yesterday. I never felt anything like that in my life. Maybe I shouldn't…"

Ruth cut him off in mid-sentence. "He told you it takes a while to take effect. You need to take it."

Lee was in no mental state to argue or put up any sort of defense, but the possibility of a repeat performance of yesterday's episode was terrifying. "But what if…"

"No. If you stick it out, things will smooth over. He said so."

Lee thought for a moment. He was not a doctor. That was Dr. Harper's job. He was the expert. He should know. It really would be wonderful to feel like Lee Lucas again. He felt a little hopeful. "Well, okay. Maybe it will be better this time."

He picked up the sample box, took out little red pill number two, and swallowed it with the remaining coffee in his cup. Surely his body would be more adjusted having already experienced the drug once. Feeling a bit of courage and some confidence, he poured another cup of coffee and went into the living room to sit in his chair.

He looked out the window at the new day. It was sunny, but the sky was grey and hazy. It looked more like a morning in August instead of June. It must have been very hot and dry here during the week of vacation because the grass on the front lawn was beginning to turn brown. He gazed at the mountain through the haze. Somehow the mountain always gave him comfort. He wasn't sure why. Maybe it was because it was big and immovable. It always stayed right there before his eyes.

Lee took a sip of his coffee and tried to focus on the day. Today was the Lightfoot reunion at Caledonia Park. Although he didn't care much for reunions or any type of social gathering, there would be lots of food, and he loved to eat. He typically said as little as possible and just listened to others talk. He had always been that way.

As he was contemplating what he should do before getting ready for the reunion, he noticed that familiar strange feeling lurking in his lower abdomen. In a moment, as if a switch had suddenly been thrown, he was overtaken by terror and rocking back and forth in his chair. It was back, and it was as strong as the day before. His thoughts immediately turned to survival.

He felt like he would explode. He went upstairs and put his sneakers on and hurried out the front door. For the next two hours he walked the same course he had walked only yesterday. Lee was exhausted, but he had to move. Ruth saw him leave but didn't know what to do or say. What was happening to her husband?

When he returned, he sat down on the chair beside the living room door fatigued but still rocking from side to side. His hands were shaking as he bent down to untie his shoe laces. He could barely grasp the strings, not so much because of his shaking hands, but more because he could barely sit still long enough to do it. It felt as though his brain was forcing him to keep moving.

While he was bent over fumbling with his shoes strings, Ruth came into the room. Lee stared up at her with wide, terror-filled eyes and a look that must have revealed how hopeless and confused he felt. He wanted to cry, but he couldn't. He was completely baffled. He had no idea what was happening to him. Ruth felt as though she had betrayed him by insisting that he take that antidepressant. Yet, was it the paroxetine or something else? She was as confused as Lee, but she had been trained to follow doctor's orders. It had to be this way. Surely Dr. Harper knew what he was doing.

Lee finally got his shoes off and sat back in the chair. He looked into Ruth's face with tears in his eyes. He had no words. She had no words. They just stared at each other for a moment.

Lee took a deep breath and exhaled. He shook his head and said, "What am I going to do?"

Ruth didn't know what to say but thought that, if Lee could somehow focus on something else and get through these next few hours while his body adjusted, he would be okay. She proceeded with her answer to Lee's question, "Maybe if we go to the reunion, you can eat and relax and get your mind off this."

The thought of going anywhere, especially somewhere with people, sent chills down Lee's back. "I don't know. I don't think I can."

"We said we would be there. We can just go down and stay a little while, eat and come back home. You can just sit in the car, and I'll drive."

Lee cringed at the idea. He thought about trying to convince Ruth that he could stay home alone while she went with Michael and his friend, but he didn't want to be alone. He was afraid of what he might do to himself.

"Okay." Lee yielded to Ruth's suggestion and tried to convince himself that he could do this. He had no idea how that was possible.

Three hours later Lee found himself sitting at a picnic table among dozens of family members. He was in a mental daze. He was flanked by members of his more immediate family as though he was being protected. Maybe he was. He didn't know.

Ruth brought him a plate of food – hamburger, potato salad, baked beans, and some chips. He stared at it. He had absolutely no appetite. None. He simply could not eat this. He forced himself to take a bite of the hamburger as tears fell from his cheeks. His hands were shaking, and his mouth was parched. He could barely swallow. He knew that he loved these foods, and that only added to his certainty that something was severely wrong with him. He did his best to make it look like he was eating.

Somehow he managed to eat about half the food on the plate in silence. He sipped a soda with each bite so he could swallow. One of Jerry's sisters came by and wanted a picture of Jerry and Pat with their family. So Lee walked with the rest of the family to pose for a picture at another location. Lee wondered if those viewing this picture in years to come would notice the overwhelming sadness on the face of the tall guy standing in the back row. He had had the same thought about the picture taken by the lake only a few days earlier. He felt even worse now than he did then. That didn't seem possible.

Somehow he survived the family reunion and the ride back home. After Ruth parked the car in the garage, Lee went inside the house, put on his sneakers, and went outside to walk the walk he would repeat hundreds of times in the next eighteen months. He tried to reflect on the day and all that had happened, but all that came to his mind was feeling like a zombie in the car, the plate of food he could not eat, and the picture taken of his family that included the saddest and sickest man on earth. He was numb. He had no answers and was too tired to continue the hunt for them. He simply walked without hope or purpose. He walked because he could do nothing else.

The next morning he woke up with no desire to meet the day or to do anything. His hope that the little red pills would help him was a thing of the past. He simply could not wait weeks through this much misery for the paroxetine to "kick in." How could someone be expected to go through such hell on earth before getting to a good place?

Maybe the pills were designed or formulated to make a person so utterly miserable that, once the brain adjusted to their effects, life would seem wonderful. Perhaps they worked on the basis of mental and emotional relativism. Maybe feeling "good" was the same thing as feeling "less bad." Less bad would feel wonderful now. Lee didn't think it was possible to feel worse than he currently did. The thought crossed Lee's mind that taking this drug was similar to his years of smoking. When he started smoking, he coughed and hacked and felt miserable, but once his body adapted, he liked it. Maybe taking an antidepressant was the same thing. Misery followed by enjoyment. Of course, there was the addiction part too. If Lee could just feel normal again, addiction would be a small price to pay – at least for now. Still, even the misery of the first few cigarettes he smoked back in the day was pretty benign compared to this variety of anguish. He didn't think he could survive another day if this agony continued. There had to be another way.

Lee got out of bed and went downstairs. Ruth was already up and sitting in the living room with a cup of coffee.

"Go ahead and get a cup of coffee. I made a full pot," she announced to Lee.

"That's okay. Don't feel like coffee today." Lee could not remember the last time he turned down his morning cup of coffee.

"What's wrong?" Apparently Ruth couldn't remember the last time either.

"I don't know. Just feel weird." He already felt shaky and knew coffee would only enhance that feeling.

"Weird?"

"Yeah. Just…uh…shaky and antsy. Weird."

Lee hoped Ruth would not mention the pills. He wanted to explore other options once his brain cleared up and his edginess settled down.

His hope was short-lived. "Don't forget to take your pill."

"I don't know if I can," Lee's voice was filled with dread.

"I think you should. It's only been two days."

Lee felt like crying. He honestly didn't believe he could handle three days of feeling this way. The last forty-eight hours had been the next thing to humanly unbearable. "I don't know. I feel so strange."

Ruth went to the kitchen and got the third paroxetine tablet from the dry sink. She brought it to Lee with a glass of water. "Here."

Lee knew there was no use trying to explain how indescribably bizarre the paroxetine made him feel. Ruth could not possibly understand. He took the glass of water and pill from her while looking at her with pleading eyes and hoping that she could see the utter anguish in them. Maybe he could get a reprieve. He had no energy to argue. He swallowed the pill.

He waited to see if the results would be different this time. Third time is a charm. Right? Wrong. In twenty minutes, like clockwork, the inner explosion of extreme agitation returned. The restlessness from yesterday's pill had not worn off yet. "Oh, God, please help me!" was all he could say. He sat for a moment and rocked back and forth thinking that maybe it would pass this time, but it did not dissipate. He wanted to explode. He had to move.

Upstairs. Sneakers. Out the door. Ruth could only watch.

Lee was certain he would lose his mind completely this time. This was worse than the first two days. He walked and walked and walked until he was too exhausted to go on. He went inside and sat in the living room. He was totally fatigued, but he still had to move. Something inside would not let him be motionless. He was being tortured. He rocked back and forth.

Ruth came in and sat in the chair on the other side of the room and watched Lee without saying a word.

"If I have to take another one of those pills, I am going to go outside and kill myself." It was not a threat. It was a statement of fact. Lee would simply walk out to the highway and throw himself in front of an eighteen-wheeler. End of story. End of torture.

All Ruth could say was, "Okay. No more pills."

The rest of the day Lee did anything he could to survive. He paced. He walked outside. He sat and rocked back and forth. He could not rest. He could not eat. He could not focus on anything but this never-ending anguish. Tomorrow he would call someone who knew how to deal with this. He wasn't even sure who the experts were. Psychiatrists? He didn't like the thought of seeing a psychiatrist. That would give him a label, but right now he didn't care. He would take help from anyone and deal with the stigma later. It could not be worse than this. Tomorrow he would search for help. He just had to survive until then. Maybe he would feel slightly better tomorrow.

Somehow Monday morning did arrive. Going to work was out of the question, so Lee called the office and told the secretary he was not well and would not be in today. He sat in the chair by the front door and wondered who he should call about his problem. He was certain that the paroxetine had thrown him into this downward spiral that seemed to have no bottom and no inclination of allowing him to slow down. He had taken an alprazolam last night before bed, but it didn't seem to do any good. The relentless restlessness that enveloped his body and mind was punctuated by short episodes of fitful, broken sleep that may have totaled an hour or two. He seemed to be even more restless than he was yesterday. He wondered how that was possible.

As he sat in the chair shaking and rocking, he thought that he might feel better gradually over time if he just stopped taking the antidepressant. He wondered how long it would take the drug to clear his body completely. Surely he would begin to feel better then – or at least not as bad. He remembered that he had taken the first little red pill because he felt like he was losing his mind. This was light-years beyond the fear of insanity. This was purely survival mode. Maybe if he could get back to just the dread of going insane he would feel comparatively normal. Perhaps surviving this torment would "cure" him in a sense. One thing was certain – he could not exist in this state of mind for much longer.

Lee thought that it was probably time to talk with an expert, so he shuffled to the kitchen and got the phone book. He opened it to the yellow pages as he began pacing back and forth between the kitchen and living room. He simply could not get his body to be still, and his mind was racing even faster. But, if he wanted to find a source of help out of this torment, he had to concentrate as best as he could on the words in the phone book. Somehow he found something called "psychological services" and decided that was a good place to start. There were only a few names to choose from. He settled on State Counseling Services. He was shaking, and his mind was not cooperating at all. He wanted to run out the door and never stop.

He tried to focus on what the next step was. Okay. He had to write the phone number on a piece of paper. He placed the phone book on the counter and opened the drawer to the dry sink. He grabbed a small sheet of scrap paper and a pencil and closed the drawer. He returned to the counter and placed the paper and pencil beside the phone book. He leaned on the counter with his head down and waited for his brain to discover the next step in the process.

After another twenty minutes of going step by step through the process of writing down the phone number, he was finally sitting in the chair by the front door with the paper in one hand and the phone in the other. His brain went through countless scenarios of what he might encounter on the other end of the line after he dialed the number. He struggled to decide what he should say for each of those scenarios. He finally gave up and looked at the phone. He did his best to hold it steady as he slowly pushed the buttons. He listened as it began ringing. He was startled as the ringing stopped and a voice began talking. "State Counseling Services is not open for business at this time. If this is an emergency or if you are suicidal please hang up and call 911. Our offices will be open at nine a.m. Thank you."

Lee's whole body was shaking and his brain felt like it would explode. Making that first call was monumentally difficult, and he only got to listen to a machine. He would have to do it again. He didn't know if he could. He felt like he should call 911 and just be put away somewhere where they might put him out of his misery.

It was only 8:35 so he put the phone on the stand beside the chair and got up and paced. He tried to fathom how he would be able to make another call. The first one had been almost impossible to make.

He paced for another forty-five minutes until he was exhausted and returned to his chair. It was 9:20 so someone would surely answer this time. He picked up the phone again and pushed the same numbers. He closed his eyes immediately in an effort to focus on whatever he was about to hear and how he might respond to it.

On the fourth ring came that voice again making the same 911 announcement and then proceeding through a list of options that Lee had no chance of following. He hung up after all the options had been announced. He knew he didn't want to talk about billing or insurance, and he had no idea which of the several counsellors and therapists he should see. He was irritated in a confused way. If these people were experts in helping individuals with anxiety and other emotional sensitivities, why would they make the process of getting help so difficult?

The mental health system had not been very kind to Lee thus far, and he was painfully aware of it. He was quickly developing a displeasure for this whole ordeal, but he knew he had no choice. There were no other options (except for the ones he had just heard on the phone). Surely the individuals working in the system had more compassion than this. Didn't they know how desperate he was?

Lee felt completely defeated. He stared at the wall across the room with tear-filled eyes and wondered how this could possibly end well. He had exhausted all of his mental strength and energy trying to make a simple phone call. He was too demoralized to pace so he sat there shaking and wishing he could be anywhere but where he was. He wasn't even sure where he was – inside his head somewhere trying to get out…but he couldn't do it.

Ruth came into the room and saw Lee sitting there in a state of quiet agitation and wearing a glazed expression. She saw the tears in his eyes.

She proceeded delicately. "Did you get through to them?" She didn't wait for the answer that she knew would not come. "Would you like me to call?"

Ruth had a way of knowing what Lee needed without him even asking. "Yeah. Please. I can't do it."

Ruth let that statement pass because she knew it was true. She reached for the phone and pointed at the sheet of paper with the number scribbled on it. "Is this the number?"

Lee nodded. "Yeah."

Ruth looked at the number and began pushing buttons on the phone calmly and without hesitation. Lee watched Ruth's face as she listened to the voice on the other end of the line. He could see that she wasn't particularly thrilled with the long menu of options either, but she must have been able to make some sense of it because she pushed another button. In a few seconds, Lee could hear another voice through the receiver.

Ruth spoke. "Yes. My husband is having some problems with anxiety and depression. No, not suicidal."

Lee acknowledged to himself that her statement was true for the moment but would not be if he didn't soon get some help.

The conversation continued. "No. He's never been there. I don't know. Let me ask my husband."

Ruth turned to Lee and asked something about insurance coverage. Lee took a moment to process the question. He walked out to the dry sink to get the insurance card from his wallet. He could hardly hold his hands still, and his brain was in fast forward. He wanted to give the wallet to Ruth and let her find the card while he went somewhere else, but he managed to persevere and found the card. He pried it out with shaking fingers and handed it to Ruth who was once again engaged in conversation.

"On the back of the card? The mental health care provider. Okay."

She put her hand over the receiver and directed Lee to look on the back of the card for the name of the mental health care provider. Lee complied and stared at the tiny print on the back of the card. He reached for his glasses on the dry sink. He tried to slow his brain down enough to find the name. He handed the card to Ruth. One more failure.

Ruth scanned the card quickly and spoke to the person on the phone, "Behavioral Health. You do? Good. I don't know. Just a moment."

Ruth turned to Lee. "She wants to know who you want to see – which therapist."

Lee was agitated. What was wrong with these people? "How am I supposed to know? I've never had a nervous breakdown or whatever this is. Don't they understand that?" He was shaking. He felt bad about yelling at Ruth.

Ruth put her hand up for Lee to be quiet. The lady on the phone was talking. She must have heard Lee. Ruth responded to her voice, "Okay. You do? She is? Okay. Hold on."

Ruth looked at Lee again. Lee felt guilty that Ruth was stuck playing middle man in something that was his own problem. "She recommended one of the therapists there, Jenn Franklin. What do you think?"

"Yeah. Okay. I don't care," and he really didn't. He just wanted to get things moving.

Ruth was on the phone again. "That's fine. Yes. As soon as we can. Tomorrow at two? Okay. Thirty minutes early. Okay." Ruth hung up the phone.

"You have an appointment tomorrow at two with Jenn Franklin. We have to be there early to fill out some paperwork."

All that Lee heard was the part about the paperwork. How would he do that?

Tuesday afternoon found Lee and Ruth sitting in the waiting room of State Counseling Services completing forms. When they had arrived, Lee checked in with the receptionist who directed him to a clipboard on the wall. Lee noticed that each clipboard had the name of some sort of drug on the clip part. Sertraline, valproic acid, and venlafaxine were foreign to him, but he knew paroxetine personally and had certainly heard of fluoxetine. He recognized olanzapine as the drug Ruth took for schizophrenia. The clipboard he chose held a plethora of papers about a quarter inch in thickness. This was the dreaded paperwork Lee had been concerned about and which he was now trying to complete to the best of his ability and mental state. Somehow he did manage to answer all the questions. He hoped he wouldn't be graded for the content or his penmanship.

As he sat there, he looked at his surroundings. The room was small and shabby and had too many chairs for its size. The chairs were of assorted sizes, colors and conditions. Some had obviously been there for many years. There were a couple small tables with magazines haphazardly strewn across them. Lee noticed a Gideon Bible that he had grown accustomed to seeing in doctor offices and hotels. He was actually a dues paying member of the Gideons. He had been an active member at one time but was now reduced to having only long ago and far away memories of something that he once enjoyed.

Lee returned his attention to the waiting room. One of the first things he had noticed upon entering from the outside was the sliding glass window between the receptionist area and the waiting room. A sheet of paper was taped to it with the following warning printed in large letters: "DO NOT KNOCK ON WINDOW." Lee thought it was a very unfriendly way to greet people who were clearly having emotional and mental difficulties. The receptionist was even less friendly than the sign in the window. Maybe it was a toss-up. Lee wasn't sure.

Lee scanned the walls of the room. The walls beside the door and in the front of the room were covered with all kinds of posters, pamphlets, and brochures with information about all manner of mental and emotional conditions, illnesses, disorders, and problems. Lee wondered what the proper term was. It was as if someone wanted you to know that there was something obviously wrong with you if you were sitting in this waiting room. Major depressive disorder. Generalized anxiety disorder. Bipolar disorder. Panic disorder. ADHD. These were the most popular disorders. It seemed like "disorder" was, indeed, the proper term for mental and emotional pain and anguish. Lee wondered which of these disorders he had. Maybe he had one that they hadn't found a name for yet – a new classification. He hoped not because he was certain that these disorders must be treatable since they were so popular. In fact, every bit of literature on the wall said, without exception, that that disorder was treatable and that there was hope. Lee knew he should be heartened by those words, but this place certainly didn't give the impression that it was first rate or even second rate. It was third rate at best and had a very strange, musty odor to boot.

Lee glanced at some of the other clientele in the room with him. There were men and women, young and old. They all had one thing in common. Not one of them smiled or showed any type of emotion. Nobody was making eye contact. Everyone was looking down at the floor or peering around nervously. No one appeared happy – not even the receptionist. It felt like a morgue with breathing corpses. Lee felt sorry for each one of them because he knew how they felt. He looked like they looked. If there were such great hope and successful treatment as the posters on the walls proclaimed, why was not one person in that room even remotely happy? Lee had a very eerie feeling. This place did not improve his wavering perception of the mental health care system. He sat there without expression with his comrades-in-suffering and waited to see a therapist.

At 2:01 the door beside the receptionist area opened, and a woman of perhaps fifty years questioned, "Lee Lucas?"

Lee and Ruth both stood and walked toward her. She smiled as she greeted them, turned and walked back a hallway. Ruth and Lee followed her to her office. For the next ninety minutes Jenn Franklin and the Lucas's talked and learned a little bit about each other. Jenn was very pleasant and quite attractive – at least to Lee. She had experienced some very difficult things in her own life and described some of those to Ruth and Lee. She had certainly known anxiety and depression at different points in her life and was not reluctant to share that information. That put Lee at ease. He felt that he could trust her. Lee was pleased, but he couldn't understand how such an impressive, professional woman could be employed in such an unimpressive place.

Ruth did nearly all the talking for Lee which Jenn noted during this meeting and many of the sessions to come. Lee couldn't respond to her questions somehow. Many of the questions were about his past and his opinion on various things in his past. He didn't care about his past, and he could form no opinions on anything except how bad he was feeling. He knew she was searching for causes of his current mental and emotional distress. He certainly had his share of issues and baggage from his childhood, but he was sure he had dealt with that long ago. No use dredging that up again. He really was not interested in talking. He was interested in feeling well, and the only way to do that was to find out what was causing his anguish. It was nothing from his past. He had no doubt about that.

At some point, the conversation turned to medications. Finally, this was something that interested Lee. Now he had some words to offer and launched into a discussion about alprazolam and paroxetine. The alprazolam had worked well for a week or so but then fizzled out. The paroxetine made him feel like a shaking, terrified less-than-human creature who wanted to kill himself. Lee was very clear about that.

Jenn listened intently. When Lee was finished, she mentioned that a consultation with a staff psychiatrist might be helpful. She gave Lee a card with the name, address, and phone number of Dr. James Rosenberry. Now they were getting somewhere. Lee felt a twinge of hope knowing that he would be seeing someone who would sort this out for him and get him on the road to recovery. He wasn't sure exactly what he needed to recover from, but it didn't matter as long as he could be well again. Lee scheduled another appointment with Ms. Franklin for next week with the understanding that he would be seeing Dr. Rosenberry as soon as possible. His first meeting with a mental health care professional ended on a high note. Soon he would be entering the world of psychiatry and psychotropic drugs. Lee thought he was ready.

Chapter Six

July 1997

There was a distinct feeling of déjà vu as Lee sat in one more waiting room with Ruth. In the last three weeks he had been in four different waiting rooms for what he presumed was a medical condition. He had no idea what the condition was or where it came from. All he knew was that it was playing havoc with every aspect of his life and every part of his being. It consumed his thoughts from the time he opened his eyes in the morning until he closed them at night. It was inescapable both physically and mentally.

He had hoped that the time between his first visit with Jenn Franklin and this visit with Dr. Rosenberry would have been uneventful and that he might even improve enough to have no more of those incapacitating mini-attacks. He was taking the alprazolam twice a day now so he reasoned the medicine would improve his overall condition. His hopes were dashed on Wednesday as he was taking his lunchtime walk across the river to City Island. He had the same disconnected, floating feeling that he had had often in the past few months. It was something like dizziness, but it also gave him a sense of being lighter than air. It was very unpleasant, but he had grown somewhat accustomed to it.

On Wednesday as he walked across the Walnut Street Bridge and around the island, he began to obsess over the dizziness which made him feel panicky. He tried to push it out of his mind as he walked back across the bridge to the city. As he looked down through the metal grates of the bridge, he suddenly became extremely dizzy. He stopped in place and froze. He was shrouded in pure terror. He could only stand there in the middle of the bridge while people walked by him on both sides. No one asked him what was wrong. He looked over at the handrail about five feet to his left and wondered if he could get himself to it without passing out.

He wanted to shout, "God help me!" but managed to whisper it instead so as to not draw attention to himself. Somehow he made it to the handrail and grabbed it tightly with both hands. He took deep, long breaths as quietly and inconspicuously as possible while he stared downriver at the sparkling water. How could this happen on such a gorgeous day, and how would he get back to the office? He stood there alone for several minutes clutching the railing and planning the remaining portion of his return trip.

He would first have to go another quarter mile to get off the bridge and then another quarter mile through the city navigating across busy streets. What if he passed out on one of the streets? What if he couldn't make it back? There wouldn't be anything to hold on to once he reached the city.

He turned and slowly resumed walking while touching the handrail. He thought that, if he at least felt his hand in contact with the railing, he would be stable enough to continue. In a few minutes, he was at the end of the bridge and stopped in a stiff-legged posture to assess the next part of his trip back to the office. Front Street was about twenty or thirty yards from him. It was a busy street, and there was nothing to hold on to. He would have to find some way to walk there. He settled on the gait that he had seen drunks use many times and that he had employed himself more times than he liked to admit. Yes, the "drunken stagger" would work. He tried not to shuffle his feet too much or spread his legs too widely and look as sober as possible. Maybe others would think he had a physical disability.

He made it all the way up Walnut Street past Raspberry Circle and turned right onto Fourth Street. Then came the next obsession. He worked on the fourteenth floor of the Wilkins Office Building and had developed a sudden fear of riding in an elevator. What if he passed out in the elevator? He knew it was irrational, but that didn't prevent him from being afraid.

As he slowly ambled down Fourth Street, he decided that he would walk up the thirteen flights of stairs instead of chancing the elevator. What if he had a heart attack on the stairs? No one would know where he was. He took the stairs every morning for the past several months, but he was never in this sort of mental state when he did it. He would chance it. He went in the side door and through the lobby past the security guard as he approached the door to the stairway. He was keenly aware that his heart was already racing. It felt like it was going to beat through his chest. He proceeded up the stairway and took each step very slowly. It was not an extremely hot or humid day outside, but the level of heat and humidity in the stairway felt suffocating.

After three flights, Lee's heart felt like it was going to explode. He stopped in the stairwell outside the fourth floor and put his hands on the wall with his arms extended. He was filled with terror that he was going to have a heart attack and die on the stairs. Why was this happening? How was this possible? He still had ten floors to go. How would he get to the fourteenth floor? He decided to try to get to the eighth floor where the snack bar was. He could take the elevator the last six floors. Maybe no one else would get on the elevator there. He walked as slowly as he could for the next four floors stopping on each to calm himself, catch his breath, and let his heart rest.

He took one last deep breath on the eighth floor stairwell and pushed the door open into the cool air conditioned atmosphere. He had emerged in a small, dark hallway on the other side of the elevator bank. He walked as nonchalantly as he could over to the elevators and pushed the up button. There was only one other person there. She glanced at Lee, and they both acknowledged each other's existence with a smile and a nod. The bell announcing the arrival of the elevator dinged. Only six more floors between Lee and his cubicle where he could hide and try to pull himself together. The elevator bell rang again declaring his safe arrival to the fourteenth floor. Lee headed for his chair.

He sat down and wanted to bask in his success in making it back to his seat, but it seemed like a pathetic accomplishment. He had taken that same walk hundreds of times without a thought. It was routine. There was no success in this effort. As Lee removed his sneakers and reached for his loafers, he realized there was no answer to his woes – or at least not one he could identify. He had tried countless times. He was suddenly hit with a feeling of sheer panic. These mini-attacks terrified him. They were becoming more and more frequent. Why?

He reached into his pocket for the bottle of alprazolam. He removed the cap with a shaking hand and decided to take two of those little white pills. He put them in his mouth and quickly swallowed them. He waited for them to work their magic, but there was no magic to come. His panic was escalating, and he felt like he was losing control. He was physically shaking. What would he do? He still had three hours to go. If he could make it that long, how would he ever make it to the bus stop and survive the long ride home?

He picked up the phone and called Ruth. When he heard her voice, he said in a not-so-quiet voice, "I can't take this anymore. I can't do it. Can you call Jenn Franklin?"

Thirty minutes later Ruth picked Lee up outside the building. In another thirty minutes they were once again sitting across from Ms. Franklin for Lee's first emergency counseling session.

Lee tried to forget the events of Wednesday's meltdown as he sat in Dr. Rosenberry's waiting room. He decided to focus on something else. The waiting room itself was much smaller than the one he sat in on Monday and again Wednesday at State Counseling Services. It was darker but not quite as dingy. There were no posters on the walls. Instead there were pictures on the walls of tranquil nature scenes. Magazines were neatly placed on the two end tables. It did not really have a comfortable, homey feel to it. The atmosphere was more one of a subtle, quiet passivity. The outside of the building gave no clue as to its purpose, and the building itself was far from the beaten path. It was as though the existence of this building was meant to be a secret except to those who had a need to visit it.

The contrast with the State Counseling Services building and waiting room was stark. Lee rolled that around inside his head for a while trying to conjure up a reason for the great dissimilarities. It would be nearly impossible to drive by the State Counseling Services building without noticing its name spelled in huge silver letters across its front. It sat right along the main road. Maybe the word "counseling" had something to do with the difference. People could go to counseling for a variety of reasons that had nothing to do with a psychiatric problem or mental disorder. For all anybody knew, it could be a center for people trying to quit smoking or those needing some sort of assistance. Lee had driven by the building many times and did not know what kind of counseling took place there. He thought it probably had something to do with financial counseling. He was obviously wrong.

    The sign outside the building he found himself in now was very small – almost too small. They had driven by it the first time and had to turn around. The lettering on the sign was simply "Office of Psychiatry" followed by the names of the doctors who practiced inside. There was no doubt about the nature of what went on in this building or who the clientele were. This was a place for people with emotional and mental problems. Even in his current mental state, Lee was aware of that. Right now he was having some kind of mental issue that was sufficiently debilitating to require professional help. Even though he always prided himself on his mental and emotional strength, he was now a pathetically helpless man. He was already attaching a stigma to himself. No doubt others would do the same when they found out. Lee really didn't care what anyone thought. It was irrelevant to him whether he was getting counseling or psychiatric help. He only wanted to feel human again. He was desperate.

    As Lee was finally concluding the "counseling" versus "psychiatry" game in his head, a lady came into the room and called his name. Lee and Ruth followed her down a hallway to an office just as they had followed Jenn Franklin to her office on Monday. Lee was about to meet a psychiatrist as a patient for the first time in his forty-three years.

    Dr. Rosenberry welcomed them into his office and, as they were seating themselves, he got right to the business at hand. Over the course of the next hour, Lee explained in great detail what he had been experiencing in the last several months. He talked about the mini-attacks that started in his sleep and later occurred while driving. He mentioned the extreme fear that he was going insane and how he was completely and constantly consumed with this entire situation. He described as best he could the horrific effects the paroxetine had on him and that, if he had taken it one more day, he felt certain he would have killed himself.

When Lee had finished sharing the horrors of the last several months, he fully expected Dr. Rosenberry to flash a look of incredulity and maybe even scratch his head in amazement. Surely he had never heard of such bizarre symptoms.

Instead, Dr. Rosenberry calmly nodded his head. Lee wasn't sure how to evaluate that reaction. Did the doctor think Lee was insane, and he was just appeasing Lee? Was he trying to put Lee at ease? Was this something he had heard hundreds of times before and was genuinely unmoved? Was he hiding his emotions and compassion or did he have neither? Lee wasn't sure if he should be uneasy or not.

"So, the paroxetine didn't work for you?"

Lee was stunned by the question. "Didn't work for you?" Was he joking? There was not a hint of humor on Dr. Rosneberry's face. Lee had just told him that the paroxetine made him suicidal. It was not an exaggeration. Lee felt too shaky to pursue the matter and didn't want to antagonize the doctor whom he hoped had the answer to his dilemma.

"No, that was a very bad experience," Lee replied.

The doctor made a note of that on his notepad and launched into a series of questions about sleep, appetite, paranoia, hearing voices, concentration, energy, memory, guilt, hopelessness, periods of overexcitement, worry, and thoughts of suicide. He seemed to have no emotion at all as Lee answered each question. Maybe Dr. Rosenberry had asked the questions so many times and received so many varied answers that nothing surprised him anymore. This appointment clearly had nothing to do with therapy or counseling.

The doctor then changed the line of questioning to family history primarily with respect to emotional problems. Lee explained that his mother died when he was eight. The cause of death was not clear, but there were those who believed she had committed suicide. Lee had been too young to know. He did recall his mother spending a lot of time in bed during her last year or so of life and also that she took many pills. His father had always blamed her death on the pills.

Lee also mentioned that he had been told all of his life that his mother was never well after he had been born. He was born seven years after the last of his siblings. He had always carried a bit of guilt about that. It was like his siblings were telling him that his mother would still be alive if he had never been born. He knew it was not said with ill intentions, but it was still a bit painful.

His father had died of lung cancer when Lee was twenty-one. He had struggled with bouts of depression during his lifetime and had even received shock treatments when he was young and later shortly before his death.

Dr. Rosenberry said something about genetic predisposition as he took notes while Lee spoke. Lee didn't like the sound of that, but maybe it was true.

The final questions concerned his current family and work life. There was a significant degree of pain in both of these areas in the past couple years. His reputation and how he was perceived as a technical professional had taken an enormous hit two years earlier through no fault of his own. To be blunt, he had been set up and was not permitted to defend himself. He still carried resentment about the situation. Then there was Lynn. When she turned thirteen, her relationship with her father began deteriorating very rapidly, and his current mental distress was only accelerating that trend. He could not pull himself together enough to try to mend his relationship with her. That only created more guilt for him to manage.

Lee didn't like to dwell on those two topics. In some way, those recollections made him feel like he had already all but destroyed his own life and would end up destroying Lynn's life as well.

As he was looking down at the floor in emotional defeat, Dr. Rosenberry interrupted his thoughts. Maybe he felt sorry for Lee and wanted to pull him out of the mire that was quickly swallowing him, or maybe he wanted to get this over with in the allotted one-hour appointment.

"You are on alprazolam right now and nothing else?"

"Yeah. That's all. Alprazolam."

"Okay. I'm going to switch you over to clonazepam because it has a longer half-life. It will stay in your body longer."

Lee nodded absently. He had no idea what clonazepam was.

Dr. Rosenberry continued, "It can be addictive to some people, but you will need to take it for the rest of your life for panic disorder."

Lee thought about that momentarily while the doctor scribbled on a pad. If he had to take it the rest of his life and if it pulled him out of his mental turmoil, it didn't matter if it was addictive.

"Here is a prescription for clonazepam. A half milligram three times a day." He continued. "Since the paroxetine didn't work, we will start you on sertraline. It's an antidepressant and will help the depression. It usually takes four to six weeks to be fully effective. Take it in the morning because it can affect sleep in some people. If you don't have any questions, you can make an appointment for two weeks to see how you are doing. "

With that, Dr. Rosenberry stood. Lee's first psychiatric visit had officially come to an end in exactly one hour.

On Monday, Lee returned to work. He had taken the sertraline for four days and seemed to be slowly declining from lousy to miserable. His appetite, which he had lost as an effect of the paroxetine and which had slowly returned during the four days between the last dose of paroxetine and the first dose of sertraline, had once again disappeared. Despite the large dose of clonazepam, he could barely sleep, and the horrid restlessness was returning. He was feeling "paroxetine-ized." He also realized that he had absolutely no sexual desire. His libido was buried somewhere in his past. Even if he had any sort of desire, the sexual dysfunction was complete. Nothing could possibly happen down there. Lee hadn't expected the new drugs to be a panacea for his problems, but he had hoped they'd bring him some relief. Instead he felt worse. To add insult to injury, Lee was now constipated.

In fact, he had no desire at all to do anything. He felt like he was slowly dying while at the same time he was growing more restless every day. Nevertheless, he managed to take his morning dose of sertraline for six more days until he could no longer tolerate it.

For the next five days he took no sertraline, his appetite returned, and he was once again successful on the toilet. The extreme restlessness subsided, but he still could not sleep even with the clonazepam. He still had that underlying pervasive panicky feeling. In fact, it seemed to be growing instead of shrinking.

Sometime during those five days, Lee received a call from Dr. Rosenberry's office indicating that Dr. Rosenberry would no longer be seeing Lee. He would now be seeing Dr. Inmet whose office was in the State Counseling Services building. At least Lee would have no trouble finding him.

During the next seventeen months, Dr. Inmet would leave no stone unturned in his quest to find a drug or drugs that would make Lee feel well again. The first one was something called nefazodone. This one was not as debilitating as the paroxetine or sertraline, and Lee was able to tolerate it for eight months. He still didn't have much of an appetite, and the insomnia remained. He had no energy at all and no desire to live what most people would call a normal life. The drugs had no effect whatsoever on the original problem of the pervasive fear and mini-attacks.

The nefazodone did have one particularly bothersome effect on Lee. Every morning he would get up and go into the bathroom to shower before work. For some reason he would always see two showers with two doors. It was very much the same sort of visual effect he recalled from boyhood when he would cross his eyes. After the first few mornings he discovered that if he walked between the two openings of the two doors he could actually get into the shower without too much trouble provided that he lifted his legs high enough to get his feet over the bottom ledge. He had only skinned his shins a few times.

That strange effect on his vision also followed him to work. He was an environmental scientist and spent a great deal of time in front of a computer writing spreadsheets. He had been attempting to write a spreadsheet for calculating safe levels of chemicals in various environmental media based on accepted exposure assumptions for those media and chemical-specific toxicological data. This was the type of work he had done for years using the default ten-point font of the spreadsheet software. The drug had affected his vision so much that he found it necessary to use a thirty-six-point font. Even then he had to sit close to the monitor.

After eight months it was clear that the nefazodone was not improving Lee's symptoms of anxiety. The mini-attacks were ever-present and debilitating. The lack of sleep was wearing him down. His overall mental condition was rapidly deteriorating. He complained persistently to Dr. Inmet who finally decided to try another drug which led to another drug and another drug.

Over the next four months Lee was prescribed valproic acid, citalopram, and buspirone. Each one created its own bizarre, debilitating effects. He even tried olanzapine at twice the dose Ruth was taking, and she was the one diagnosed with schizophrenia – not him. Lee felt like a guinea pig. Dr. Inmet admitted that some of these drugs were developed to treat other types of disorders – not major depressive disorder, generalized anxiety disorder, or panic disorder. This was called "off-label" use. Lee realized that this was not remotely similar to any scientific approach he had ever studied or practiced, but he really didn't care. He would have drunk mercury at this point if he thought it would make him feel even slightly better.

In midsummer of 1998, Dr. Inmet increased the dose of a drug called mirtazapine which was something he had given Lee earlier for sleep and appetite but at a much reduced dosage. After a week or so Lee managed to reach the maximum dose of mirtazapine and was completely non-functional. All he could do was sit and stare blankly at the walls. If there was such a thing as a zombie, he was one.

Lee remained in that zombie-like state until Dr. Inmet decided to reduce the dosage back to the initial dose. He then prescribed something named gabapentin. Over the course of a week, Lee's dose increased to twelve hundred milligrams of gabapentin a day. It whacked him out completely making him dizzy and disoriented in a very strange way only minutes after he would take it. It really made matters worse for the most part, but it did come in handy one time.

While Lee was taking the gabapentin, the time for the annual family vacation in Ocean City, Maryland had arrived. Michael had gone along with Ruth's parents to Ocean City a few days earlier, and the plan was for Ruth, Lee, and Lynn to join them on Saturday. When it came time to leave, Lynn begged her parents to let her stay home. She insisted that she could stay with her friend, Abbie, until they returned home on Monday. Neither Ruth nor Lee thought it was a good idea, but they finally gave in to Lynn's determined pleas. Something inside Lee was certain there would be a price to pay, but he was so weary from being increasingly ill for more than a year now and from the evaporation of the close relationship he once shared with Lynn that he raised the white flag. Nothing good could possibly come from the decision to leave Lynn at home. There would be consequences. They would deal with them later.

The car ride to Ocean City was uneventful. Lee had taken a couple capsules of gabapentin shortly after they departed and was in a mindless, numb daze for the next five hours. They arrived at the condominium in the early evening and went upstairs to greet Ruth's parents and Michael before unpacking the car. In fifteen minutes the phone rang. It was Lynn. She said she wanted to make sure mom and dad arrived safely. Of course, Lee knew she was making sure that Ruth and he were hours away and it was safe for her to get into whatever mischief she desired. Lee had hoped he was wrong, but he knew he was right. He was even more uneasy than usual for the rest of his evening imagining what kind of trouble Lynn was getting into. He took two and a half milligrams of clonazepam, the mirtazapine, and a couple capsules of gabapentin before he went to bed. Hopefully, he would get his usual three or four hours of sleep.

The phone rang at seven in the morning. Lee had a feeling it was Lynn, and he was right. Maybe they didn't like each other anymore, but

Lee knew his daughter very well. Ruth answered the phone and barely reacted to the news Lee had expected. Ruth had been worn down in the past year with Lee's failing mental and emotional state and Lynn's defiance. She was no longer surprised by bad news. It had become commonplace.

Lynn said that she was in some kind of trouble and the police were involved. Within thirty minutes Ruth and Lee were on their way home. This had to be a family record for the shortest vacation ever – less than twelve hours. Lee took two capsules of gabapentin before they left and two more about halfway home. He was dazed.

When they pulled up to the house, Lee saw Lynn and one of the three or four Ryans she hung out with sitting on the front porch. Lee had no appreciation for any of them as individuals. Maybe it was because they all had the same first name. Lee jumped out of the passenger side door before the car had stopped and was in Ryan's face immediately. He was smiling smugly at Lee as Lee pointed directly at him and said through gritted teeth, "You, get out of here." Lee wanted to grab him, but Ryan complied and was gone in moments.

Lee's eyes were on Lynn in a flash. She got up and Lee backed her into the living room all the while staring directly into her eyes with a seething anger. He had his left hand at her throat as she was backed against the closet. He wanted to squeeze the life from her. Instead, he uttered a guttural noise from the depths of his being and removed his hand. He turned his attention toward the living room. There had obviously been a party last night.

He walked into the kitchen which looked worse than the living room. Lynn feebly mentioned that Ryan and she had been cleaning up, but nothing appeared to have been touched. Empty beer, wine, and liquor bottles were strewn throughout the living room, kitchen, and family room. There were cigarette burn marks on the kitchen table and floor. Someone had apparently not been satisfied with the burn marks because the wooden kitchen table had also been keyed.

Even in his drug-induced stupor, Lee was filled with rage. He knew if he searched the rest of the house more closely he would find evidence of activities that would throw him over the edge. He knew he would spend the rest of the day having panic attacks. So he pulled the bottle of gabapentin from his pocket and took four more capsules. That should send him far enough into oblivion so that he could focus totally on the mundane task of picking up bottles. For the next two hours he concentrated on cleaning up and nothing else. He felt like he was hovering dizzily from bottle to bottle with a type of search and destroy attitude. There was no thinking. There was no feeling. There were only bottles. Lee was uncomfortably numb.

After he managed to carry the seven garbage bags of bottles out to the garage, he went back inside and sat in the living room with Ruth. She had been talking to Lynn and learning what transpired the night before. Lee tried to fix his mind on what Ruth was saying. Lynn had received a citation for underage possession of alcohol while having a party at their house with over a hundred guests. Of course, she didn't invite them all. Many of them showed up on their own Lynn claimed. Someone had been arrested for punching a police officer. Lee simply listened until Ruth sat there in silence.

He decided he would search the rest of the house right now while he could feel nothing. He went down to the laundry room and noticed the screen was ripped out of the window – probably from some kid attempting to make his or her great escape from the cops the night before. Lee opened the door to the storage room where the entrance to the crawlspace was. The sheet of plywood that closed off the hole to the crawlspace was missing, and the hole was right there gaping at Lee. He grabbed the flashlight from the top of the water heater and shined it into the space. He noticed something sparkling on the floor so he crawled in to get a better view. He found several of Ruth's earrings and other pieces of jewelry. He picked them up. He noticed a very strong odor of urine. Whoever tried to make off with Ruth's jewelry must have been lying in there a very long time. Although Lee didn't care, he wondered if the person or persons who relieved themselves in the crawlspace had escaped the police or had been arrested.

He went outside on the porch and sat for a few minutes trying to peer through the fog of his memory. The last nearly twenty-four hours were just a continuation of the past year. He thought of all that Lynn had done over that time to hurt him. He thought of the dozens of green slips Ruth and he got in the mail informing them that Lynn cut classes or entire days of school. He thought of the nights that she stole his car and picked up friends for a joy ride. They called the police many of those nights to report that she had taken the car. The same young officer would always come by to speak with them. It was like having one's own personal police officer. Lee recalled the last episode when he brought his supervisor with him. He was a tough-as-nails cop who wanted Lee to sign papers to have her sent to the Schaffner Detention Center once they picked her up.

Lee had called the crisis center several times to try to get permission to kick Lynn out of the house. He was informed every time that he was responsible for her until she was eighteen. She was only fifteen. Lee couldn't imagine how he could survive three more years if things didn't change. He would surely die. Still, he had heard horror stories about rape and brutality at Schaffner. No, nothing good would happen there. He could not send Lynn to that place. Even in the haze caused by all the drugs he was on, he could not sign the papers.

Lee stood up on the porch and went back into the living room. Ruth was sitting in a chair and was visibly upset. "They were in my jewelry box. They were in our bed. Someone was in our bed."

Lee played that in his head for a moment and could only give a matter-of-fact, "Probably just hiding from the cops." He wasn't even sure why he said it.

"But I feel violated. They were in our bed. I should burn the sheets."

Violated. Yeah, Lee felt violated. Violated by all the drugs he had taken in the last year. Gabapentin was just the latest one. Right now Lee was numb. He was glad he was numb. Gabapentin was good for something after all.

Shortly after the failed vacation and Lynn's party, it was apparent that the gabapentin was not helping. Dr.Inmet finally had no more tricks up his sleeve and recommended that Lee see another psychiatrist in the city. Her name was Leah Michaels.

Lee wasn't sure what Dr. Michaels might be able to do for him that Dr. Inmet could not do. Surely they both had the same psychotropic drugs in their arsenals of treatment options. Dr. Inmet had described her as a "specialist" concerning Lee's condition, so she must have something other than drugs to offer.

Lee sat with Dr. Michaels for several minutes and explained his symptoms. He emphasized how bad each of the drugs he had taken up to this point had made him feel without giving him any relief from the original condition of anxiety and panic attacks. In fact, he was progressively sinking into a place that was becoming very difficult to accept. He stressed his inability to get more than a couple hours of sleep a night even on a low dose of mirtazapine and two and a half milligrams of clonazepam.

While Lee was talking, Dr. Michaels was busy taking notes. When he had finished his description of the effects of the drugs he had tried, Dr. Michaels took a few moments before she spoke. Now she was scribbling something on a small pad as she said, "I think this will help you sleep better." She peeled a prescription from her pad and handed it to Lee. She began scribbling on her pad again as she continued, "It's a drug called trazodone. It's technically an antidepressant, but this dosage is not high enough to have an effect on your depression. It's one of the older drugs. It will definitely improve your sleep though. You can stop taking the mirtazapine."

Lee sat there for a moment. More sleep would definitely be welcome. He wasn't sure though. Dr. Inmet had made similar claims about drug after drug he prescribed. None of them had been helpful. If Dr. Michaels was so sure this drug was the "right" one for better sleep, why hadn't Dr. Inmet prescribed it?

Before he could give trazodone any more thought, Dr. Michaels was handing him another prescription. "Here, this one is for venlafaxine. It's one of the newer drugs and works in a different way than anything you have taken so far."

"A different way?" was all that came to Lee's mind and then his mouth. He hadn't sufficiently evaluated trazodone yet and here was something else to analyze.

"Yes, it's an SNRI and works differently than anything you have taken. It targets norepinephrine."

Lee had no idea what an SNRI or norepinephrine were. He didn't have an intelligent response to that last statement so he said, "I see." He was still concerned about why Dr. Inmet hadn't prescribed these if they were so effective. Yet, they were two drugs that he had not tried. He was so desperate that he pushed his doubts aside and questioned, "You really think these will help me?" He prayed she would respond affirmatively and give him some hope. She did not disappoint him.

"Yes, you will sleep, and after a few weeks the venlafaxine will give you relief from depression and anxiety."

Just hearing those words made Lee feel a little better. She sounded so confident like she had no doubt that what she was saying was true.

"Okay," Lee said with a bit of hope in his voice. Certainly he was getting off the path that was leading to nowhere. It had been well over a year since he had that horrendous experience with paroxetine. He had exhausted Dr. Inmet in his quest to find relief. Lee was tired. This had to be the answer.

"You can follow up your treatment with Dr. Inmet." With that, the appointment was over and Dr. Leah Michaels excused him from her care after only one meeting. How could she be that good to be able to see the errors of Dr. Inmet and correct them in just one hour? Lee wasn't sure, but he had two new prescriptions in his hand and was off to the drugstore.

During the next five days, Lee took the trazodone and venlafaxine as prescribed. The trazodone did much more than make him sleep. It felt like it put him in a coma. He woke up for absolutely nothing in the night – not even to empty his bladder. His wet sheets for three of the five mornings had been evidence of that. He also felt like he had a huge hangover each of those five mornings and was so groggy he could barely get out of bed and walk. Not being a fan of wet bed clothes or hangovers, Lee discontinued the trazodone after five days and resumed the mirtazapine.

The venlafaxine was a different story. Lee started out with a very small dose and gradually worked up to a much higher dose over a few weeks. This drug made him feel fidgety and somewhat nauseous. One very strange and disturbing effect of it was that, if he was even an hour late in taking a dose, he would get what he called "brain flips" that made him feel like his brain would go offline for a second and "reset" bringing him back to the same place but leaving him in a daze. It was similar to the eyes' reaction to the flash of a camera where one has to momentarily refocus after getting zapped by the flash. It was extremely unpleasant, so Lee tried to be very careful about not being late for his daily dose.

Even without the brain flips Lee noticed that, once he reached a much higher dose, he again returned to the familiar zombie state where he would sit and stare. He had no thoughts or feelings about living life. His only focus was surviving the day. Lee imagined it felt very much like being dead but still being able to move and breathe. Nevertheless, Dr. Inmet insisted that he needed to continue to increase his dose and that the venlafaxine would become effective at some point. He would never venture a guess as to when that might be even though Lee pressed him for an answer.

At the end of 1998, Lee felt like he had had enough of the venlafaxine and decided that he needed to reduce the dose to something he could tolerate better. He thought about all that he had been through in the past eighteen months trying to find the answer to why he felt so miserable. Ever since the horrid experience with the three doses of paroxetine in the summer of 1997, he had spiraled downward at an accelerating pace. He never fully recovered from whatever the paroxetine did to him. He wasn't allowed to recover. He was kept in a constant state of misery with other drugs that only served to keep him in anguish. He was being worn down mentally, emotionally, and physically.

During these eighteen months he had seen Jenn Franklin dozens of times. She had helped him try to sort through some of the thorny issues in his past in an effort to find something that might improve his mental and emotional state. Lee's father had been less than faithful to Lee's mother, so Jenn explored that aspect of his childhood. She instructed Lee to write a letter to his father, who was no longer alive, in an effort to get Lee to let go of some of his baggage from the past. Lee complied, but, if it helped, it wasn't significant.

Jenn gave Lee the Minnesota Multiphasic Personality Inventory (MMPI) test for some reason that he never really understood. It included hundreds of questions that Lee found to be more torturous than relevant to helping him get well. His anxiety level was so high when he took the test that he wanted to jump out of his skin. He could barely sit still long enough to complete the task. When she received the results of the test, she told Lee he was the most depressed person she had ever met. He wondered why a therapist would tell that to a client. It only served to make him more depressed and terrified that he might never be well again. Maybe she was trying to "snap" him out of it with that bit of knowledge. Perhaps it was supposed to have shock value. If so, it didn't work. Generally, the therapy had little positive effect on Lee. He continued to sink more deeply into a quagmire of fear and despair that he did not understand.

In the first year of this illness, Lee had undergone many different non-psychological tests for symptoms he was having. He was certain that there was something wrong with his heart. He had had that weird feeling of movement in his chest many times and thought a stress test would reveal some sort of abnormality. During the stress test, as the incline of the treadmill increased, so did his heart rate. He was certain he would a have a heart attack. That thought brought on a terror that gripped him causing a mini-attack. He was confident that the test would indicate a cardiac irregularity. To his surprise he was told that he had a very strong heart with no abnormalities at all. The mini-attack did not even register. Lee was relieved that his heart was normal, but he was still worried about what was wrong with him.

Since Lee was not responding to either therapy or psychotropic drugs, Dr. Inmet thought his problem might have its origins in his sleep patterns. Lee had great difficulty sleeping, so it seemed like a possibility. During the sleep study, Lee was instructed to take his medications before the test which didn't seem to make sense to him because the medications were being taken for sleep. He took them. He slept. The study revealed that he had no abnormal condition with respect to sleep.

Then came the upper GI test and gastric pH study. Lee had developed an extremely painful, constant heartburn that nothing seemed to alleviate. It had started right around the time he was originally prescribed alprazolam. He had tried many different over-the-counter antacids with no relief. He even cut a few inches from the legs at the foot of his bed to prevent nighttime reflux. That did no good and only caused Ruth to be irritated with him. He had to admit that the shortened legs gave the sensation that Ruth and he would slide out the bottom of the bed. It was not one of his better decisions.

The upper GI indicated that Lee had a small hiatal hernia but not severe enough to cause reflux. The gastric pH study showed that Lee definitely had gastric reflux. For two days Lee had an electrode in his throat which dangled from a wire that entered his throat through his nose. The other end of the wire connected to a meter attached to his belt that read pH. Whenever Lee would experience heartburn, he would press a button on the meter which then read the pH in his throat. It was an extremely depressing two days that filled Lee with anxiety. Lee was later prescribed various drugs for the reflux. He would take these for the next fifteen years.

At the end of 1998, there really was very little of the year that Lee recalled. It was the only year of his life, up to this point, that seemed like he hadn't even been alive. He had used over one hundred days of sick leave because he could barely function at work. The days at home were always the same. He would take the same walk every day. In the house he would watch The Weather Channel hour after endless hour. Nothing much on the weather channel changed either except the weather they reported, and that seemed to constantly recycle itself. For some reason that he never understood, he developed a fondness for Vivian Brown. He liked her voice. Maybe that was it.

When he could cajole himself to go into the office, he was not particularly functional. His mind was foggy and he was completely unmotivated. Nothing mattered to him. Every morning his friend, John, would visit his cubicle for a while, and Lee would complain about how bad he felt. He could think of nothing else. His brain was self-absorbed and paralyzed with the fear that it would always be that way.

He lived with many different physical sensations during the year. Of course, there was that constant feeling of being disconnected from everything and the dizziness that seemed to be its companion. He was constantly cold. He had spent most of the summer at home walking and watching Vivian Brown and her coworkers on The Weather Channel. He went back to work in early September on what he would normally have considered a sultry day. But he was no longer normal. He wore his old Air Force field jacket with the liner in it. It was the warmest coat he had ever owned, and he was wearing it in eighty-degree weather. He stood at the bus stop in the morning pulling the collar up under his chin while the other guy waiting with him wore a t-shirt. Lee tried to explain that the medication he was taking was causing him to feel cold, but he was always met with a blank expression. In years past they had talked animatedly about the Pittsburgh Steelers, but that seemed like another lifetime to Lee. So, he stood there shivering and wallowing in depression. That was all the animation he had left.

On Sunday, January 3, 1999, as he was walking with his brother, Ed, Lee tried to recall if there had been anything in the previous year that might give him a glimmer of hope – anything even remotely positive. Ed had come to visit Lee many weekends during the past year and a half trying to help him out of his mental and emotional dilemma. Ed tried relentlessly to pull Lee out of the pit, but Lee could tell his brother was losing his grip on Lee's hand. Lee was slipping away. He was nearly out of mental and physical strength. His hope was all but gone.

Lee thought back on the phone calls he would often get from Pat, his mother-in-law, and Steve, his brother-in-law. He had married into a good family. They were very kind people, and their phone calls did lift Lee for a while, but the magic was wearing off. As Lee continued sinking further into depression, the phone calls became fewer. No one knew what to do for Lee. If they had known how to rescue him, Lee had no doubt they would have moved mountains for him.

Then there was Michael. Michael was thirteen and met Lee every day when he would walk in the door from work with "How do you feel today, Dad?" On the many days when Lee didn't work, Michael would ask the same question when he came in the door from school. Sadly, just as the question was always the same hopeful expression of Michael's love for his father, Lee's reply was always the same hopeless expression of his sorrow and self-absorption.

Michael possessed something very special inside – a tender, childlike compassion for others. He seemed as though he was incapable of hurting anyone else. For this Lee was grateful. When Michael was small, he had a book entitled *Big Goof and Little Goof* which Lee and he read many times. They would often refer to each other by those names. Tears came to Lee's eyes as he walked along with Ed. The days of feeling goofy were long gone, and he feared they would never return. Yet, he was thankful for those memories. They were very tender ones. Michael would always be ten feet tall to Lee. That would never change as long as Lee was alive. He was not sure how much longer that would be. Probably not very long.

Lee remembered the hope he had felt at the beginning of 1998 when Dr. Inmet changed the medications he was taking and told Lee that one of the drugs would eventually pull Lee out of his funk. As each of the drugs failed and actually made Lee feel worse, his hope eroded more and more. In the spring of 1998 Lee had done a search on the internet about the effectiveness of antidepressants for depression and anxiety. He had been reluctant to do so because he didn't want to lose the little bit of hope he still clung to. Surely he was some sort of "statistical outlier" who, for whatever reason, was not responding in a positive way to the several drugs he had been prescribed. Certainly most people must get significantly better on these medications. For some reason, he feared what he might find. He hoped and prayed that his fears were unfounded.

To his utter dismay, the results of his inquiries were always the same. Again and again he read that in clinical trials the drugs were barely better than a useless placebo – maybe five percent more effective. He was paralyzed with dread. He had, at best, a one in twenty chance of improving on the drugs? He searched and searched but continued to retrieve the same results. He was devastated. Still, he had no choice but to keep hoping he was the one person in twenty.

Ed was rambling on about something or other as Lee was considering his glass of hope. It was not even half-full anymore. It was completely empty. It had shattered into pieces months ago, and now, as Lee tried to pick up the pieces, he was harmed even more by the shards. Therapy had been somewhat meaningful at the beginning of this journey, but it had soon lost all value. Jenn Franklin had poured a lot of effort into helping Lee, but his brain could not respond in any positive way anymore. It felt like his brain was incapable of doing so – as though something had taken it hostage and would not release it. Lee had always prided himself on being rock solid mentally. His mind was now a heap of rubble and he had been unable to determine how or why it had happened.

The journey had become seemingly endless for others in his life as well, Lee imagined. He was sure everyone had written him off as being hopelessly mentally ill. Lee himself had no recourse but to come to the same conclusion even though he continued to grope for the answer to the seemingly unanswerable question. He knew there must be a solution, but he had no idea what it was. The only person in his life who seemed to hold out hope was Michael.

Lee thought about all the different drugs he had taken in the last eighteen months. With the exception of the first two weeks he had taken alprazolam, the drugs made him progressively more and more depressed, anxious, and lethargic. They had finally worn him down completely and sapped the very last molecule of hope from his soul. He had given up living long ago. Lee was now merely existing, but he decided that it was time for that to end as well. The drugs would then be able to take nothing more from Lee Lucas.

Lee's attention turned to Ruth and, more specifically, her work schedule. She worked on the night shift every other weekend at the nursing home a couple miles from their home. She was working this weekend, but Ed was here, so Lee would not have an opportunity to act on his idea this weekend. Besides, Lee needed to plan this out. He had only contemplated such a thing one other time in his life. That was eighteen months ago when he had taken the paroxetine. Jumping in front of an eighteen wheeler would be too messy and painful. He had two weeks to plan this time. That was certainly enough time to come up with something less painful and violent.

Ed continued to talk as they walked having no idea what Lee was devising inside his head. In some macabre way, Lee felt somewhat invigorated and reluctantly hopeful. His thoughts turned to the garage. That would be the perfect place to do this final deed. The garden hose was in storage directly above the garage. He could easily pull it down with the garage door down and the car in the garage. Everything he would need would be right there, and no one would discover what he was doing until it was too late. Too late. The words hit Lee hard in the stomach. Someone would be the first to discover his lifeless body. Lee cringed at the thought and felt like retching.

He shifted his thoughts to something else. He thought of the pure misery of the year that had just passed. He could not endure another year like that. There weren't many more drugs to try, and they had almost no chance to work anyway – based on his brief research. He knew he had started the drugs because something was "not right" inside him. He knew that he had tried obsessively to resolve the initial problem without any success. But all the drugs he had taken for the last eighteen months were destroying him. He could not think. He could not feel anything but misery. He was trapped inside his own head and could not escape. He thought of the words to a song he had heard long ago but had never understood until now. It was as though the words were written for Lee for this time in his existence.

It was a song about a lobotomy and the patient being trapped inside his head. Yet, it wasn't that person who was incarcerated inside his head but someone else – a stranger. Lee wondered if whoever wrote the lyrics to that song had ever known someone who had a lobotomy. They must have. There was someone inside Lee's head trying to get out, but Lee had no idea who it was. It had no resemblance to the Lee he knew in a long ago and far away life. If there was such a thing as a chemical lobotomy, Lee felt as if he was in the midst of one.

Soon, whoever the intruder was inside Lee's head would have to leave. Then Lee would have peace. Lee was comforted by the knowledge that he had a plan to evict his unwanted guest. He would know when the time was right.

Chapter Seven

January 4, 1999

The next day was the first workday of the new year for Lee. He met it in much the same way he had met the first workday of last year – without the slightest bit of anticipation or motivation. He had lost even the tiny bit of hope he had one year ago and had no desire to go to the office or to stay home. He had forgotten what desire was or that he had ever wanted to do anything at any point in his life. He existed. That was the sum total of his being on this day and had been for as far back as he could remember.

Lee got out of bed and shuffled through the darkness into the bathroom. Somehow he mustered both the mental and physical energy to get a shower, dress, and make his way slowly down the stairs where he flipped the switch on the wall that turned on the lamp in the far corner of the living room. He squinted as his eyes adjusted to the light. He trudged slowly toward the counter in the partially illuminated kitchen as he had done hundreds of mornings before this one. He picked up the little yellow clonazepam tablet and the pink and black capsule he took for heartburn from the counter and popped them into his mouth as he reached for the door of the refrigerator to get his bottle of water.

The morning routine never changed. Lee walked into the living room and plopped into his chair to read his morning devotional. He sat quietly and contemplated the silence. He could hear the ticking of the clock on the wall across the room. He looked at it for a moment and thought about the person on the other side of the wall who was sleeping peacefully in her bed – his daughter, Lynn. She had created such havoc for Lee and the rest of the family in the last eighteen months. Lee was trying very hard not to hate her, but he was failing. He wanted more than anything to push her out the door and dismiss her from his life. The little girl he had loved so completely for thirteen years was gone. He had no idea who was now residing in that bedroom. She was an unwanted stranger. He loathed her. He knew he should be ashamed, but he could feel no shame.

In the past few days Lynn had not been feeling well and legitimately stayed home from school. Lee assumed she had a virus, or maybe it was something she had eaten, taken, or smoked. It was hard to tell. Whatever it was, Lynn had been nauseous over the weekend which was unusual. Even as a little girl she hated to throw up and would do absolutely anything to keep from doing so. Somehow it gave Lee slight relief. Lynn was more subdued when she was sick. There would be no phone calls from the school or visits from the police while she was lying in bed. There would be a modicum of peace, at least until she was well again.

Lee reached for his devotional booklet and rushed through the reading as he usually did. He was incapable of relating to much of what he read except when the subject was about the pain and difficulties of life. He put the booklet back on the stand and prayed the same Bible verse he had prayed thousands of times in the past year and a half. It had become his mantra every night as he lay in bed trying to fall asleep and every morning as he sat in his chair before work – "Rest in the Lord and wait patiently for him. Rest in the Lord and wait patiently for him. Rest in the Lord and wait patiently for him." Lee was tired of being patient and never felt at rest. Nevertheless, he kept repeating it. Maybe it would come true one day. Maybe he would be patient and be able to rest. He reluctantly got up from his chair and resigned himself to the reality that it was time to meet the rest of the day.

"So, are you feeling any better today?" Lee had known Greg for eighteen years now. They had both started their careers in the same field office as inspectors and had moved to the central office near the same time. Nearly every day they would take a one-hour walk at lunch over the Walnut Street Bridge to City Island and circle the island twice before returning to the office. Lee knew that Greg's question was born of genuine concern even though Lee was certain Greg already knew the answer before Lee replied.

"No. I don't know what to do. It's been a long time. I don't know." It was the same answer Lee had given dozens of times.

Greg talked about things he had done and seen over the holidays. Lee was silent as Greg spoke at length about his family and, in particular, about his sister and brother-in-law. Lee recalled that, in earlier years, Greg would tell him that his brother-in-law always asked for world peace for Christmas. It was always an amusing story to Lee, and they would chuckle good-naturedly and say that it was a very laudable Christmas wish. It was not amusing this year, and it had not been amusing last year. Lee found it depressing that he could not feel the humor in a story that he once found comical. Greg was a good friend to hang around for all these months waiting for Lee to bounce back to his old form.

As Greg continued with his stories, Lee was completely engrossed with how miserable he felt and how he could do nothing about it. He thought about being at home and the fact that home provided no solace from this inner storm. He thought about the decision he had made yesterday afternoon while he was walking with his brother. He had no feeling one way or another about it. He would just do it. It was a solution.

"Hello. Earth to Lee."

"Huh? What? I was just thinking about something at home."

"Guess Lynn and Michael are back in school?"

"Oh, uh, yeah. Lynn was sick over the weekend – throwing up. She hates to throw up."

Suddenly Lee had a repulsive thought. Maybe hearing his words out loud brought it to him, but it was something he could barely repeat inside his own head. It could not be true. It just could not. Surely it was merely one of those "what ifs" that Jenn Franklin warned him about. Lynn could not be pregnant. Lee was holding on to life by a thread already. That would destroy him.

"Throwing up?"

"Yeah, in the mornings." Lee felt like throwing up. "If she is pregnant, it will kill me." He was not exaggerating.

In the afternoon, Lee was able to dismiss the likelihood of Lynn's pregnancy. Jenn Franklin had been right about the hundreds of "what if" scenarios Lee had imagined in the last year and a half. This one was more far-fetched than most. Lee rejected the notion and focused on something more familiar to him – his hopelessness.

Lee pulled his brick-colored Oldsmobile Ciara up to the curb in front of the house. He sat in the driver's seat and thought about all the nights Lynn had "borrowed" this car and went joy riding with her friends or sometimes alone. Once, when she was fourteen, she had driven the car out to the truck stop along Interstate 81 to play video games. She was alone. What would possess anyone to do that? Lee had never taught her how to drive, but all the years she sat in the backseat with Michael, she had been watching Lee or Ruth as they drove. Apparently, she had learned by observing. Lee marveled at her bravery – and stupidity.

Lee sat there and shook his head. What had happened to him and his family in the past couple years? Everything had fallen apart, and there was no indication that the downward spiral would end. Maybe, if he could send Lynn away, he would have a little peace and could pull himself together enough to emerge from wherever he was. Lee realized that, wherever Lynn went, she would still be a problem for which he was responsible for two more years. Lee could not imagine living this way for two more years. It was simply beyond his human ability.

He opened the car door, trudged into the garage, opened the door to the kitchen, and entered the house. As he stood there with his briefcase, he heard a soft noise in the living room. He put his briefcase on the table and walked slowly toward the refrigerator. He peered into the living room and saw Ruth sitting in the tulip chair by the front door sobbing and holding a tissue. Lee stood motionless for a moment and tried to assess the situation. Before he had become ill, he would have immediately hurried to her side and comforted her. That sort of compassion for anyone, even Ruth, had been lost to him for many months. Ruth had faithfully stayed by Lee's side throughout this struggle without shedding tears. For Ruth to sob like this meant there was something extremely amiss.

As Lee peered down at the floor as though he would see the answer written there, he heard other sounds coming from the room. Someone else was in the room with Ruth hidden from Lee's sight. Lee hadn't noticed any cars outside other than his own so whoever was there was not a visitor.

Suddenly, Lee felt sick. He looked into Ruth's eyes and, with no emotion, he asked, "Morning sickness?"

Ruth nodded without saying a word. His immediate thought was one of relief. This was his chance to send Lynn away. He could now justify his disdain for her and tell her to pack her things and go live with the losers she had been spending her time with these past months. He would be free of her at last by her own doing – not his. For a moment, he imagined himself saying to her, "and don't let the door hit you in the butt on the way out."

He walked to the threshold between the living room and the kitchen and looked over to his right. Michael was sitting on the chair by the far wall with tears in his eyes. Lynn was sitting in the middle of the sofa to Lee's immediate right. She was sobbing uncontrollably and looking down at the floor. She wouldn't even look at Lee.

From somewhere deep within the recesses of his soul, he hurt for his little girl. Compassion that he had not known for more than two years welled up inside of him. It was as if someone or something inside Lee was taking control and casting all the hatred that he had accumulated for Lynn over these months into a place of forgetfulness – or at least forgiveness. Lee was quietly dumbfounded at what was happening inside him. It felt completely foreign to him, but he had to let go of it all. He had no choice.

Without a word, he walked over to the sofa and sat beside Lynn. She appeared so pathetic as he looked at her. Then something even more amazing happened. Lee raised his arm and put it around Lynn. He was trembling. Tears were coming to his eyes. He said, "It will be okay. We are all going to get through this together." Even as he was saying it, he could hardly believe it was his arm and his voice.

It was as if the Creator was speaking directly to Lee and Lynn, "Okay you two. The chasm between you is far enough. It's time to come back out of the pit."

This was apparently not the response Ruth expected from Lee. She was overcome by the scene playing out before her and cried, "That's why I love your father."

For the first time in as long as Lee could remember, he had felt some strength and shown some gumption. He was still the husband and father, and he felt like it again – at least enough to recognize it.

There was talk about "fixing" the problem at hand immediately. Even in his still weakened mental state, Lee knew that decision would only result in regrets for months and years to come. Lynn wanted to keep the baby, but Ruth and Lee objected and would not even consider the option. The only outcome they could envision from such a choice was them raising a grandchild while Lynn continued living as she had these past two years. No, that was definitely out.

Conversation turned to adoption. Everyone seemed to agree with the idea. The specifics were much more difficult. Lee insisted that Lynn would have to go away for the next several months and have her baby elsewhere, after which she could return home. He could not fathom living in the same house with his daughter while she was pregnant. He did not anticipate an improvement in her behavior. Ruth agreed with Lee, but Lynn was adamantly opposed to Lee's proposal. She began to sob again.

Lee was moved again by her tears and offered a compromise. They would simply play it by ear and see how things went in the household over the next few weeks. If Lynn could abide by the rather minimal rules of the home and be respectful, she could stay. At first Ruth held out for Lee's original proposal of having the baby somewhere else, but she eventually bought into the compromise.

Later in the evening, Lee thought about the events of the afternoon. He was trying to discern what had happened. Earlier in the day he had told Greg that, without a doubt, if Lynn was pregnant he would be incapable of surviving any longer. Yet, the reality was that her news, in some way and for some unknown reason, probably saved his life – at least temporarily. It was some sort of supernatural encounter that he could not understand. The feelings he had had during the afternoon were indescribable. It felt like some sort of spiritual experience – unlike anything he had ever known. It had been a very powerful occurrence that was satisfying, and even comforting, in some strange way.

Over the next few weeks, not a whole lot changed. Lynn was still hanging around with her group of friends, known as "undesirables" to Lee. The compassion and tenderness of that tearful, soul-searching afternoon weeks earlier were gone and had been replaced with the more familiar distrust and anger of the previous two years. Life was back to the normal dysfunction to which Lee had grown accustomed.

One evening Lynn was in her room talking on the phone. Lee was sitting in the living room trying to simply get through the evening when he heard Lynn become very loud and agitated. Lee had heard that this particular friend was a drug dealer and that Lynn liked him at some level Lee didn't care to know about. Lee assumed this guy didn't know Lynn was pregnant yet, so he thought it would be best to end the conversation for Lynn. He went to her room, grabbed the phone, and walked downstairs to hang it on the wall. Lynn was right behind him breathing fire.

Lee sensed this was going to be the showdown that would make or break him and determine the direction their relationship would take. He walked into the living room and stood. Lynn's face was inches from his and she screamed as loudly as she could, "If I had a baseball bat, I'd kill you!"

Without blinking or hesitation, Lee fixed his eyes on Lynn's eyes and bellowed into Lynn's face with everything he could muster, "You go ahead and get a baseball bat and see what you can do!"

His heart was pounding. He knew he was either going to get well tonight or die trying. Lynn called him a few unsavory names. He slapped her face, and she ran outside into the dark night. He had just confronted the thing he feared most and was still alive. He knew he would be well again one day.

Days passed, and Lee was able to see that he was becoming more functional than he had been in the previous year and a half. Lynn was a junior in high school but had missed so many classes during the year that it was nearly a certainty that she would not be a senior next year. In fact, Lee had already assumed that she would simply fail and drop out of school. Maybe one day, if she could get her attitude and behavior together, she would get a GED.

For some reason that Lee could not understand, the principal of the high school contacted Lee and Ruth with information about an afterschool program for kids with "academic difficulties." The principal saw the same potential in Lynn that Lee and Ruth had known she had since she had been a child. Her intellectual potential was never the problem. It was her deteriorating behavior that began when she became a teenager.

For the first time in many months, Lee was able to sit in the company of others and participate in the role of a father without feeling completely overwhelmed. Ruth and he joined the principal and the teachers to discuss the afterschool program. This really seemed to be the only hope for Lynn if she was going to graduate from high school. The program outline was very simple. Lynn would be employed by a business in the area for half of each school day. Later in the day after regular school hours, she would be attending classes at the high school with others who were in the program.

Lynn started the program and seemed to have a completely different attitude. She was going to work and attending class. Things were going very smoothly compared to the previous two years. Lee's emotional state had improved greatly as well. He was more functional at work and able to enjoy life for the first time in many long months. He had weaned himself off the venlafaxine over a few weeks and was no longer ill from his body's struggle to tolerate it. He still experienced those brain flips from the withdrawal from the drug. They lasted for six months and were extremely disturbing. He was sure that getting off the venlafaxine had helped greatly. He also discontinued the mirtazapine and was taking only the clonazepam. He had started drinking again on Friday and Saturday evenings. That seemed to take the edge off. While he drank, he would often sit in his chair in the living room with his headphones on, his feet up on the coffee table, and the smooth jazz filtering into his brain. It didn't get better than Wes Montgomery, Lee Ritenour, and Fourplay. Lee was starting to feel almost human again.

Over the next six months, Lee and Lynn spent a lot of time together re-establishing the relationship they had once enjoyed. The love that had been temporarily clouded by hatred had not died. It had only been dormant until it could re-emerge and blossom again. They had some truly special times over those months enjoying their renewed relationship.

One evening Lynn sat in a parking lot with Lee for two hours while he tried to repair her car. He never did get it running, but the time together with Lynn was priceless. They laughed and joked and reveled in each other's company. It didn't matter that Lee had to pay someone to fix the car the following day.

During the hot summer days of Lynn's pregnancy, Lee and Lynn would often go to Rita's for Italian ice. The trips were more frequent as Lynn's belly got bigger. They would often act goofy as they stood in line. Sometimes Lee wondered what the other people who looked at them were thinking, but he didn't care. A pregnant sixteen-year- old girl and a middle-aged man who was acting like he was sixteen was probably a sight. Life felt good for the first time in a long time. Lee wanted to share it with others. Maybe intense pain was a prerequisite for such unbridled happiness and joy. Lee didn't know, but right now his life was brimming with the delight he felt for his daughter. He loved her again.

One evening during that hot summer, Ruth and Lee were having dinner with a couple they had attended church with years earlier. Lee and Jerry used to golf together frequently, and Ruth and Penney would often have lunch and visit the shopping outlets together. The conversation was one of old friends reacquainting themselves once again and "caching up" on things that had occurred during the years they hadn't seen each other.

Over the course of their conversation, Penney mentioned that a young lady in their church, Brenda, had recently committed suicide. Ruth and Lee remembered her from years past when they attended that church, but Lee also knew her from his frequent visits to the drugstore across the main road from the development where he lived.

Brenda was a very attractive, young lady with an amazing smile and sweet demeanor. One day in 1998, Lee had visited the pharmacy of the drugstore where Brenda worked. He was picking up his prescriptions and was in his barely functioning, too-sick-to-cry mental state. He got the drugs from the pharmacist in the back of the store and went up to the checkout counter at the front of the store to pay for them. Brenda was standing there smiling and waiting to help him. Lee was sure that she didn't remember him, but he was certain she was Brenda. Her name tag confirmed what Lee already knew.

As Brenda scanned the two prescriptions, Lee looked at her and imagined what her life must be like. She was beautiful and intelligent with a whole lifetime ahead of her. She had one of those smiles that seemed to never completely fade from her face. She appeared to be without a care in the world. In one way, it irritated Lee. It didn't seem fair that anyone could seem so happy while he felt so miserable. In another way though, he wanted to blurt out how awful he felt. She seemed so cheerful, almost like an expert in happiness. Maybe Brenda would have some notion about how to rescue Lee from his inner turmoil. He almost said something, but he didn't have the courage. She would probably think he was a strange middle-aged man. He paid her the money for the prescriptions, thanked her, and left the store.

Lee sat at the table with his wife and friends and internally chided himself for not speaking to Brenda that day. If he would have spoken, she might still be alive. Lee promised himself he would never remain silent about such matters in the future. Maybe behind her smile, Brenda had been struggling with her own issues. A few words might have made a difference. Lee would never know. He'd never have that opportunity again.

Lee couldn't get his mind off Brenda and was immersed in that encounter inside his head. He could hear Ruth, Jerry, and Penney chatting and laughing, but he was far away. He thought about the two times in his own life when he was so distraught that he had planned his own suicide. They were both caused by the effects of prescription psychotropic drugs. There was no doubt about that in Lee's mind. The suicidal ideation from the paroxetine was extreme and almost immediate. The relentless poly-drugging over the next eighteen months put him in the same place of despair and hopelessness – so hopeless that even death seemed more desirable than continuing in the hell that his life had become. Only nine months ago, he had discontinued the antidepressants, and the hopelessness had vanished. Lee wondered if Brenda had been taking psychotropic drugs and surrendered her will to live to them. He would never know. It was so sad.

One night, as the summer of 1999 was nearing its end, Lynn's pregnancy was reaching full-term. She was having labor pains, and these seemed like the serious ones. It was time to head for the hospital. Lee, Ruth, and Lynn got in the car, picked up Will, the father of the baby, and headed for the hospital. Lee dropped everyone off at the front door of the hospital, and he parked the car.

He walked back to the hospital building and settled in at a lounge area outside the delivery area. He was feeling rather decent and was pleased with himself for being able to stay relatively calm. He could smell coffee brewing at the snack bar. The aroma resurrected a desire in him that he hadn't known in quite some time. He hadn't had a cup of coffee in well over two years. He had developed a fear of caffeine in 1997 at the beginning of his struggles with anxiety and panic attacks. He thought about the possibility of having a cup. The fragrance was beckoning him. So what if he had a panic attack? He was in a hospital. What better place to be? They would rescue him if anything happened.

He gave in and purchased a cup. It was delightful and brought back feelings that had been long forgotten. It gave him that special energy that he had not experienced in a very long time. He felt a kind of release from the mental and emotional prison he had been in since he took that first little red pill in June of 1997. The first of thousands of pills. What a long time to be incarcerated for a crime he had no recollection of committing. He had a sense of confidence and freedom – so much so that he decided he would write a letter to Jenn Franklin telling her that he was among the living once more. He thought she might appreciate knowing that one of her former clients was well and living a real life.

As Lee sat there in a deeply satisfying mood, sipping his coffee and penning his thoughts on the back of a napkin, Ruth came into the lounge and sat in a chair beside him. He looked over at her and saw an exhausted woman with a disconcerting expression.

"How's it going in there?" Lee inquired.

"She's delivering now. I couldn't stay and watch."

"She's having the baby right now?" Lee continued to question.

Ruth nodded. Lee knew that Ruth had been upset about the whole pregnancy and, even more, the fact that her granddaughter would never really be hers to hold and cuddle and love. There would not be sleepovers at Grandma's house or reading stories or playing "This Little Piggy" or baking cookies or...anything. Her granddaughter would belong to and be raised by others. All the dreams a grandma has for her granddaughter would remain dreams forever. There was no reason to get attached to a little one to whom she could never be close. They would be strangers to each other on this earth.

Lee had experienced similar emotional turmoil from loss throughout his life. In fact, this event felt like one more episode of the same television series. It was not that he did not care but rather that he had so much numb scar tissue from past injuries in his life that only the most profound suffering by others could move him. He had developed his own perspective on life and loss.

Over the years he had concluded that all the losses early in his life would serve as an advantage in his later years. He was not a rookie in such matters. Maybe it was preordained that it would be this way so that he could be strong for others. He really didn't know, but that seemed to be how his life had played out.

Yet, he understood Ruth's pain, and her pain was his pain. That's how a marriage was supposed to be. He spoke, "Yeah, hard stuff." They waited together.

Several minutes later, a nurse came into the lounge and told Lee and Ruth that they could go in and see the baby. As they made their way into the room, Lynn was holding the baby, and Will was standing beside her. Lee took a mental picture of this new family that would not exist for more than just a couple days. Lee felt a twinge of sadness deep inside.

Lee moved to the side of the bed and peered down at the little pink face peeking out from the soft, white swaddling blanket. She wasn't more than a few minutes old. Her eyes were closed. Her lips were tiny just like he remembered Lynn's lips nearly seventeen years earlier. Lynn raised her toward Lee. He put his hands gently under the blanket and raised her to his chest and held her close. It seemed like only yesterday he had done the same thing with Michael and Lynn. Some things a man never forgets how to do. This was one of them.

Lee held her in his hands and prayed for this little one who would be his granddaughter for only a few days. He thanked God for this precious one. He prayed for her health and safety as she grew. He prayed for wisdom for the parents who would be coming to take her to their home. He prayed that she would be blessed and that she would be a blessing to her parents and others. He prayed for his own family and for the continued healing of hurts. Amen.

There were tears of course. It was sad, but there was also peace in knowing that, because of a wise decision by his own daughter, two other people would have a baby to love, cherish, and raise. They would see this tiny one grow from a sweet baby into a young lady, and their lives would be blessed because of the unselfish choice of his daughter. Lee was proud of Lynn, and he knew he would be proud of this little one as well. She would always be a special part of both Ruth and him. That could never change.

Three days later Lee returned to the hospital. Lynn and Will were standing at the curb of the pickup area waiting for him. They got in the car, and Lee slowly pulled away. Although there was silence in the car, their thoughts were almost loud enough to be heard. Someone was missing, but no one said a word. On the way home, Lee contemplated the silence and the atmosphere in the car. There was a sadness. He could feel it. He felt it inside himself. He marveled that this sadness was markedly different from his struggle of the previous eighteen months. Then he had lived with a black depression that was a kind of sadness but much more. It had combined with an anxiety, a fear, a hopelessness, a total lack of believing life had any meaning. It had felt like being pulled into a black hole with no chance to escape. It was an unnatural, unwholesome, manufactured type of depression that was thrust upon him when he took that first antidepressant in 1997. It was only by God's grace that he had somehow escaped after eighteen months.

No, this sadness was different. It felt real and wholesome. It felt like it was supposed to be happening in him. In a strange way, it felt good – maybe because he was once again feeling human with normal human emotions. He could feel life again. He was alive. He smiled as he drove home simply because he was sad and he knew the reason why.

One evening later in the week, Lee was sitting in the living room pondering the last two years and basking in the happiness that he was no longer in the grips of the anguish he had endured for so long. In fact, he called those two years the "blank" years or the "black" years. Both were equally valid descriptors of that time of his life. He had almost no recollection of specific events that had happened in those years. He could only remember the torment. It felt almost as though those years never occurred for him. Maybe others had lived life during that time, but he hadn't. He had simply existed.

He recalled the trouble at work and the simultaneous beginning of Lynn's teenage rebellion. Although he was rock solid and he had thought he could handle anything that would come his way, he was obviously wrong. He had been completely unprepared for either of those problems, and he had cracked. He remembered the jitteriness and shaking during that period in time and that he quelled those feelings with large amounts of alcohol. Then came the panic attacks in his sleep and while driving. He still could not grasp what had caused the panic attacks. Surely it was not just the trouble with Lynn and the problems at work. The answers eluded him now just as they had during all those months in 1997.

Next came the alprazolam, which helped momentarily, followed by the paroxetine that spiraled him into the abyss of hopelessness. Now he knew the vile, suicidal depression was caused by eighteen months of psychotropic drugs. Two years later that was very clear. Yet, he still could not determine the reason for the initial panic attacks. No matter. He felt human once again. The depression and panic attacks were in the past. It was no longer important to find their cause.

As Lee mused over these thoughts, Lynn came into the room and sat across from him in the chair by the front door. Lee was feeling calm and reflective. He wanted to start a conversation with his daughter about the life they had both lived these past few years. They had been hard years for both of them, each struggling with their own internal issues. Regrettably, they had fed off each other's negative emotions. The more emotionally ill Lee had become during the blank years, the more rebellious and angry Lynn had become. This always made Lee more emotionally unstable, and the continuous cycle spiraled both of them into a vortex from which they narrowly escaped.

Interestingly, they continued this pattern, but happily it manifested itself in positive changes. As Lee continued to feel well and become stronger again, Lynn's rebellious demeanor eased, and she began to "see" the father from her childhood. Her perspective of Lee changed, and her behavior began to revert back to the Lynn whom Lee had known in her first twelve years. In time they became friends again. Maybe they always had remained friends and just lost sight of it. There was some saying about hurting the ones you love. Perhaps these past two years were proof of that for Lee and Lynn.

"So how's it goin'?" Lee thought that was a pretty general question to start with. He hoped it would evolve into more.

"Good. A little sad."

"The baby, Marie Lynn?"

"Yeah. I hope she is okay. I mean…" Lynn sighed.

"I'm sure they will take good care of her. They are good people. You made a good choice." Lee had watched the videos with Lynn of prospective couples who wanted to adopt her baby when it was born. Lynn had chosen the same couple Lee would have chosen. She had made a wise choice.

"But it's just so…" Her voice faltered.

"It hurts. I know. It hurts." Lee's words trailed off, and they sat there silently for a while absorbing those words and feeling the hollowness of the hurt. Nine months is a long time to carry another's life inside one's body. Although he had never known that feeling, he imagined it must be very difficult to part with one you had given life to. He searched for words with deeper meaning. "I am proud of you Lynn – for making the decision to have her and for allowing her to be a blessing to someone else. That was very unselfish." He really meant it. Lynn had changed a lot in these past nine months.

"Yeah. I couldn't keep her. I have to go to school. I couldn't…"

"Do you remember the day when I came home from work and you were in here crying with Mom and Michael?"

"Yeah. That was terrible."

"I don't think I ever told you this, but the day before that I was…" Lee had to stop for a moment and collect his emotions. Trying to speak of that time always brought tears and made it hard for him to speak. "Um…I was thinking of killing myself. I had a plan. I was going to…" It was almost impossible for him to say the words. "…uh, commit suicide." He hated the sound of those words because he vividly remembered that place of pure hopelessness – the loneliest place he had ever been. He was looking down at the floor.

Lynn rescued him. "You never said."

"When I came in the room and put my arm around you that day, something powerful happened. It was from God. I knew I was going to be okay. We were going to be okay. I knew we were both being pulled out of the pit at that very moment." Lee started crying quietly. It was always difficult to get through the raw emotion without breaking down a bit. "Marie Lynn saved my life."

Lynn sat there for a moment in deep thought. "She saved my life too. I was drinking and taking any drug that I didn't have to inject. When I found out I was pregnant, I quit all that and started to take care of myself. I didn't want anything bad to happen to her."

They sat in silence considering these revelations. The Lucas family would have been destroyed if Lynn had not become pregnant. Lee and Lynn could both be dead. How would Ruth and Michael have coped with a suicide and a drug overdose in their family? Marie Lynn had saved two lives before she was even born. Lee and Lynn would never forget the little one who was part of an amazing miracle in their lives. She would always be part of them. The whole Lucas family would always be grateful for that gift.

Lee and Lynn sat together a while longer each enjoying the feeling of their own special freedom. The only psychiatric drug Lee was taking anymore was a little clonazepam. All the other drugs were long gone. Lee suspected that he would have to take the little yellow pills the rest of his life to keep the original panic attacks at bay. Surely he would never have to revisit the world of panic attacks, anxiety, and suicidal depression as long as he was careful to take the clonazepam.

Chapter Eight

January 17, 2010

Lee opened his eyes and had to wait a few moments in order to get his bearings. Where was he? Obviously he was not sitting in his living room talking with Lynn and feeling good about life. He was lying on a bed. He tried to figure out where he was without moving. He stared at the ceiling and tried to focus. Nothing. He let his eyes drift over to the right side of the room. Another bed with someone sitting on it. That did not register. He glanced at the door to the left of the foot of his bed and noticed it was open. On the other side was a hallway. He heard loud voices. Dr. Ingerson's face flashed across his mind. Oogden Institute of Psychiatry. He was in a mental institution? Stark reality slapped him in the face. Yes, the voices beckoning him to end the anguish yesterday. The trip to Community Hospital. Wendy's. Paul.

This was no dream. Was the trip back to the 1990's a dream? No, that happened. That was true. He had lived all of that. Hadn't he? He moved his arms and legs in an effort to return to the present. Okay. Yeah. He had been trying to find a hint from his past that might help him discover a solution to his current state of insanity or confusion or…he couldn't find the right word. That was the problem. He had been depressed and suicidal back in 1997 and 1998. He came out of that in 1999. He remembered. Lynn. A baby, Marie Lynn. A miracle.

But what else? There was something else – something more tangible. He had quit taking all the drugs except clonazepam, and he started drinking again. He started to feel better in 1999. It was the drinking. It helped him feel better at the time. But drinking was not the answer now. The drinking had escalated over the past ten years until Lee knew he had to stop or die. He could feel it killing him. He had stopped the drinking just three months ago – on October 20, 2009. That was when the nightmare of 1997 and 1998 returned. Lee realized this was what triggered this new painful episode of panic attacks, anxiety, insomnia, and depression.

    Lee had struggled with alcohol for a very long time. He had been a drinker since he was a young teen, but his intake had increased greatly after he began to feel well from his alcohol and drug-induced nervous breakdown over ten years ago. In 2008 he had become concerned about the countless blackouts from his drinking and considered the possibility that he might be an alcoholic. He had discovered the fourth edition of *Alcoholics Anonymous* (more commonly known as "The Big Book") and read only a few chapters until he was sure his own story could legitimately be written in that book.

    He began attending AA meetings in February 2008 and even managed six months of sobriety. During those months, he knew he would drink again, and he did. He didn't want to drink, but he wanted to drink. It made no sense. He had no control. He could not suppress his craving for booze no matter what he tried. He had tried writing drinking rules for himself which he could not follow. He bought books and listened to subliminal messages. He exercised more. Nothing worked. In the spring and summer of 2009, he went to the altar at church nearly every week asking God to help him quit drinking. He drank even more. In total desperation, he went to the altar one last time and asked God to make him quit drinking and to do whatever was necessary to bring that about. When Lee got up from his knees after that last plea of complete surrender, he was deeply afraid. Somehow he knew that the method God would use would include what he went through in 1997 and 1998.

    A few weeks later, Lee was on his way to see his two sisters for a few days. As he was driving to their home, he began to feel very anxious. He didn't give it too much thought believing that it would pass. He stopped to get a case of beer and then continued on his way. The next forty-five minutes became one continuous panic attack. He arrived at his sister's house and was an anxious, shaking mess. He spent the two days there in a state of fear and anxiety with a constant dizzy sensation that made walking nearly impossible. As he drove home, the panic attacks returned. Just minutes away from his home, he crossed the Market Street Bridge shouting, "God help me! God help me! God help me!" He was terrified that he was going to pass out. He knew that last prayer at the church altar was now being answered. This was not going to be easy.

During the next two weeks, it seemed like the extreme anxiety might be plateauing. Lee hoped it would subside on its own, but it didn't. At the beginning of the third week, it felt like his life was falling completely apart. He couldn't eat. Sleep was impossible. He could barely go to work and was virtually non-functional while there. For six weeks he tried with every ounce of courage and strength he possessed to beat this demon. He had searched alcohol withdrawal on the internet and learned that there was something called post-acute withdrawal syndrome (PAWS) that alcoholics often experienced after getting clean. The symptoms of PAWS typically got much worse after a couple weeks and often peaked between four and six months of sobriety. He knew he couldn't make it that long without some kind of help. He had lost thirty pounds in six weeks and felt like a zombie from the extreme insomnia. The one milligram of clonazepam that he was still taking wasn't helping at all.

He tried to rationalize that, if this was all being caused by the absence of alcohol, maybe he could up-dose the clonazepam until the anxiety subsided and then discontinue it when he felt well again. So, he was off to see the doctor. Lee remembered that he took a low dose of an antidepressant back in 1997 and 1998 which helped him eat and sleep. Mirtazapine. That was it. He reminded Dr. James about the mirtazapine he took years earlier for sleep and appetite. Dr. James agreed and handed Lee a prescription for mirtazapine. Okay, the sleep and appetite were covered. How about the incessant anxiety? He explained to Dr. James that he had also taken up to four milligrams of clonazepam back in 1998 when he was at his worst. Dr. James obliged him a second time with another prescription – four milligrams of clonazepam in three divided doses each day.

Lee was as hopeful as he had been in weeks, when he left Dr. James' office with the two prescriptions. Ruth and he stopped at Barnes and

Noble on the way to the drugstore. Lee purchased a couple relaxation CD's and a book. He was pulling out all the stops in hopes of beating this PAWS monster.

The pharmacist at the drugstore was a bit concerned about the dose of clonazepam written on the prescription, but he filled it anyway. Lee felt uneasy as the pharmacist looked at him. Maybe this was how a drug addict felt. No matter, he was confident that he would soon be feeling much better. Lee felt as though he was carrying two bottles of gold as he walked out the front door of the store. Now he would be able to eat and sleep. The clonazepam would surely reduce his anxiety to a manageable level.

He rushed home and took one milligram of clonazepam as soon as he got in the door. He hadn't felt relaxed in many weeks. He lay on the living room floor and waited for the pill to do its magic. Maybe he would fall asleep. Sleep would be welcome. After thirty minutes, nothing had happened. He became afraid and could feel his anxiety level increasing from the fear. He tried to calm himself. He rationalized that one milligram was the dose he had taken for nearly thirteen years. It was only his normal dose which hadn't worked for the past six weeks. Tonight he would add two more milligrams plus a low dose of mirtazapine. That would do the trick. He would definitely sleep. He felt a bit less anxious armed with a plan.

That night he took the two additional milligrams of clonazepam and the mirtazapine. He slept like a baby. He didn't wake up even once during the night. In the morning he didn't really feel rested, but he knew he had slept over ten hours. That fact helped his outlook even though he physically felt very tired and sluggish. After he took his morning dose of one milligram, he felt drowsy and fell asleep for a few minutes.

That was the last of the good sleep for the next six weeks. Even though he was taking a high enough dose of drugs to knock a horse out, he could get very little sleep. He continually woke up in sweats and panic when he did fall asleep. The days were an unending parade of increasing weariness, anxiety, and dark depression. He felt like he was being sucked into a black hole. He would soon be destroyed if something didn't change.

He emailed Jane and described his situation with the clonazepam. She responded with an email and an attachment listing the side effects of clonazepam. Depression and increased anxiety were on the list. His level of anxiety was off the charts, and the depression was devouring him. It was clear; he needed to get off the clonazepam. He did his own search and learned that it was very difficult to get off clonazepam and other benzodiazepines. If not done properly, it could result in seizures and death. He had no idea how to do it properly. He also read that withdrawal from benzodiazepines could take as long as two years.

Lee was instantly terrified. How would he get off the clonazepam? It was obvious that he needed to, but, if he did it wrong, he could die. If he did it properly, whatever that meant, he might have to suffer for two more years. That was something he knew he could not do. He didn't know how he made it through these past three months. Two years. No way. He did a quick review of his two choices – death or two years of suffering if he didn't die. They didn't seem like choices at all. He knew that up-dosing wouldn't work. That's what got him to where he now was. Getting off meant two years of suffering unless he died first. This was the rock and the hard place. This was not a proverbial dilemma. This was reality. It couldn't get more real than this.

He got up from the chair at the computer and went upstairs pacing back and forth with that dizziness that comes from a brain that is numb with dread. He could not imagine a way out. He sat down in exhaustion and defeat. The voices in his head started.

"And here I am at Oogden," Lee muttered as he looked up at the ceiling. He was now in the midst of that mental breakdown that he somehow knew would arrive. Lying on his bed in Room 702 of Oogden Institute of Psychiatry was proof. He whispered to himself and to anyone who might be listening, "I can't drink. That's why I'm here. I can't up-dose. That's why I'm here." He had no more words.

Once again he was stymied. He did get well, or at least he thought he did, in 1999. Did he do it with booze and clonazepam? He might have thought it worked before, but it wasn't going to work now. Booze and benzodiazepines were what got him into this place. It didn't make any sense. Nothing made any sense. Maybe he wasn't well these past ten years. Perhaps he only assumed he was well. Maybe the alcohol kept his mental disorders at bay for those years. That must have been it. Well, he hoped he was in the right place to get help. He just wanted to feel normal again – or at least be functional. He was not optimistic, but he had no choice. For him to be resurrected from this place of mental pain, he would need another miracle.

Lee sat up and walked over to the door. He wondered what time it was. He peeked out into the hallway, but he saw no one. He was relieved and disappointed at the same time. He wasn't sure why he wanted to know the time. He obviously wasn't going anywhere. It was not like he was going to be late for an appointment or for lunch. He had no appetite anyway. He cautiously walked into the hallway and looked to his left toward what he believed was the community room. He shuffled his feet in that direction. When he got there, he looked through the glass window in the door. There were a few people sitting in the room staring up at the television on the wall. He bravely pushed the door open and sat in the second chair along the wall. He sat there with no particular thought in his head, but his mind was racing. He looked through the bars on the window across the room toward the balcony outside. There was life out there, and people were feeling normal emotions and doing normal activities. Nobody was doing anything normal in here. Lee wondered if this existence could even be called life. Maybe there was no life in here. He felt like he had no life. He didn't want to be alive, but he was. He didn't like this kind of being alive.

While Lee was sitting along the wall playing games with himself inside his head, he noticed a young lady in a white lab coat rushing through the doorway beside him. In seconds she had made her way to the door on the other side of the room and disappeared. Lee assumed she was Dr. Richards. The lab coat gave her away. She was apparently very busy on this Sunday morning that didn't seem like a Sunday morning. In fact, it didn't feel like any morning in particular. It was a generic morning like every one of Lee's mornings in the past three months. They had all been dismally the same.

Lee's mind drifted from his ground hog day existence to the television. He tried to focus on what appeared to be a movie. He couldn't remember the last time he had watched a movie. He tried to recall some of the movies he had watched in his life. He couldn't think of even one. He knew he had seen movies in his lifetime, but that's as far as his movie knowledge went right now. His memory was almost totally shot. He knew he had a past, but he couldn't seem to access any of it. It felt like one huge three-month-long blackout.

The movement on the television screen bothered him. It was too fast and too busy. It created something that felt like fear inside him, but not really fear. It seemed more like an inner agitation that gave him a sense that he was losing his mind. The sound was even worse. His hearing was extremely sensitive. He wanted to scream at someone to turn it down. The pictures, the color, the movement, the noise were driving him insane. He turned away from the television, got up, and started walking back to his room. He didn't want to go back there, but he had nowhere to go and nothing to do. He had to get away from the television. It was too much sensory input for him.

"Room 702…702…702," he muttered as he trudged back down the hallway toward his room. He knew he should have some sort of expectation or some slight hint of what he would do when he got to his room. Nothing. His bag of desires was completely empty. It was more like the bag was lost. He couldn't even remember what it was like to want anything. Did he ever really have such a bag. He tried to push his thoughts backward to another time…any time. There were lots of bags in his past, but now when he peeked inside each of them, he found only misery upon misery. He decided to change the channel inside his head. He was better off without a bag right now. He would look for it later.

When he spied the 702 on the wall by the doorway of his room, he could not bear to enter the room. He decided to pass by and continue walking. If only he could walk and walk down the hallway through the doors and the walls and just keep going until he was far away from whatever this demon was that had control of his mind. The only problem was that the demon had somehow gotten into his head and would not leave. Lee could not evict it. The demon controlled the very thing that Lee would normally use to eject it from his brain. His brain. Channel change.

For some reason the double doors that had been locked last night were unlocked today, so Lee pushed on them. It took a great effort because he had become very weak since this whole mental debacle began in October. It was hard to remember when he had enjoyed working out. He had been a strong workout freak for years. Now he not only had the physique of a skeleton but also the strength of one.

His ankles were very sore as he ambled along. He could not bend them without severe pain so he walked as though his ankles were fused. He imagined it made him look even older than he was, but he cared nothing about his appearance or what anyone thought. To be honest, no one in the place looked very good. He continued walking slowly with his ankles throbbing and that unrelenting feeling of dizziness and unreality in his head. He made his way around the entire hallway to the double doors that opened to the community room area. He turned and began walking back from where he came. He did this three more times until he was too exhausted to continue. He finally surrendered and entered room 702 where he sat on his bed for a moment and then reclined. He didn't know what to think about, but it didn't matter because his mind immediately began counting the ceiling tiles for the hundred twenty-first time. He had to make sure there were still one hundred fourteen of them. He counted them in rows. He counted them in columns. He even counted them diagonally but had to do it three times to get a total of one hundred fourteen. He wondered what he would do if the number had changed to something else. Probably have a panic attack. Big deal.

"Mr. Lucas?" It was the voice of someone coming through the doorway.

Lee looked over at the door and noticed a middle-aged woman in a white lab coat. The garb gave her away. She was a psychiatrist. Lee simply mumbled, "Yeah."

"I'm Dr. Richards. I am the on-call weekend doctor. I will be seeing you today until you see the psychiatrist tomorrow who will be assigned to you during your stay here. He or she will have your records."

Lee stared at Dr. Richards for a moment and tried to process what she had said. She was his doctor for one day? What was the point of having a doctor for only one day? He was on a suicide watch lockdown floor. They were going to keep him from killing himself. He would be safe from himself until he was assigned a doctor tomorrow. He was sure of that because a staff member was looking at him every fifteen minutes or so to make sure he was still alive. What could a doctor do for him in only one day? She didn't even have his records.

Lee was about to find out. Soon he would be embarking on the next leg of a journey that would take him to places far worse than anywhere he had yet been – dark places existing in the infinite depths of unimaginable mental and emotional anguish. If he had known what was in store for him, he certainly would have found a way to kill himself.

Part Two

Chapter Nine

Summer 2014

The mountain was a very dark green except for a few lighter patches where the morning sunlight had found its surface. The sky was gentle blue with some lingering wispy, white clouds that seemed as though they were guarding the tranquility of the mountainscene below. Ruth had been out for the first leg of her early morning walk returning to announce that it was very warm and humid for 6:30 in the morning. She had just gone out the living room door to resume her walk, leaving Lee to sit alone in his chair in the living room. He had been there for quite some time sipping his cup of coffee and regarding the day ahead of him. This was his favorite part of the day now. Unlike Ruth, he had never been a morning person. If it were not for his coffee, the early morning hour would not appeal to him at all.

There was something about that first cup that opened his mind to the world. He had always wondered why that was. It was as though the coffee unlocked the door to deep thoughts that his brain must have produced while he slept. It lured them out into the light of day but not before translating them into crystal clear perceptions of the wonderment of life. It was hard to understand because, as the day wore on, those discernments usually became less vivid and often faded from his memory. They always returned the next morning as new perceptions that were equally amazing. It was much like reading the same book or looking at the same beautiful painting every morning but perceiving it differently each time. Lee used to think that he should record all these different insights so that he could draw on them in the future in case this goldmine of his ever stopped producing. Awakening to such wondrous ideas had not failed him for even a day in the past two years, so he eventually decided that it would not be wise to write them down. They might become stale, or he might rely on them too much and stop producing fresh insights and especially the dreams from those insights. He definitely should just let his mind freely wander to present him with new ideas without chasing after the old ones. He didn't understand it, but he sensed it was special.

He knew it definitely had something to do with his personality. In the past year he had taken one of those personality tests. For years he had considered them to be not only a waste of time but also meaningless and without any scientific merit. After all, he had been a scientist and mathematician for many years and liked to look at things as either black or white. He especially liked mathematics for that reason. Numbers never lied. The answer was the answer except, of course, for statistics. That area of mathematics seemed to be a way to manipulate numbers using techniques that he perceived to be beyond proof.

The purpose of the personality test he had taken was to first determine the various personalities of the members of the church board on which he sat. This information could then be used to explain why each member thought and acted in certain ways and could ultimately help the members of the board relate to each other in the most beneficial ways. Lee found himself to be what he viewed as the "statistical outlier" of the group. He was the "dreamy idealist" who was concerned more with trying new and different ideas rather than studying the details *ad infinitum*. He was a "just do it" type of person. The others were more cautious and oriented toward facts and details. As a scientist and mathematician, Lee was very capable of working with details, but he was oddly more interested in the "big picture" which was composed of those details. The exercise with the personality test explained a lot to Lee about himself, but, more importantly, it was a "light bulb" moment of enlightenment for him about human beings in general.

In his mind, it was evidence that everyone is "wired" differently. He envisioned the nervous system with its billions of neurons and trillions of synapses as an incredibly complex electrical wiring system. The probability that any two humans were or ever had been wired exactly in the same way was infinitesimal. The wiring was responsible for each person's personality. Each unique personality would perceive the things of life in its own unique way. Lee even thought about how he would perceive the very same thing differently at different times. It didn't mean his personality or wiring had changed or was somehow compromised. It meant that something else in his environment had affected how his wiring was functioning and caused him to perceive and react differently.

Of course, this was only how Lee perceived the reason for differing perceptions and behaviors. Every person on earth would perceive it at least a little differently. No wonder there was so much disagreement and even controversy over whether a given perception, mood, or behavior was the result of a "mental disorder" caused by some biochemical or physiological defect or deficit or was simply the result of a unique personality coping with something amiss, or perceived as amiss, in its environment. Lee was certain of one thing. Each person's wiring diagram was far too complicated for anyone to completely understand it.

As Lee sat in his chair holding his cup of coffee, he had a peaceful feeling. He remembered the previous evening. He had been listening to some jazz with the headphones and came upon a song that elicited some intensely poignant feelings. It was a song that he had heard at one of the turning points during his withdrawal from benzodiazepines, clonazepam to be exact. The song came to his mind again this morning. He dwelt momentarily on the anguish of that time of withdrawal with a thankfulness that it was now far in his past. In fact, it would soon be four years since he had taken that last little bit of clonazepam. It would be his fourth anniversary of being "benzo free." He smiled at the words. "Benzo free" was something of a victory cry for many people getting off benzodiazepines. Lee thought back on the first day he was "benzo free." That was only the first victory. It signified the winning of a single battle. For many, like Lee, there would be many additional battles in the war to be waged. It had been impossible to predict how brutal the battles would be or how long and seemingly eternal the war would last. Much of Lee's war had been spent not with what felt like great strength and valor but with tears, shaking, screaming, and unbearable, indescribable physical and mental pain. It had been like waging war while being tortured.

Lee shook his head as he looked across the room to the place he sat four and a half years ago. The voices in his head had told him to go upstairs and end his life. It was not a gesture of disgust or even regret. Instead, it was an acknowledgement of how extremely ill he had become on benzodiazepines and a near disbelief that he had survived the next two and a half years. Those years had been filled with a relentless suffering that was so intense, bizarre, and all-consuming that only those who had experienced it or were currently experiencing it could even begin to fathom. A slight smile came across his face. He had not only survived the minute-to-minute torment but was now mentally and emotionally more capable and stronger than he had ever been in his life. He was well. He was thriving. He remembered what had happened and always would – not out of fear or some kind of post-traumatic stress but rather out of gratitude and a sense of necessity to help others. He knew there were many people who needed help as they waged their own wars during withdrawal from benzodiazepines. He would help them get to safety – to the haven where he now resided. He wanted more company, and he knew he would get it.

His eyes once again returned to the mountainous scene outside his front window. It was so calm and peaceful and seemed to reflect Lee's mood. He took a sip of coffee thinking about the twenty-eight years he had sat in this very spot looking out the same window at the same view. Actually, this was not the original window. This was a replacement window that was installed in February 2010 while he was a resident at Oogden Institute of Psychiatry. That was nearly four and a half years ago now. His sense of serenity and comfort this morning was in stark contrast to his intense anxiety, depression, and distress then. He wondered how it was possible for a mind that was so extremely ill to heal so thoroughly, so perfectly. He knew he had lived through it, but it still seemed impossible.

Although nothing much changed outside over the years, his perception of all that he was seeing was vastly different. He looked at Pastor Dave's house across the street. He had probably viewed that home tens of thousands of times over the years without thinking much about it.

Now, every time he looked at it he thought of his conversation with Pastor Dave in October 2009. Lee had been in the midst of intense and increasingly worse anxiety caused by what he thought at the time was some kind of withdrawal from alcohol. Pastor Dave had prayed for him. Lee would always remember that encounter.

Lee's eyes moved to the house directly across the street next to Pastor Dave's. This house belonged to Bennett and Trudy now but had been the residence of several different owners over twenty-eight years. The one he remembered in particular was the couple, Mark and Sue, who lived there in 1997 and 1998 – his "blank" years. In the winter of 1997 and 1998, someone had apparently backed into Sue's car which was parked along the curb across the street. Lee had noticed that her car was dented but didn't think either Mark or Sue was home because there had been no activity at the house for days. The dented car had slipped his mind, but it was brought to his attention by Mark several days later. Apparently, Sue was home with the flu at the time. Mark had been furious with Lee for not telling Sue about the damaged car, so that it could be investigated. Lee could only stand there listening to Mark's barrage of verbal abuse toward him and all that he believed about life and the Creator. Lee had feebly tried to defend himself by explaining how ill he himself had been and still was, but Mark continued to spew hatred at him. As Lee sat there now looking at that house, he wondered if Mark still hated him.

Lee looked at the huge bush growing at the corner of Bennett and Trudy's property. This bush had its own special story in Lee's mind. Before he had quit drinking, it was Lee's custom to come home from work and get in a good workout before planting himself in that chair and drinking whatever alcoholic beverage was on his menu for that afternoon and evening. He would listen to jazz or seventies music and look out the window. After a few drinks, he would become fascinated with that bush. One evening he noticed that the bush appeared to have another plant growing out of it. For some reason probably having to do with his increasing inebriation, he would contemplate sneaking over there at dark on his hands and knees to cut down whatever was growing inside the bush. Of course, by the time it was dark enough, Lee was in no condition to follow through with the plan. In fact, he had usually forgotten about the plan, the bush, and whatever was growing inside the bush.

Lee smiled as he gazed at the bush. Five years later, Lee was still curious about that bush. In fact, one day last week he had walked over to the bush in the middle of the day out of curiosity. He pushed back the outside branches to discover that a twenty-foot high tree was growing inside the bush. The bush itself appeared to be some sort of honeysuckle. For some reason, even though he hadn't had a drink in nearly five years, Lee still wanted to cut the tree out of the bush or the bush from around the tree. It didn't really matter to him. Maybe it was the coffee. He chuckled as he took a sip from his cup.

He turned his attention to his own front yard and a Japanese maple tree that he had planted about a month or so earlier. Its delicate branches appeared to be trembling in the breeze that had replaced the stillness of the morning. It had a certain kind of beauty and elegance that he liked. Lee had planted a purple plum tree in that very spot nearly twenty-eight years ago. At the time, it was no bigger than the Japanese maple. Over the years, the purple plum had grown into a beautiful tree with a nearly perfect shape. In the spring, the pink blossoms covered the tree completely. It was gorgeous.

But the years had taken a toll on the tree. Ice storms in recent years had destroyed several of the limbs changing the shape of the tree. Borers had made their way into the root system and traveled up the trunk and into the branches sapping the tree of its life. Lee and Ruth had talked about replacing it for a few years, but it was always granted a reprieve thanks to their affection and sentimentality for it. This spring the blossoms were sparse and many branches and twigs were lifeless. Lee and Ruth thought it was best to put it out of its misery, just in case trees had feelings.

Lee tried to put it into perspective as part of the "ebb and flow" of life. The only constant in life on earth was change. What a seemingly strange paradox Lee thought. For years Lee could hardly bear change because he had feared what would replace the comfortable and familiar.

At the time he would have denied such a notion calling himself a realist. Now, having gone through the experience of benzodiazepine withdrawal, he realized he had always been a pessimist who expected the worst. He even acknowledged that the cause of that pessimism was purely based on his fear of change. Fear was a thing of the past now. What was left to fear after enduring and surviving the minute-to-minute terror that had defined him for over two years while he was in withdrawal?

Lee had decided that he would remove the purple plum tree himself. It was only about twenty-five feet high, so one Saturday morning he got out the ladder and rip saw and began the task. During the course of the job, many of his neighbors stopped to greet him and watch. One neighbor had even offered to lend him a razor saw which Lee gladly accepted. In a couple hours, the entire yard was covered with limbs, branches, twigs, and leaves. As he was taking a break, Bennett and Trudy came from across the street and offered to cut up the limbs and help Lee reclaim the lawn. He gratefully accepted the help. By the end of the afternoon, all that had remained of his beloved purple plum was a three-foot stump. Lee had been too exhausted to even think about the stump.

The following week he had decided that he would remove the stump by hand. Of course, he could easily hire someone to come and remove it, but he wanted to do it himself for a few reasons. It would replace his daily workout because it would be quite an aerobic effort. Additionally, Lee had always enjoyed a tough physical challenge. He imagined this would give him a great sense of accomplishment. After all, in the twenty-first century, how many people remove tree stumps by hand? A third reason had to do with others who were going through the same experience and struggles of withdrawal from benzodiazepines. For the past three years, he had been in contact with hundreds of men and women in various stages of withdrawal. Each person had his or her own set of physical, mental, and emotional symptoms. His successful removal of this stump would be evidence that his suffering had ended and theirs would as well. This act would show that one could return to accomplishing normal activities again. Okay, maybe removing a tree stump by hand was not exactly normal. His hope was that they would see his success as proof that the battle against benzodiazepine dependency and withdrawal could be won.

Over the course of the week, Lee had attacked the stump with a mattock and axe. Finally, he had removed it and rolled it, with great effort, out of the yard. He posted "before" and "after" pictures of the purple plum tree and the newly planted Japanese maple online with some text explaining what he had accomplished hoping that it would give a nugget of hope to other withdrawal sufferers. Hope was the precious metal of benzodiazepine withdrawal. It was the one thing that little by little got Lee from a state of praying for death to reveling in the joy of life. It would surely do the same for others.

Beside the Japanese maple was a bird feeder that Ruth and he had put out during the long months of Lee's withdrawal. Lee recalled the countless hours he had sat upstairs looking out the window watching the birds land on the feeder. It was simply something to do to pass time while his ailing brain was slowly healing. It had no other meaning or purpose. He had watched the birds to burn time. There had been no pleasure or amazement – only anxiety, depression and waiting for better days to arrive. Now Lee enjoyed watching them. The birds which had seemed only grey to him during withdrawal were now vibrantly colorful. The cardinals, blue birds, gold finches, and many others Lee could not identify were sources of amazement. They were proof that life is astonishing – that life is alive. The red and white vincas and violet petunias planted on either side of the bird feeder attested to that fact. The grey squirrels gathering the seeds falling from the feeder added to the impression that the small cutout island on the front lawn was an island of life teeming with hope and beauty. It had taken Lee most of his life to truly see and fully appreciate such simple things. It felt like a reward for having survived a period of nearly total hopelessness.

Although the neighborhood still looked much like it had when Ruth and he moved into it twenty-eight years ago, the occupants of most of the houses on their street had changed several times. The only exception was the house where Pastor Dave and his wife lived. When Lee and Ruth had arrived with Lynn and Michael in 1986, Pastor Dave's son and daughter were teenagers. Now both were grown and gone. The empty lot adjacent to the Lucas' on the east side now had a house, and the house on the west had been owned by a young couple whose names Lee could not remember. For some reason, Lee could only recall the name of their dog, Stingray.

Lee remembered the couple that had moved into that house not long after Stingray and his owners moved out. They were a young couple, Jack and Kristina. Jack was a fairly quiet guy who took great pleasure in his car. Lee thought he probably washed and waxed his SAAB a little more than necessary, but it was a fine looking vehicle. Kristina was a very energetic, outgoing young lady with one of those sweet smiles that never seemed to leave her face. Lee found her very easy to look at and talk to. In a few years, Kristina had a baby girl and later a boy. They seemed to grow into a happy little family over the years.

One Sunday evening in the fall of 1998, Lee had been struggling with his daily demons of anxiety and depression and went for a long walk around the neighborhood. As he was returning home, he noticed Jack washing and waxing his car. At first Lee wanted to cross the street to avoid eye contact or any form of greeting or conversation, but something inside him wanted to talk to Jack. Maybe Jack would have some insight into his mental and emotional state if Lee would mention something to him about it. Lee walked slowly by, and Jack said hello. Lee stopped and started a bit of small talk about Jack's car, his lawn, and other trivial subjects. He was terrible at small talk, but he felt a sense of desperation this evening. Somehow he got around to expressing what he had been going through in the last year with the anxiety, depression, and prescription drugs. Jack stopped what he was doing and looked right into Lee's eyes in what appeared to be amazement. Lee soon learned that Jack had been struggling with the same things and was also taking psychiatric drugs.

Sometime over the next several months, Lee had begun improving and he was able to return to work. Life became fairly normal. Jack was still struggling with depression. Lee had spoken with Kristina a number of times about her husband's trouble and how difficult it was for him. Lee was amazed at Kristina's compassion and "tough-it-out" attitude.

In the next few years, Jack continued to struggle, and Kristina seemed to get worn down. Lee remembered a conversation he had had with her one time about something she had read. It had to do with everyone being a god and deserving to be happy. To Lee it was simply an admission that she was tired and wanted something different – a chance at a happier existence. Shortly after that, their marriage dissolved and they were no longer together. It was very sad.

Lee could understand how she felt. During his years of struggle with anxiety and depression, he had been certain that Ruth would leave him. In his mind, it was not a matter of "if" but rather "when." He had known Ruth was getting worn down by his constant whining about how miserable he felt. It had become his total existence. His whole world was agony. There had been nothing else to talk about because he was aware of nothing else. He had been completely self-consumed.

But Ruth had a strong faith in her Creator and found strength in Him. That was the difference. Kristina was just as compassionate and kind as Ruth, but her focus had apparently become herself. It's hard to stay strong in the face of great adversity when you only have your human strength to draw from. Even the strongest people can run out of energy for dealing with others when the battle seems unending. At least that had been how Lee explained the demise of their relationship to himself.

Even now Jack lived nearby. Lee had spoken with him over the years and tried to convince him that the drugs he was taking for his anxiety and depression might actually be causing the symptoms of his diagnosed illness. Lee had explained that he had successfully gotten off clonazepam and was finally living life again. Jack, however, was convinced that he was mentally ill. There was no changing his mind. Lee would continue to hold out hope for his friend.

Lee got up from his chair and went into the kitchen to pour another cup of coffee. He had learned in the last three years that it was hard to convince some people that there could be happiness and goodness in the future. He had been one of those people. For years he had dwelt down in the dark valleys and, when a mountaintop experience arrived, he viewed it as an anomaly that would soon disappear and he would return to the ravine he had made for himself. It was a self-fulfilling prophecy in many ways. He would not let himself climb up to the mountaintop. He suspected he had been afraid of falling, so he stayed in his self-made abyss drinking and taking his little yellow pills to make certain he stayed there. He had been unwilling to take the risk. He had been afraid. No more. Those days were in the past.

Since this was Saturday, he had plenty of time to drink coffee and ponder. He poured the last cup of coffee, removed the soggy filter from the coffeemaker, and dropped it in the sink. He rinsed the carafe and refilled it to the four-cup level. One scoop of fresh coffee grounds into the new filter and once again off to his chair in the living room with his cup. He would return in a few minutes when the coffeemaker had cooled to flip the switch for the next pot. He ambled back to his chair and resumed his daydreaming.

The mountain attracted Lee's gaze one more time. There was something almost hypnotic about the mountain since Lee had begun feeling well more than two years ago. He could stare at it on clear days and notice things he had never seen before. For the last seven years or so, he would often look at the silhouette of the trees at the crest of the mountain against the blue sky in the background. Different parts of the silhouette reminded him of certain objects much like seeing objects in the shapes of clouds. In his mind he had observed six separate objects – a lion (which was starting to resemble a bear more and more as the years passed), a moose, a buffalo, Mr. Snuffleupagus from Sesame Street, a helicopter, (which now looked more like a guy riding a cow because one of the trees had died), and a jalopy.

During the two years of Lee's withdrawal from benzodiazepines after he had quit drinking, he did not look at the silhouette of the mountain at all. For those years, Lee had had no real interest in anything outside except the bird feeder which he watched from one of the upstairs bedrooms. He had preferred to keep the window blinds closed in the living room because even looking outside made him fearful – not of anything in particular but of everything in general. Lee would try to rationalize the fear away, but he had always failed. So he had simply accepted it as one of the countless, inexplicable symptoms of benzodiazepine withdrawal. The fear had been irrational. Period. There was nothing else to say about it.

His vision dropped to another area of the mountain in search of something he had first discovered in the autumn of 2012 when the leaves of the trees on the mountain were turning color. At the time, he regarded it as something that was unusual but had given it no more thought. The following year he noticed it again and tried to "mark" its location so that he could identify where it would reappear in 2014 – this year. He had mentally recorded its location from his chair. It was located at a spot that appeared to be directly above the tip of the crest of Pastor Dave's garage. Of course, it was actually located a half mile or more from the garage.

His discovery was a very small tree, or at least it appeared to be very small compared to the other trees on the mountain. In the fall, it was the first tree that changed color that could be seen from Lee's vantage point in the living room. Even more remarkable was the extraordinary color of the leaves. They were a vibrant, brilliant red unlike the color of any of the other trees on the mountain. Lee thought the tree resembled the burning bush at the side of his house, but, to be visible so far away, it was surely much larger than a shrub.

Even though he had marked its location last fall, the tree had disappeared into the various shades of brown-grey over the winter because its leaves had dropped. All winter Lee tried to imagine where it would be if he could see it. He wanted to be able to "predict" where it would pop up this autumn. One morning last month, to his surprise, he rediscovered it. It was a significantly lighter shade of green compared to the other larger trees surrounding it. Even though it was small, its shape was unmistakable. This was the tree.

This was obviously a special tree in Lee's mind. The first time he had spied it in 2012, he had just passed his two-year anniversary of being free of benzodiazepines. At the same time, the last of all the mental and emotional symptoms of his withdrawal had finally faded along with that relentless dizzy, disconnected feeling he had had for years. That was a symptom he had expected to haunt him the rest of his life. Even though he had always hoped it would leave, he really did not believe that it would.

For that reason, Lee had claimed this particular tree as his own personal tree. It would forever remind him that miracles happen. In the last four and a half years, he had been the recipient of many miracles. He never wanted to forget it, and this tree would help him to always remember the gifts he had been given. He called it his Tree of Hope.

In many ways, this tree was very much like the hope that had helped him survive withdrawal. For many consecutive months, the hope within him had been nearly imperceptible. It had felt small and insignificant compared to all the other overpowering feelings of fear, despair, guilt, shame, paranoia, weakness, anger, defeat, and even hopelessness. He had kept a tiny ember of hope alive every day by reading success stories of others who had survived withdrawal and who promised that there was a rainbow of wellness at the end – a wellness with a greater intensity of satisfaction, happiness, and peace than anything he had ever known. He had hoped that those stories were true, and his hope had paid off. Those success stories were truer than he could have imagined. Even though the hope had seemed small, it had been enough.

Lee could not see the Tree of Hope during the winter months, but he knew it was there somewhere among the rest of the trees. It had simply been camouflaged from his sight. It was much like the many times in withdrawal when his brain lied to him that he would never be well, that he was mentally ill, and that he would always be sick. Sometimes it said that he should just give up. At those times, his brain would not allow him to "feel" any vestige of hope, and he felt no hope. But there had always been that tiny spark inside his very being that refused to cower to the lies of his ailing brain. He might not have felt the hope, but he knew it was there within his spirit against which his brain could mount no attack.

At some point in Lee's withdrawal, he did start to feel the depression and fear lifting. This glimmer of wellness had fanned the flames of his hope until it burned brightly – just as his Tree of Hope seemed to burn brilliantly in the autumn. As time went on and Lee's recovery accelerated, he began to share that hope with others so that their hope would not be extinguished. As each person's hope grew and was shared with others who needed it, more and more people who were struggling would be helped. The Tree of Hope was the first tree to show its brilliant colors in the mountain each fall. That color soon spread to the rest of the trees in the mountain that Lee could see from his house. Just as the colors of autumn were spreading, Lee's hope was reaching many who needed it.

Lee thought that one day he would like to physically touch his Tree of Hope, but he wondered about the possibility. It was far away, and the closer he would get to it, the more it would be lost from his view. He would probably not be able to find the tree for the forest. Maybe it was just as well. Hope also cannot be touched, but it is still there. He would have to be satisfied to view the tree from a distance in full array in the autumn. It was enough just to know it was there and always would be as long as he was alive.

Chapter Ten

He took the last sip of coffee from his cup and went back to the kitchen to hit the switch on the coffeemaker. As he waited for the coffee to brew, he looked out the window of the back door in the kitchen toward the yard. In the past two years the backyard had changed dramatically. For two years the symptoms of his withdrawal from benzodiazepines had not allowed him to do any work outside except mow the lawn. Even that small task had taken every speck of mental and emotional energy he could muster because he had been afraid to go outside.

The forsythia bushes at the bottom of the yard had grown into a jungle. The arborvitaes at the east boundary of the yard had not been trimmed, and branches were split and broken from the weight of winter snow and ice. Weeds had overtaken the shrub beds until they looked like beds of weeds with a few out-of-place shrubs in them. But the worst feature had been the vegetable garden. Lee had planted it two years before the withdrawal. It had been overgrown with weeds, and the vegetables from the last growing season had lain rotting on the ground. The fence was also on the ground as a result of hungry deer and burrowing groundhogs. It had been an eyesore. His neighbors had probably thought he had died. They would not have been far from the truth.

In the past two years, he had trimmed the forsythias, removed the arborvitaes, taken a mattock and hoe to the shrub beds, cleaned up and removed the garden, and planted lots of grass. He was pleased as he looked at his rejuvenated backyard. In his mind's eye, he reflected back into his blank year of 1998. He remembered feeling the same fear of going outside. He recalled an overcast day in the fall of 1998 when he had been on a very high dose of mirtazapine. He had decided he should stain the small back porch. He had been so confused and felt like a terrified zombie as he tried to complete the project. His hands shook as he gave all his effort to the task. The grey, overcast sky of that day had matched his mood perfectly. For some reason, that particular day had stuck in his memory for sixteen years.

Lee's musing was interrupted by the sputtering of the coffeemaker signaling that his next cup was nearly ready for consumption. He poured the steaming coffee from the carafe into his cup and decided to go downstairs to the family room and check his email on the laptop. In the first few months after Lee had gotten off the clonazepam, Ruth and he had refurnished and re-carpeted the family room. Actually, it would be more accurate to say Ruth did it. She had picked out all the furniture and carpet. Lee had tagged along little more than a disinterested bystander who knew he should be an interested participant. He could not summon the motivation, courage or mental clarity to do so. He had managed to paint the family room before the furniture and carpet came. At the time it had meant nothing to him and had given him no sense of accomplishment. In fact, it had made him feel worse because he knew he should feel a sense of satisfaction or achievement. His ill brain had taken every opportunity to turn everything against him – even good things. This had been only one of many.

Lee sat down in the easy chair in the corner of the room, placed his coffee cup on a coaster on the stand beside the chair, and logged into his laptop. He would often get emails from others who were in the grip of withdrawal from benzodiazepines, and today was no exception. Many of these individuals were in extremely dire straits and grasping for the tiniest morsel of hope. Lee remembered those days very well. For months he had groveled for even a slight bit of hope – just a word of encouragement from someone who had survived it – someone who would tell him he would make it. It had been something he had to hear over and over and over. He understood the pleas of these people very well. They were going through something beyond horrendous. It was impossible to not reach out and help. Hope was the elixir that helped others endure suffering while time continued the slow process of healing.

Lee was humbled that he could use his experience to help others who were suffering. He knew he hadn't survived withdrawal by himself, and that made the humility and gratitude even greater. He could now look back on his entire journey with a calm clarity and ease that he had not had at any time during his fifteen-year trek that started with anxiety and panic attacks. The journey had taken him through countless psychiatric visits, more than a dozen psychotropic drug prescriptions, numerous individual and group counseling and therapy sessions, and other forms of ineffective and questionable treatment all of which had nearly resulted in his demise. If he had not, by sheer accident, stumbled upon others who were not even affiliated with the mental health care system, and, if he had not been rescued miraculously at other times by supernatural means, he would not be alive to contemplate his journey. He would be dead by his own hand. He had had specific plans to commit suicide four separate times in the last fifteen years – not in spite of the mental health care system – but because of that system. He still marveled at how his initial trust and reliance on the system increasingly grew to fear of that same system until he had finally been released from the "care" of the eighth psychiatrist.

He acknowledged to himself that a small fraction of individuals seemed to benefit from the system. Some seemed to be permanently trapped within the system extracting no benefit from it. Unfortunately, still others had been and were still being severely adversely affected by it. Some had died as a result of the treatment they received in the system. Sadly, Lee had known some who did not make it out alive.

Lee knew relatively very few people in the category he now occupied – those who had been adversely affected by the mental health care system but who escaped and regained health and happiness. He knew many who were trapped within the system and who were not really living life. They were merely existing just as he had for many years until he had stumbled upon the truth.

Now he was seated right here in his big easy chair in the family room. He wondered how he would have reacted to himself as a patient. What if he had been sitting in the chair of any one of the eight psychiatrists or more than a dozen other specialists, therapists, and psychologists, he had seen throughout his trip through the mental health care maze? He had survived some of the most hellacious mental and emotional suffering that he could ever imagine. This was a luxury that he knew was afforded to a rather small minority of individuals who had experienced or were currently undergoing treatment within the same mental health care system in which Lee had also been snared. In other words, he was one of the lucky ones.

He envisioned himself entering the office of Dr. Rosenberry. He would see an anxious, nervous middle-aged man take a seat in front of him. Of course, Lee would ask him how he felt – a question from which he could glean very little useful objective information. Mr. Lucas would describe his anxiety, panic attacks, inability to eat or sleep, inability to focus or think clearly, sense of hopelessness, exhaustion, restlessness, and all the other symptoms that an anxious, depressed person would describe. Lee would listen and understand why Mr. Lucas had come to see him. This would hopefully give Lee a sense of empathy – something that Lee had sensed in only one of the psychiatrists from whom he had received treatment.

Lee's additional questions would become more objective and would be directed by a sense of both compassion and logic. Being a mathematician and scientist, Lee viewed things of this complexity much like a series of mathematical equations with many variables – each of which must be assigned a value or answered in some appropriate fashion in order to solve the series of equations and come to a conclusion. In this case, the conclusion would be the reason or reasons why Mr. Lucas was feeling so poorly. Only then would Lee be able to construct a plan to aid Mr. Lucas' brain in helping itself to adapt to whatever caused its mental and emotional anguish and discomfort. Lee would suggest some sort of therapy or therapies to assist his brain to return to its normal condition.

Lee took a break from his game-playing and contrasted this to the questions he had been asked by Dr. Rosenberry and the other seven psychiatrists he had met in his journey. Nearly all the questions addressed symptoms – not for the purpose of finding compassion for a hurting soul or discovering the root cause of those symptoms – but rather to conjoin those symptoms into multiple mental disorders so that one or more anthropogenic psychotropic chemical agents could be prescribed. The intent of the questioning had seemed to be directed toward destroying or masking the symptoms without seeking the cause of those symptoms that might lead to ways to help his brain naturally address and eventually resolve the cause or causes. This was perplexing to Lee and seemed neither compassionate nor logical. It had surely seemed to be strange science – if it was science at all.

Lee returned to the role of doctor and the questions he would ask of himself. He would certainly ask Mr. Lucas what psychotropic drugs he was currently taking. He would ask this based on his own personal experience and the experience of thousands of others whose stories he had read or heard. He would want to ascertain whether or not the drugs themselves could be the cause of Mr. Lucas' symptoms and whether or not Mr. Lucas would be able to respond to non-drug therapy. Lee knew that he had been incapable of responding to therapy in any effective way while he was on all the various drugs that had been prescribed for him. The drugs themselves had made him very ill with different symptoms many of which were the very symptoms the drugs were supposed to treat. He had read and heard the same story thousands of times.

Lee would also ask Mr. Lucas about his family history especially with respect to others in his immediate family having depression. This was a question that had been posed to Lee many times in his interviews with psychiatrists. The intent of the question was obviously to determine whether or not a genetic component was involved in Lee's depression and anxiety. Lee had acknowledged that his father had suffered a nervous breakdown at two different times in his life. He had undergone electroconvulsive therapy both times. In addition, although Lee was only eight when his mother died, he recalled that she rarely smiled and often did not get dressed during the day, especially toward the end of her life. She had spent much of her time in bed. As an adult, Lee had been told by a member of the family that his mother committed suicide.

Lee had disclosed all of this information to Dr. Rosenberry and the other psychiatrists over the years. He had been told each time that his depression was genetic. There was no further questioning about it. No tests had been ordered to confirm such an assertion. It was as if the medical professionals believed it to be a foregone conclusion. Lee recalled that he felt doomed every time that declaration was made. He had been too sick, so he had no choice but to trust their expertise and believe them.

Eventually Lee had begun to get well. It was then that he could see that not one of those doctors had addressed the genetic issue properly. Yes, his father had suffered with depression two times in his life. The first episode was after he got home from the Korean War where he had contracted malaria and suffered terribly. Over the years, his father had become an alcoholic. He had often worked out of town and had ample opportunity for having a good time – which he took advantage of. He had reason to be depressed, and it had nothing to do with genetics.

Similarly, his mother had life issues as well. She had four children, the first out of wedlock prior to marrying Lee's father. Her husband travelled for work and was often away from home leaving her with the full responsibility for tending to the daily needs of four children. She had been aware that her husband was unfaithful. She had no driver's license or means of transportation to go anywhere. She had apparently suffered postpartum depression when Lee was born and was taking psychotropic medications for it. She never recovered from the depression which Lee's father blamed on the drugs. A very sad story but one with no evidence of a genetic predisposition for depression.

Now that Lee was well, he could see that the expert opinions of the doctors had been completely wrong. They had taken a small amount of true information and used it to justify an incorrect diagnosis. It had simply not been true. Lee did not have general depression – genetic or otherwise, and he certainly did not need psychotropic drugs.

No, Lee would be interested in Mr. Lucas' family history, but he would ask many more questions than he had been asked. He would save Mr. Lucas the terror of believing he was permanently and genetically sentenced to a life of anxiety, depression, and drugs. He would not read the words on the jacket of the book of Mr. Lucas' life and pretend he understood everything about the cracks and crevices contained in his life's tome – a story that had been written minute-by-minute and day-by-day over fifty-some years.

Since Lee had survived the onslaught of the multiple psychiatric drugs prescribed to him and the withdrawal from those drugs and was now very well, he found a fascination with the thousands of stories he had read and heard. Stories of others suffering either while on psychotropic drugs or withdrawing from them tugged at his heart. He had even spoken with many who had heard his story and who were put at ease enough to share their own stories. Each was a mathematical equation containing many of the values for the variables Lee had imagined. There were many variables that had little or nothing to do with symptoms of anxiety, depression, or any other mood or behavior. In reality, the variables had more to do with the reason for the symptoms rather than the symptoms themselves. The values for each variable would help to unlock the reason or reasons for the symptoms.

Lee had heard many times that everyone has a story. Certainly, most, if not all, of the answers were contained in a person's life story. The story had to be told to someone willing to spend the time to listen and to respond when needed. Lee had found that the mere act of listening to someone in mental or emotional distress often had a surprisingly quick, positive effect. The reason was very simple. Hurting people usually responded to others who would take the time to "sit in the mud" with them. The positive effect seemed even greater if that person had experienced the same sort of pain. Lee envisioned it as simply allowing the brain of the one in distress to synthesize or release its own natural antidepressants and anxiolytics by natural means.

Yes, every person he talked to had a unique, fascinating story. It was that story of each person's life, and within that story was the key to the mystery of why that person felt and behaved the way he or she did. Each story was complex and wondrous. It was a puzzle made up of many pieces – each one distinctly unique in its own way. Lee thought that it was certainly in the systematic unraveling of that story that the reasons for a person's mental and emotional state could be found.

During the first seventeen years of Lee's employment as an environmental scientist, he had a very creative, innovative mind and spirit. He had the privilege of working on many projects that required "outside the box" thinking with others who were very talented and energetic. Then came the panic attacks and anxiety. More importantly, that had been when the prescribing of psychotropic drugs also began. Although he had been functional for about ten of the next fourteen years, that zestful, inquisitive spirit of innovation and new ways of looking at problems had disappeared. The drugs had all but destroyed it. It was not until he had discontinued the benzodiazepine and struggled through two years of withdrawal that his mind and spirit had begun to return.

Contemplating all he had endured and his harrowing experience in the mental health care system, he smiled. His mind, spirit, and abilities had long since returned. Somehow his horrendous experience and the recovery from it had honed them so that his mental and emotional acuity seemed even greater than they had been prior to his thirteen-year sentence on psychiatric drugs.

His mind wandered to his experience in the mental health care system and all the things that could have been done differently to reduce the amount of time he had suffered or even to prevent his anguish. There were very few positive things he could say about that experience. In fact, the only one that he could think of was that they kept him alive while he was at Oogden Institute of Psychiatry. They had made certain that he did not commit suicide. Yet, he had felt like he was being tortured in countless ways while he was there. He had never understood that. Had they kept him alive merely for reasons having to do with liability? Could they truly not perceive the indescribable mental and emotional turmoil within him? How could one explain the seemingly cruel treatment he received? Lee seriously wondered if they had cared at all. That was simply how he felt about his whole experience. One day he would write about that painful part of his life.

Yes, there clearly was a problem with his experience in the system. He had read and heard about countless other similar experiences. He knew of very few people who had actually benefited from their encounter with the mental health care system. Most had been harmed. The system certainly didn't run like a well-oiled machine. It didn't run at all. It seemed more like a prison into which those who suffered with mental and emotional distresses were thrown – a human dump heap of individuals who were not understood. It seemed to be human nature for a person to either be incapable of feeling another's suffering, unless he or she also knew such suffering, or to refuse to acknowledge that such suffering was possible. Lee had been such a person prior to his experience in the system. He had been changed by the seemingly indifferent system. He now knew better. He had lived the truth.

Lee surmised that this would be a good place to begin to exercise his mind and spirit of innovation. A chance to sink his teeth into something new and different. The system was certainly broken and in need of repair. In fact, Lee thought it was in need of a complete overhaul. There was virtually no science involved anywhere in the system. Lee found this very strange considering the fact that those trapped in the current system were biological organisms – humans. The keepers of the system seemed to give the science of biology only lip service. They spoke of "chemical imbalances" but would often use wishy-washy disclaimers especially with respect to many of the psychotropic drugs they marketed. Lee found it ironic that no such disclaimers had ever been presented to him when his mental condition was explained to him by any of the psychiatrists he had seen. He had always been told with blunt certainty that he had a "chemical imbalance."

One of the psychiatrists he had seen pulled out a Venn diagram with three circles on it with each circle representing one of three neurotransmitters – serotonin, dopamine, and norepinephrine. That was the extent of all the science that had been used to explain the cause of Lee's condition to him. At the time, he had been so ill from the effects of the drugs and withdrawal from clonazepam that he assumed she knew what she was talking about. Lee was no longer ill. His mind was working properly. He was amazed that, even though his mind did not work during that time, his brain had still been taking notes to which he could now refer.

Lee truly wanted to learn about the science behind the assertion of a "chemical imbalance" in his brain. He wanted to study it and think about it. He wanted to dissect it and understand it. He loved mathematics and the sciences – especially biology in which he had a college degree. He wanted to know more than the paucity of information on a simple Venn diagram. He didn't want to hear about mental disorders being like diabetes and psychotropic drugs being like insulin without some logical foundation. If there were a true scientific basis for it, he wanted to see it. He wanted to examine actual chemical and physiological data and study biochemical equations. He wanted to read studies that considered the body's specific biological compartments and how they affected and were affected by the central nervous system. He wanted to see any other germane information that possessed objectivity.

He had begged for such information at the outset of his journey, but he had become so drug-sick that he had no longer been able to think about anything except his own misery. He had seen it many times in writing: "It is thought that such and such disorder is caused by a chemical imbalance." What did "thought that" even mean? And who thought that – other than the desperate ones to whom the story had been told? If you tell a lie big enough and long enough, will you begin to believe it yourself? Lee no longer gave the lie any credibility. The spell had been broken.

Psychiatrists, at least the eight Lee had seen, seemed to be incarcerated inside their own prisons with no desire to break out and think for themselves. They all mouthed the same mantra of "chemical imbalance." Surely, they could not believe that Lee's deteriorating condition over time had just been a worsening of some "chemical imbalance" which was making the disorders that he had never had worse. Did it never occur to them that the unrelenting drugging and ensuing withdrawals were creating a toxic backlash in Lee's brain or, perhaps, more properly, causing a chemical and physiological crisis for which his brain could find no answer? Lee was certain that he was not the only one who had responded to drugging in this way.

He would not be satisfied to see data from clinical trials of psychiatric drugs or discussions of statistical interpretations of such data. He had read the arguments on both sides of that coin. There was no way to know what the true data were or if such data had any validity. The data were based completely on subjective endpoints anyway. There was nothing objective about the data. He had read stories of thousands of people and communicated with hundreds of others who had taken or were taking psychiatric drugs. He had his own database. He didn't have to decide whether he needed to trust someone else's data. The vast majority of individuals he knew were not helped by the psychiatric drugs they were prescribed but were harmed in one way or another. If the "chemical imbalance" assertion were correct, this should not be the case.

He didn't want to hear high-sounding words from well-educated, well-dressed men and women with impeccable vocabularies unless they spoke of objective things. He had read enough psychiatric evaluations since he had gotten well to understand that psychiatric jargon, when boiled down to the language of the common man, was simply based on subjective opinions and without objective merit. Lee had always believed that language was created as a tool to help people communicate ideas, concepts, feelings, and so on in an understandable fashion – not as a tool to confuse one another. Abstruse verbiage was not the same thing as clearly stated wording. Whether by design or by accident, it gave the listener or reader the perception of being talked down to – of being inferior to the speaker or writer. It was intimidating.

It seemed to Lee that everything in psychiatry was subjective and based purely on opinion – on feelings. Every question in the countless interviews he had had with psychiatrists was subjective. Everything focused on how he felt and what types of thoughts he was thinking. The true and false questions on the Minnesota Multiphasic Personality Inventory did the same thing. He didn't know if he did well or poorly on that test. After Jenn Franklin scored his MMPI, she declared Lee the most depressed person she had ever met. He had been even more depressed after that announcement. He assumed he had probably done poorly. The questions that had been used to evaluate the effectiveness of the electroconvulsive therapy treatments he had been given at Oogden were all subjective as well.

During all the evaluations, Lee's brain continually played mind games that seemed very much like a battle or war between two parts of his brain. One part felt absolutely miserable and worse with each successive visit and line of questioning, but the other part was trying to convince Lee that he felt better – at least a little bit better. That part had tried to be hopeful and make Lee feel better. Lee would often sit for quite some time before answering the questions until his brain finished its "back-and-forth" discussion after which he was always confused and had no idea if he felt a smidgeon better or a lot worse. In frustration he would usually just give any answer. It hurt too much to try to "get it right." He desperately wanted to feel better, but he didn't want to acknowledge to himself that he didn't feel better and often actually felt worse. The process had been purely subjective. There was nothing objective about it. It was a system of evaluation devoid of any scientific merit.

Chapter Eleven

Lee's thoughts were suddenly interrupted by a noise. Ruth had apparently come down the stairs with a load of laundry and walked past Lee into the laundry room adjacent to the family room only a few feet from where Lee was sitting. The noise he heard was the washing machine. He picked up his cup from the table and took a sip. The coffee was cold. He had been so deep in his contemplations that he had forgotten about his coffee. Oh, well, cold coffee and loud noise. It was a signal to get on with the day. He grabbed his cup, ascended the stairs into the kitchen, and poured the cold coffee into the sink. Time to sweat.

Exercise was an activity that made Lee feel alive. It was excellent for his mood and mental clarity, especially with some nice loud fusion jazz playing. This morning it would be Return to Forever's *Hymn of the Seventh Galaxy*. He changed into a pair of sweatpants and went into the room that was once Michael's bedroom. It had been converted into a combination sewing room and exercise room five years ago when Michael moved out. It now contained a quilting table, an elliptical machine, and a Total Gym. Lee picked up the remote, hit "play," and the music began.

As Lee was going through his routine on the Total Gym, he could feel the endorphins doing their job. It was very nice. In between sets of five separate exercises, Lee would usually rest for about forty-five seconds. This was when his mind felt the most active and clear.

His thoughts returned to the subject of "chemical imbalance." He was still trying to make sense of it. All eight of the prescribing psychiatrists whom he had seen offered only one solution to his mental and emotional difficulties – psychiatric drugs. He had always been prescribed at least one drug. Usually counseling and therapy were recommended as adjuncts to the drugs.

Now that Lee had run the gauntlet through the mental health care system and was well, he could see that therapy and counseling had been useless for him. His brain had been so overmedicated that he was completely incapable of gaining any benefits from counseling trying to tolerate the drugging (and withdrawing from the drugs) that it was completely incapable of helping itself. He was unable to resolve issues from his past. He couldn't. His mind would just not allow it. Perhaps if he had received therapy and counselling without drugging, he would have had a chance at a quicker recovery, but that was not how it had played out for him.

Psychiatrists seemed to go straight for a "pharmacological approach" prescribing drugs for "chemical imbalances" whether or not there appeared to be any supportive, objective data or information. If that theory had been corroborated by objective data, Lee was certain that psychiatry would share it with the rest of the world immediately. Their silence on the matter seemed to be more evidence that most of their diagnoses and treatments relied on mere speculation.

Lee tried to think of an analogy. In his mind, it was like taking a car to a mechanic for repair. This particular mechanic's repair repertoire consisted of only three types of repair. He could replace the engine, replace the transmission, or replace the tires. For every automobile brought in for repair, the mechanic did only one of these things, irrespective of what was wrong with the vehicle. Of course, you would take your car somewhere else if it didn't need a new engine, transmission, or tires. Unfortunately, all the other repair shops did exactly the same thing. To make matters worse, the repair shops only had engines and transmissions available for ten different models of vehicles, and they sold only two sizes of tires. All the engines, transmissions, and tires were chosen randomly from the shop's inventory. It was a grab bag of sorts.

If you wanted your car repaired, you needed to assess the probability that the mechanic would fix your problem. Of course, there was a greater probability that you would leave with a much bigger, more difficult problem. Maybe your car wouldn't work at all. If your car's problem had nothing to do with the engine, transmission, or tires, you were out of luck. Anything the shop did would not help your problem. If the mechanic replaced your engine or transmission with parts for another model or tried to force the wrong size tires onto your car, you would be in for a rough ride home from the repair shop – if you got home at all.

The probability that you would be a completely satisfied customer was low but still possible. The likelihood that the repair would do something to harm the performance of your car and still not affect the original problem was high. You were left with no other options. You wouldn't want to keep driving the car until the problem got so bad that the vehicle no longer functioned properly.

You had heard that there were automotive repair courses where it might be possible to learn how to perform the repairs yourself using any parts that were needed – not just engines, transmissions and tires. It would undoubtedly take longer, but the chances of a proper repair would be much greater. Perhaps there would be others in the class who would be able to help you. You could help each other. If worse came to worst, there was always a professional mechanic, but that was a last resort.

This had been Lee's experience with psychiatrists and psychiatric drugs. It was also the experience of multitudes of others. A patient made an appointment with a psychiatrist for a mental or emotional problem that they had been struggling with for some time. There was only one "repair option" for the problem termed "chemical imbalance." That "repair option" was the prescribing of one or more psychotropic drugs by the doctor. In Lee's case and in the case of many others, the drugs did something other than "repair" whatever the problem was. More often than not, the drugs caused even greater problems resulting in more "repairs" with drugs. The original problem soon became dwarfed by increasingly much more difficult problems to fix – problems created by the drugs themselves. In some comparatively rare instances, the drugs did seem to have a beneficial effect on whatever the problem was. Lee had met very few people who attested to such results. His own wife, Ruth, was one of them. Her symptoms of schizophrenia had been diminished over the years from taking an antipsychotic drug, but she was also left with some bothersome and unpleasant effects from that drug. For every Ruth, Lee was certain he could find ten individuals who had been adversely affected by psychiatric drugs. This was not a success rate of which to be proud.

Lee was equally certain that, if those who had been adversely affected by psychiatric drugs would have taken the time to get counseling and therapy first, they would have had a better chance of obtaining a positive outcome. Lee looked at therapy and counseling as "self-help" that was taught and directed by someone else. He imagined it as the brain learning to adjust to or cope with distress with the guidance and aid of one or more other individuals. Perhaps it was a sort of chemical or physiological anomaly that only the brain itself could fix by producing its own natural chemicals and making appropriate adjustments. These adjustments were somehow enhanced or optimized by the mere presence or input of others.

The eighth and final set of exercises was over, and Lee sat on the Total Gym listening to the music. He knew he could think about the various theories of psychiatry forever and point out many weaknesses and fallacies, but what was the point of it? What benefit would it offer to anyone who was now trapped in the system or who would become its prisoner in the future? There were already dozens of opinions and arguments being bandied about by the "experts."

Lee had always found the word "expert" to be both confusing and amusing. In his mind, an expert was someone who knew a great deal about some subject – much more than the average Joe. If this were true, why wouldn't all experts have similar opinions on the subject in which they were expert? He had seen experts do battle in the courtroom many times. He, himself, had been one of them. It didn't take long for him to conclude that, if there were such a thing as an expert, his or her expertness was only as good as his or her bias. Everyone had a motive, and it was that motive that tinted and often tainted the validity of the expert opinion he or she rendered. We are all human – even "experts." Lee was glad that he had never become a judge who had to listen to opposing "expert" opinions. Judge Lucas would probably have carried a coin to flip in order to render any decision based on opposing expert testimonies.

No, delving into the nuts and bolts of psychiatry was a rather fruitless endeavor except for the mental exercise it provided. There was obviously something amiss with the mental health care system. Even those members of society who had never had the opportunity to be part of it, either as a worker or a patient, knew something was clearly wrong. If it were working properly and if people were getting well, wouldn't there be less so-called mental illness as time passed? If we were making great strides in psychiatric treatment, wouldn't the problem be diminishing instead of ballooning? Lee thought about it as he sat listening to Stanley Clark's bass. There must be a better way. He could think of several possibilities off the top of his head – alternatives to the current processes and methodologies. Surely someone had already tried these, hadn't they? In Lee's mind, they were only common sense. Had they ever been explored? Lee wondered.

He looked back on his experience with the mental health care system. It had not treated him well at all. It had literally forced him into retirement three years ago. The withdrawal from benzodiazepines had rendered him non-functional and brought him to his knees – literally lying face-down on the floor at one point. He could no longer work. He had not even been well enough to gather his belongings from his office when he retired. His colleagues had to bring them to his home – to a terrified, depressed zombie – a far cry from the high-functioning, respected scientist and mathematician with whom they had worked for many years. He had not planned to retire for a few more years, and certainly not in such a manner or condition. The psychiatric system, its drugging, and its failure to acknowledge or even understand what it had done to him ended his career, took away his self-respect, and nearly killed him. Its only response had been prescribing of more drugs, recommending more ECT treatments, and billing him for whatever monetary fee his insurance company wouldn't pay for his "care" at

Oogden Institute of Psychiatry. There was no acknowledgement that any wrong had been done to him.

Nevertheless, Lee was not bitter and had no resentment about his treatment by the system. He had escaped with his life. That was something that many did not do. He retired with a decent pension and did not lose his family or friends or his home. That was something thousands did not do. He once again possessed his physical and mental health. That was something that many thousands, and possibly millions, in the system would never do as long as they stayed in the system. No, Lee had no reason to be bitter. Others did. It was for them that Lee was angry. He would use his resources to balance the equation in their favor and help them escape, survive, and thrive. There was life to live, and everyone should be given the opportunity to live it without being incarcerated in a prison when they had committed no crime. They should be permitted to walk out of the matrix if they so desired just as he had done.

Lee looked out the window at nothing in particular and spoke, "A better mousetrap. Build a better mousetrap. They will buy it." He grabbed the remote and turned the music off. He had thoughts to think and ideas to ponder. He had perspectives to examine. This would be interesting, and, if it was anything like the old brainstorming, think-tank days, it would be fun. Lee was up to the challenge.

It had been seventeen years since Lee had done anything technically innovative with respect to logic, science, and math and he had been chomping at the bit to return to such endeavors. He would surely need others to join him in this quest because it would require input from multiple disciplines. Now that his brain was working well, he honestly couldn't understand why an approach based on logic and the scientific method had not been developed as an alternative to the current practices employed by the mental health care system. It was a wide open field as far as he could tell. Even those who had never had experience in the system knew there was a problem. Perhaps they simply did not understand that the system itself was a large part of the problem. How could they? If Lee had not experienced the workings of the system firsthand, he would never have had an inkling of what was wrong or how to improve it.

For the moment he would develop his own ideas about how to approach such a multi-faceted project. He would assemble and organize those ideas into a coherent and logical methodology for some respected colleagues to review and consider. Yes, it would be a "white paper" of sorts.

There was something else that Lee needed to do before diving into this new project. He had wanted to get started on it for quite some time, but he never found the time, or he never made the time. Maybe both were true. He really felt as though he should write about his journey for others to read. Although his greatest concern was for those enduring benzodiazepine withdrawal and those struggling with bad reactions to psychiatric medications, he wanted to reach out to anyone who felt stuck in the revolving door of the mental health care system. Additionally, he wondered if his story might offer hope to the "supporting cast" – those friends and family members who were also experiencing feelings of frustration, confusion and anger.

Lee had done a great deal of writing on blogs and in forums over the last three years. He had talked with and emailed hundreds of people either going through withdrawal or helping a loved one through withdrawal. Certainly, many individuals going through withdrawal didn't go to the online forums or blogs, so maybe they could be reached through writings in the form of a book or novel. It could make a difference for some of them. They would know that they were not alone. They would discover that what they were going through was very real and that there were others experiencing the same pain. Most importantly, they would see that it is possible to get through the misery and live again.

First and foremost, Lee wanted to make it clear that withdrawal from benzodiazepines was very real, and it was often physically, mentally, and emotionally devastating. It was often completely debilitating and rendered the one enduring it helpless and hopeless. The intensity of the suffering could be brutal, and the duration of the anguish could be years. But, for him and for literally everyone he had communicated with who was withdrawing from benzodiazepines, the absolutely worst part of withdrawal was not knowing when, or if, the suffering would end. It was commonly stated in withdrawal forums that everyone healed differently with respect to both symptoms and time. Even though this was common knowledge, the pure terror generated by withdrawal was so persuasive that the one in withdrawal was certain that he or she would be one who would never get better. There was no way for anyone to predict how long it would take.

In the midst of his own two-year withdrawal, Lee had been certain that he would never heal. His ailing brain would not allow him to believe that the suffering would one day end. In the last two and a half years, the same fear had been expressed to him dozens of times by others in the grips of withdrawal. Each one was sure that healing and wellness were not going to be part of his or her future.

Equally terrifying was the thought that all of the mental and emotional agony was indeed a mental disorder and not a result of withdrawal from benzodiazepines. It had been pounded into Lee's head over and over by the psychiatrists and his therapists that he had a mental disorder and would need to take psychotropic drugs for the rest of his life. This was especially horrifying because Lee simply could not tolerate any of the drugs. It felt like a life sentence of doom. The experts had told him he had no way to ever be well again. They essentially declared that his life was over. He had been told that his mental and emotional distress had nothing to do with any sort of withdrawal. He had been declared, without any uncertainty, to be mentally ill.

For well over a year, Lee had accepted that he was mentally ill and maybe had been all of his life. How could he know? During those months, Ruth and he had searched for the answer in the form of a pill. He had taken several different drugs at the recommendation of the psychiatrists and even submitted to electroconvulsive therapy treatments. If a person got desperate enough, he or she would apparently agree to nearly anything if there was even a slight chance it could provide some relief. How else could Lee rationalize submitting to something so irrational and disturbing as electroconvulsive therapy?

About a year after he had been released from Oogden, Lee had discovered an online benzodiazepine withdrawal forum. He soon realized that he was not alone. Others were also in some sort of withdrawal, and their stories of poly-drugging and associated declarations of mental illness were very similar to his. Ruth and he had decided to stop the drugging and wait it out in hopes that what Lee read on the forum was true. In the final analysis, even though Lee had been directed by his psychiatrists and therapists to stay away from online forums, it had been the forums that largely saved his life and helped him to recover his mental and emotional wellness.

Even though no one in Lee's life had ever acknowledged it verbally, they all seemed to lean toward the belief that Lee had some sort of mental illness and that he should try to tolerate the drugs until they "kicked in" – whatever that meant. Lee had insisted that drugs were at the root of his problems and that he was in benzodiazepine withdrawal – even though he himself had not been absolutely convinced. It had been extremely wishful thinking and was based solely on the hope that the individuals on the forums were being honest and knew what they were saying.

Even now that Lee had survived withdrawal and was well, he often had to remind himself when he was communicating with others experiencing the darkness of withdrawal that he had also been in that forsaken place. He had to remind himself that it was not mental illness or a matter of laziness or failure to "buck up." It was purely and simply benzodiazepine withdrawal. Lee found that the constant whining, complaining, rage, and other bizarre mood swings usually began to wear down even those with an extremely strong constitution. Yet, in benzodiazepine withdrawal, these and many more seemingly inexplicable behaviors were justified. As impossible as it seemed to anyone who hadn't been through withdrawal, such behavior was part of withdrawal, and it was very common. Yes, benzodiazepine withdrawal was a very real malady. It was a place of hell.

Certainly, others going through withdrawal would want to know how Lee got through the never-ending misery. Just knowing that withdrawal was real did not necessarily provide any help or comfort except to the extent that one at least knew he or she was not going crazy – one of the huge fears of withdrawal. As Lee thought back on his withdrawal, he realized that it had started many years ago as tolerance withdrawal. The clonazepam that he had taken for thirteen years had created increasing anxiety in him over those years simply because his nervous system had grown tolerant to it. His nervous system had unconsciously craved something more to quell the ballooning anxiety. When the clonazepam was no longer "covering" his anxiety, he unwittingly began self-medicating with alcohol.

As the years passed, he drank more and more to make up for the "shortfall" of the clonazepam so that his neuro-receptors could be "satisfied" sufficiently to stave off the mounting anxiety. He would wake up in the morning feeling emotionally numb and physically shaking. That loopy, off balance dizziness was always with him and had seemed to worsen with time. His daily routine before work had been to get up, go into the bathroom and look at the person in the mirror whom he had grown to hate, shower, and get dressed, all the while shaking. He'd proceed downstairs to take his little yellow pill. After sitting in his chair in the living room for about twenty minutes, the shaking would stop. He had vowed every morning to not pick up another drink, but by ten o'clock he would be planning his drinking menu for the evening. His life had become one endless loop of anxiety, clonazepam, and booze.

In 2007, he had been concerned about his drinking which was getting increasingly out of control. He went online and found *Alcoholics Anonymous* and only had to read the first chapter or two to know he had a serious drinking issue. He was sure he was an alcoholic. As time passed, and after many failed attempts, he finally quit drinking. The fierce anxiety of alcohol post-acute withdrawal syndrome (PAWS) began almost immediately and, although he did not know it at the time, the cruel anguish of benzodiazepine tolerance withdrawal was walking hand-in-hand with the PAWS. Lee was about to enter the two most heartless and desolate years of his life.

When Lee quit drinking, the "getting through" benzodiazepine withdrawal began. Even though he did not know exactly what had caused his sudden nose-dive into the mental torment, something inside him had begun to take steps to try to get out of the pit of relentless, all-consuming anxiety. The survival instinct which everyone possesses had kicked in automatically.

Lee got up from his seat on the Total Gym holding onto the towel around his neck and shook his head in a kind of confused disbelief. "How did that happen? How did I make it through that?" he said in a voice that was inaudible even to himself. He had spent the last forty-five minutes working out all the while contemplating his views of experts in psychiatry, misdiagnosis and treatment, and addiction, dependence and withdrawal. Now it was time to determine how he got out of the mess he had gotten himself into starting in 1997. It had been a mess that no one seemed to understand at the outset and that the professionals to whom he had gone for help only made much worse. It had felt as though most of them really didn't care if he ever got well. He knew that was not completely true of all of them, but it was obviously true of most of them.

It had to be a frustrating job trying to help one person after another with mental and emotional difficulties especially in a system that didn't seem to work properly and appeared to be designed for failure. Many of the professionals he had met on his journey had appeared tired and worn down. Even though he had been extremely ill himself, his eyes could still see, his ears could hear, and his spirit could discern. Something in his brain had recorded the whole experience and was now playing the tape back. It was much easier to make sense out of it now that he was well.

Lee nodded. "Later. Later today." For now, he would continue with the tasks of his day while pondering the answer to his last question. He would marvel at his good fortune to have made it to this "happy, joyous, and free" place after spending so much time in a prison of mental desolation and despair. It was a beautiful Saturday morning. He was off to mow the lawn. He took the towel from around his neck, threw it on the arm of the elliptical machine, and went out the door like a man on a mission.

Chapter Twelve

Mowing the lawn had always been a time when Lee's thoughts would drift toward one subject and examine it from different perspectives. He suspected that it had something to do with the mindlessness of the act of mowing as well as the deafening noise of the mower. The combination seemed to produce a "stimulated calmness" in him. Thoughts would always burst through his mind like fireworks, and Lee would consider them one at a time knowing that he would miss some that had simultaneously appeared. But he was certain he would have an opportunity to reflect on them with subsequent bursts. There was never a shortage of thoughts to ponder. He already knew the theme of the display he would see this morning – the pathway through perdition. He would consider how he had survived his journey through the place of torment – benzodiazepine withdrawal. He would view some of the big bursts now and scrutinize them more closely later in the day when he was relaxing. Maybe he could even refine his memories enough to put them down on paper.

For the next fifty minutes Lee simply let the fireworks happen. He thought back to the beginning of what were essentially the two most gruesome parts of his fourteen-year trek. They had both started with total confusion and terror. He really had no idea what caused them at the time. It wasn't until he began to heal from the second onslaught that he understood the whole story from its inception in 1997. He did have an inkling of what was happening to him during the second phase. It had actually come from an alcohol and addiction blog owned by a guy named Bill. Through several emails, Bill had made it painfully clear that, even though Lee had been off the sauce for seven months, his brain still thought he was drinking because he was still taking clonazepam. Bill had claimed the brain "reads" them the same way. Lee would not accept it initially. Surely, Bill was incorrect. It did not make sense to Lee, and he had tried to rationalize how clonazepam should actually aid his withdrawal from alcohol instead of adding to and prolonging it.

It had not been until Bill told him in no uncertain words that he would never be well until he ditched the clonazepam. Never. That was one of those existential words that had an infinite aspect to it but not in a good way. Lee had chewed on that for a long time and turned it into something more palatable. "I will forever be well if I ditch the clonazepam." Okay. It was a little easier to appreciate in that light. Bill was almost always right. That had been irritating to Lee because he never agreed with Bill. Bill would always end his emails with "Keep on keepin' on!" That was even more irritating. Lee was keepin' on keepin' on, and he felt like he was getting nowhere except deeper in a hole out of which he thought he would never be able to climb. Bill had withdrawn from booze and benzodiazepines many years earlier, so he knew what he was talking about. He had suffered and made it out alive and well. He told Lee he could too. Okay, fair enough. That was good enough for Lee. He would give it a go.

Acceptance. The first burst and the first step on Lee's road to recovery. It was part of the answer to how Lee had survived. He simply had to accept that he had to withdraw from the clonazepam. He knew it would be difficult. He knew it might take a long time. He didn't know what else he might encounter on his journey to wellness, but he knew the clonazepam had to go. It was a plan. There could be no turning back no matter how brutal it might get. In hindsight he could now say, "Thank you, Bill." One day Lee would write a book about his experience and direct others to Bill's addiction website at whatmesober.com. It was the least Lee could do for one of many who had played a part in saving his life. Perhaps others would also be saved if Lee mentioned the website in his writing.

Lee knew what the next burst would be, and that it would be the biggest and most dazzling of all. It was the one thing that every human being on earth needed and possessed. It had sometimes been hard for Lee to find when things weren't going the way he would have liked them to go. It was all around him all the time, but sometimes he had to seek it. It was very much like playing hide and seek.

Sometimes he couldn't see or "feel" hope, but it would never leave. It was always hanging around somewhere, and there was an endless supply of it. It had been what got Lee through withdrawal after he was finally able to accept his plight. It was what kept him always looking forward for the "next good thing" after he had begun to get well and feel his health returning. Hope. Hope was the fuel for Lee's long journey through withdrawal. Without acceptance and hope, he would have perished.

Lee pushed the mower to the garage and let the engine stall. The fireworks were over for the day. He would go inside, get a shower and some lunch, and sit down to reflect on acceptance and hope. Hope was his favorite thing to ponder. It was his favorite thing to write about. He had written tens of thousands of words to try to give others hope. When Lee was suffering, he had read tens of thousands of words of hope written by others who had successfully made the journey through benzodiazepine withdrawal and were now standing on the same shore of recovery and health with Lee. Hope now seemed to surround him. For him, it had an effervescent quality. It reminded him of champagne. It was constantly creating and overflowing with bubbles. Bubbles and more bubbles appearing out of nowhere and bursting into the air above. It had become his duty, more like a calling, to help others see the hope.

The family room was very quiet this evening as Lee sat in the easy chair thinking about what he had accomplished earlier in the day. Exercise. Mowing. Vacuuming. Some bookkeeping. It was a nice list, but he didn't dwell on it very long because he had a newfound propensity toward anticipating the next adventure in his life. He was always looking forward. That was something he had been unable to do in withdrawal. During those long months, he struggled to believe he had any future. If he did, it was certain to be filled with misery. He had been so very wrong. This was now his future, and it was grand and getting grander. He would often say, "It doesn't get any better than this." But somehow it always did. He wondered if there was a limit to feeling good. He was sure that it had something to do with how bad his life felt during withdrawal. When one emerged from a place so bleak and dark that it could not be described or even imagined, everything in its wake seemed vibrant and bright. Everything seemed good.

Next Saturday Jayson and he would be going to see a baseball double header on City Island. They had club seats which meant a tasty pregame meal in the area above and behind home plate followed by seats right behind the plate. It was always an awesome experience that they had repeated several times in the past two years. In the fall they would be headed for a few home football games at Penn State and a bucket list trip to Ann Arbor to see Penn State play Michigan in The Big House. Then there would be Hershey Bears hockey in the late fall and winter until baseball season returned. It had become one endless cycle of carefree good times enjoyed with a friend.

Jayson and Lee had met seven years earlier in a small group class at the church. Lee had been struggling with alcoholism and asked for prayer. He wanted desperately to quit but could find no success in doing so. It was during those classes that Lee learned Jayson was a recovering alcoholic who hadn't had a drink in nearly twenty years. They immediately formed a bond. They spoke the same language of addiction and the pain that addiction spawns. Jayson had become a huge source of hope for Lee once he had finally quit drinking and had gone into PAWS and benzodiazepine withdrawal.

About two weeks after Lee had quit drinking, the anxiety of withdrawal surrounded and consumed him. In desperation, he had called Jayson for help. He needed someone who would understand his plight and tell him he would be okay. Jayson had come over right away but brought no comfort with him. He read Lee the riot act and asked him if he was serious about quitting the booze. If not, Jayson said he was not going to waste his time watching Lee kill himself. It had not been what Lee wanted to hear and not what he had expected. He wanted the kind words of an easier, softer way. Didn't Jayson see him shaking? It was the same type of approach that Bill would later use with Lee regarding the clonazepam. What was it with these old recovered alcoholics anyway? Didn't they have any tact and diplomacy? What about compassion?

In hindsight, Lee could now see that both men were overflowing with compassion. They knew where Lee would end up if he did not ditch the booze and benzodiazepines. They wanted to make sure he understood the consequences and how to avoid them. It had been their way of getting Lee to "own" his dilemma – to accept where he was and to go forward by pushing through instead of trying to go around. Lee would always be grateful to these two men. They had shown him that there was no hope of getting through addiction and its withdrawal without first accepting the addiction and withdrawal – accepting one's circumstances and moving forward regardless of how those circumstances had come about. It was lifesaving wisdom.

In the past two years, Lee had talked with many people who were in the midst of withdrawal from benzodiazepines. One of the first things he would try to get across to each one was the need to accept his or her current plight. That did not mean one had to like where he or she was. He certainly didn't like the two-year suffering of his withdrawal, but he had had no choice. His past had gotten him to the threshold of withdrawal, so there was no going back there. In his agony, he could see no future that could possibly be bearable. In withdrawal, he detested the present – the moment-to-moment anguish in which he found himself. There was only one direction to take. He had to go through withdrawal. There was no way to circumvent the problem and the pain. It was the proverbial "rock and hard place." Lee recalled the seemingly infinite hopelessness of having no way out other than ending his own life. He had almost taken that route, but something inside told him he could and would get through somehow. A tiny, hidden spark of hope remaining deep within him had been uncovered.

Whenever Lee thought about acceptance, it often triggered memories of the people he had met in the past two years who simply could not accept their difficult circumstance and its suffering. There was one woman in particular with whom he had talked many times on Sunday evenings. She had taken alprazolam for a minor sleep difficulty. She had become addicted or physically dependent and discontinued the alprazolam. As Lee recalled, she had taught psychology in a small college and could not forgive herself for becoming dependent on alprazolam. Even though she had seemed to rebound to a healthy state after a few hours of conversation, she had always been pulled back into the clutches of non-acceptance the next time she called Lee. Sadly, she had committed suicide two years ago.

Lee had thought about her often and wondered if her failure to accept her situation was linked to the failure of others in her family to accept her struggle. She had been extremely ill and she could do nothing to hasten the process of healing. She had to "wait it out" just as every person in benzodiazepine withdrawal was forced to do. Lee had talked with members of her family, and, as was very often the case, they had "suggested" things she needed to do to free herself from the extreme depression and fear of benzodiazepine withdrawal. She had shared that there had been perceived threats of divorce and forced admission into a mental institution. There was the typical "buck up" and "pull yourself up by the bootstraps" advice. Of course, she had been urged to take some other psychiatric drug because everyone believed she had a "real" mental disorder.

Lee had been the recipient of similar advice to help him make himself well, but it had all been baseless and useless. In fact, it had only made his condition worse. Lee found it very sad that often the loved ones and friends who should be the loudest and most persistent cheerleaders and hope-givers were the ones who unknowingly took the last bit of hope away and ushered their loved one into utter hopelessness and even self-annihilation. He understood the frustration of caregivers. He had been in that place many years ago with Ruth. If loved ones and friends truly understood the utter desolation of benzodiazepine withdrawal, they would not be so quick to give advice other than words of comfort and encouragement – over and over and over.

Lee sat in his chair for a few moments and reflected on that young woman who had taken her own life. There was a day when he could not understand or accept how a person could be so distraught and completely devoid of hope to commit suicide. How could life be so bad that one would want to kill himself or herself? Now Lee understood. He had been in that place. He didn't "want" to kill himself any of those times he had been suicidal. Nobody "wanted" to kill himself or herself. Everyone wanted to live. Lee wanted to live, but he felt like he could not live in that state. He had been surrounded by and infused with pure misery and hopelessness. He could not bear the thought of such an existence. He could see no future. He had felt no hope.

Though he hadn't felt hope, it was there all along. It was hope that kept him from taking his life that Saturday morning when he had been moments away from ending it. Two words, "Call Jane." That was all it took. Just a little hope. That was all that was needed to survive – just enough to keep going for one more moment and refuse to give up. Lee knew it had been hope that got him through withdrawal. It was what got everyone through. When hope died, the will to survive died with it. Hope had to be kept alive even if it was only an ember. After all, huge fires can start from tiny embers.

As Lee sat in his big, cushy chair, he knew that he had no choice in the matter. He had to get the laptop out and start to record his reflections on how he made it from a place of nearly utter hopelessness to this place of peace and joy and a life overflowing with hope. Lee was well. Sometimes he would forget how gruesomely ill he had been during his withdrawal and how wellness had once seemed to be a total impossibility. His ailing brain had not allowed him to feel hope. It had lied to him at every point and at every moment he was awake that wellness was not an outcome he would experience. It was reserved for others – not him. He had felt that he was that one person who would not heal. He would never have a life worth living again.

Yet, there had been a spark of hope hiding from view at the beginning of his journey. It had come from somewhere within his being. It was just enough hope to help him seek more hope. In some ways, it was like that first drink that always led to the next drink and many more. But the outcome of taking that first taste of hope was much different. Instead of ending in death and destruction, it never ended at all. The hope just kept growing and encouraging and blossoming to make more and more hope. It hadn't stopped growing until it filled Lee's life with health and wellness, happiness, joy and freedom. Still it did not stop. Hope kept going and finding the best things of life – things Lee had never imagined for his life.

Lee smiled. Sitting there, he was still infinitely hopeful. It had something to do with his purpose and the meaning of his life. He had discovered at one point in his withdrawal that he was being called to be one to give hope to others. He was still very ill at that time, but the message was clear. He was suffering so that he would one day be a hope-giver. It was not a message that he "should" offer hope to others when he was well. It was not a command. It was a statement of fact that Lee would give hope. It was a done deal that had not yet taken place, but it would. It had been some sort of personal prophecy for which Lee had no ability to appreciate at the time.

He recalled the tears he shed when he had heard that message. He had still been desperately ill and wanted to hear a message that he was going to be healed at that very moment. Giving hope was okay, but being healed was what Lee wanted. That was what Lee needed. That was not the message. Still, if he was going to give hope one day, that surely meant he would be well one day. He would not be that one person who was destined to a life of infinite misery before his final demise. The Creator must have been paying attention to him. He had begun sobbing again for a different reason. The tears had had a calming effect and momentarily released him from the mental and emotional bondage he had been experiencing for what seemed like his entire life on earth.

He now sat and stared out the window as he remembered that day. This was the time for the content of that message to be at least partially fulfilled. Lee had become an expert in hope – not in spite of his suffering through benzodiazepine withdrawal but because of it. He had to share how he survived – how he made it to this amazing place in his existence. He had to write about it. He had to give hope.

Chapter Thirteen

Lee thought back to the very beginning of his experience when he had started having panic attacks in 1997. At that time, his initial hope was that those attacks were merely anomalies that would simply fade. That was not to be, and he began a journey of several years in search of wellness. Little did he know at the outset that, in order to make it to that place of health and well-being, he would need to continually be on a search for hope. In some strange way that he could now sense, the hope was part of the wellness. He was now back to good health and filled with hope. He tried to imagine how his life would be if he was now satisfied with things staying exactly the way they had been. He would sleep, eat and drink, listen to jazz, work in the yard, go to ballgames, play golf, go on vacation, and on and on. In and of themselves, these things were all well and good, but they had no point and no purpose other than to give him pleasure. Without something more, his life would again be without hope. It would be meaningless. It would be a procession from one self-indulgence to the next. At the end of his earthly life, there would be no true pleasure in looking back. His eternal bank account would be empty.

Lee could see that both hope and purpose were necessary for his life to be the way he had always wanted it to be. He suspected it was the same way for others currently in withdrawal. Everyone always spoke or wrote of "wasting years of life" while suffering through withdrawal. That is what he had felt very keenly for two long years. It was terrifying – especially to think that it would never change. In hindsight, he could see that the many months of his own suffering were packed with purpose and meaning. He wanted others in the grips of withdrawal to one day come to the same realization. They would need hope to get to that place.

Of course, Lee's hope that the initial panic attacks would somehow dwindle away had been dashed each time he had another attack. He had known his quest would have to lead him somewhere else if he was going to successfully find the answer to his dilemma. As he sat in his chair now, he likened his pursuit for an answer to a game of hide and seek. Over those fourteen or fifteen years, he seemed to be constantly seeking "the answer" – the reason for what seemed to be a mental and emotional breakdown. It was very much a search for hope which, at times, had seemed to vanish. Hope was a strange thing. There had been times and places when he found hope. There had also been plenty of other times when hope was taken from him, and all he had found were fear and despair.

He had gone to the first logical place once he realized he had an apparent health problem he could not resolve on his own. That first step led him to Dr. Harper. Lee had to admit that, when he had walked out of Dr. Harper's office with a script for alprazolam and samples of paroxetine, he was very hopeful. For a couple weeks, the alprazolam had worked wonderfully, and hope was alive and well. Then came the terrifying experience with paroxetine. The alprazolam no longer helped. His hope faltered.

Over the next several months, he had undergone multiple tests in order to uncover the cause of his troubles. Sleep disorder studies. Acid reflux tests. Upper GI's. Stress tests. MRI's of his brain. Nystagmus tests. The Minnesota Multiphasic Personality Inventory. All he had been left with was a diagnosis of generalized anxiety disorder, panic disorder, and major depressive disorder. For eighteen months he had put his hope in three psychiatrists and over a dozen prescribed psychotropic drugs in an effort to treat his disorders and end the myriad of symptoms they were causing. Nothing resulted but a progressive decline into an abyss of torment and loss of will to live. Even the therapy he had received from Jenn Franklin was useless because his brain had been hijacked by the drugs and could not function properly. Ironically, the bit of hope he had left had been sucked away by the drugs in which he had placed his hope.

At the end of that time, Lee had somehow been given a dose of hope without even seeking it in the form of Lynn's announcement that she was pregnant. Her tears of fear and despair had bolstered the last vestige of hope in Lee's heart. He didn't understand it at the time and believed it to be a miracle both then and now. There was no other explanation.

He had sought hope in other places over those eighteen months. His brother visited him nearly every weekend which did provide Lee with some hope. He knew that his brother cared which was more than he had gotten from any of the drugs. He had spoken with friends at church trying to hold onto any hope that they might offer. A married couple from church, Harold and Sandy, did help him a great deal. During the beginning of his sickness, Sandy was very understanding. She had experienced a lot of anxiety and depression over the years and was able to help him navigate the rough waters. When Lee's health had grown particularly bad after several months, Ruth called Harold and Sandy to come over and meet with Lee and her. Ruth had been determined to help Lee in some way. Even though Lee had not been too excited about it, it was decided that Harold and he would go somewhere every Thursday evening. Lee hated the thought of leaving the house. In retrospect, it did help him in some way. It was not so much the fact that he went out in public but more that Harold was a compassionate friend who knew how to help him. For many Thursday nights, Harold had done all the talking while Lee sat shaking inside and listening in fear. Without Harold, Lee might never have developed a love for jazz.

Lee had even had the church elders pray over him for healing. He remembered sobbing uncontrollably while they prayed. It had provided an emotional release, and he was sure the Creator heard their pleas and would provide healing, if not immediately or soon, surely at some point in the future. He had shared his situation with coworkers hoping someone could help him. A few listened with interest and compassion, but they could not offer much in the way of understanding or useful advice.

At the beginning of his illness, Lee read and reread the book of John from the Bible. It had always been his favorite book and had given him comfort. After a few months, his condition had deteriorated so much from the drugs that he found no comfort in its words or any other words from scripture. He had known lots of scripture and believed its truths, but he could no longer feel the peace, comfort or joy from its beautiful promises. His hope had continued to fade.

For the next eleven years, Lee had not consciously sought hope from anyone. He had unsuspectingly placed his hope in the clonazepam that he was told he would need to take for the rest of his life to stave off the panic and anxiety. During the two years of being essentially a human guinea pig for multiple psychotropic drugs, Lee had stopped drinking. He could now recall drinking only one time over those two years.

He remembered it well. Ruth and he had gone to a cabin in the mountain with their friends, Dale and Ange, for a weekend. Ange had made margaritas one evening, and Lee decided a drink or two would be okay. He had gotten a very strange feeling from the two margaritas, but it certainly was not the mellow buzz he had grown accustomed to over the previous twenty-nine years of drinking. It didn't feel good at all, and Lee was disappointed because he was looking forward to some relief from the relentless mental misery that had been plaguing him. Even the two and a half milligrams of clonazepam and fifteen milligrams of mirtazapine he had taken that evening at bedtime afforded no respite from the torment. He got two hours of fitful sleep. He had been certain that the drugs and alcohol would give him at least one good night's sleep and maybe even render him unconscious, but they did quite the opposite. It was apparently anybody's guess what mixing chemicals would do to him. He recalled that evening quite vividly.

During Lynn's pregnancy, Lee had begun to drink again. The strange thing about it had been that he didn't start with a drink or two and work his way up. For some reason, which he would learn years later was very common for alcoholics, his brain seemed to remember exactly how much he had been drinking when he had quit eighteen months earlier. That volume of alcohol was the amount at which he had resumed his addiction. He would sit in his favorite chair with his headphones listening to jazz and sip glass after glass of cherry, blueberry or ginger brandy (although he preferred the cherry). He would typically pass out and get himself to bed somehow. Sometimes he would remember how he got to bed and sometimes not.

Over the next eleven years, the scenario had worsened. He took his clonazepam faithfully every morning and evening at the prescribed dose. That did not change. The alcohol consumption increased greatly in several ways. He had found himself drinking nearly every evening after work and on weekends except for Sundays which he "reserved for sobriety." He wondered if this had been an effort to help him believe he was a normal drinker rather than an alcoholic. He would drink earlier each day. His own personal happy hour had started at 4:30 early in his drinking career but had inched its way to 3:00 or earlier, if he could get away with it. He also found that he had developed an adoration for anything from the liquor store or beverage store that contained alcohol except for a beer named Pennsylvania's Best or something similar. Michael had once given him a can of that, and Lee could not drink it. It had been the only time Lee could remember not being able to down an alcoholic beverage.

During the last two and a half years of drinking, Lee knew he had a very serious problem. He had managed sobriety for a few months here and there in that time but simply could not stay stopped. The harder he had tried, the greater the urge to drink. Eventually, he went back out on an eleven-month spree that finally ended with panic and anxiety attacks. Even so, he had continued to place his hope in the clonazepam. He had been sure, if given enough time, the clonazepam would soak up the anxiety that the drinking cessation had caused. Little did he know that it was the clonazepam that had caused his voracious craving for alcohol and that it would continue to taunt him with unbearable anxiety, panic and derealization until he learned the truth about it seven months later. Even then it would be another two years of unbelievable mental torture until he would be well. Somewhere in those two blurry years, he came to realize that putting his hope in clonazepam and the many other prescription drugs had been a huge mistake. The very thing he had put his hope in had nearly destroyed him. It was a wakeup call and a realization that sometimes in hide and seek, one finds "scary monsters" that are better left undisturbed.

There had been several other monsters Lee had encountered as he sought something or someone who might provide hope. Without exception, all those monsters had been part of the mental health system – all having to do with drugs or labeling him with a dual diagnosis of mental illness and addiction. Shortly after he had stopped drinking, he had gone to an Alcoholics Anonymous meeting where, after the meeting, a young guy suggested that Lee up-dose the clonazepam. That was extremely bad advice which Lee unfortunately learned the hard way. Lee had placed his hope in an addiction specialist who would always fall asleep while Lee attempted to confide in him. During the third meeting with him, Lee had snuck out the side door while he snoozed. He had clearly gotten more sleep than Lee – even if it was during work.

There had been two more addiction specialists who did at least manage to stay awake while Lee spoke with them. The guy at West Side Hospital had been the first to declare Lee to be a mentally ill addict. A month later, another addiction specialist at Community Hospital concluded the same thing. He may have been the same guy who happened to have two jobs; Lee's mind had been foggy at the time. He couldn't be sure then, but he was now certain that the prescribed diagnoses had been quite wrong. He couldn't understand how others who were supposed to be entrusted with the well-being of suffering people could be so careless and arrogant. At the time, Lee really hadn't cared. The sad thing was that he had believed both of them simply because he had already been completely demoralized and was afraid. His mental and emotional condition had rendered him a captive audience, and they simply had their way with him.

A few weeks after Lee had quit drinking, Ruth called a detox facility in Florida that Lee had found online and explained Lee's plight in hopes that they could help. Whomever she had talked to was adamant that Lee would remain very ill and return to drinking if he did not visit their one-of-a-kind, exclusive, very expensive facility. The lady on the phone came across as arrogant and heartless without the slightest bit of compassion.

There had been the experience at Oogden Institute of Psychiatry. The answer there was plain and simple – more drugs. If the drugs didn't work for the depression, the answer became electroconvulsive therapy. Why not? Even now, Lee realized how absolutely desperate he must have been to submit to ECT. Any procedure with the word "convulsive" in it could not be pleasant. Lee cringed as he thought about it now in retrospect. Of course, there had been many counselors and therapists at Oogden who surely had compassion in their hearts. Lee was sure of that. But, even while he had been in a trembling, vegetative state during those three weeks, he could not fathom how therapy could have had any positive effect on him or his comrades most of whom had been drugged senseless. It made no sense to him.

In the weeks and months after he had been released from Oogden, he saw two psychiatrists who had told him he was mentally ill and that his condition had nothing to do with any sort of withdrawal or effect from psychiatric drugs. They had simply continued to write scripts for drugs. Even though the therapist, whom he had seen for a year after his release from Oogden, acknowledged that there was such a thing as withdrawal from benzodiazepines and that it could last quite some time, she had told him he was "married to his drugs" and would need to be medicated for the rest of his life.

No, Lee had found no hope in all of the obvious hiding places. These had all been people whose job it was to help him and others get well or at least recover sufficiently to function and enjoy life a little bit. They had failed Lee miserably. He would have to look in the nooks and crannies to find others who could help him – individuals in online group forums from whom he had been told to stay away. He had been told they would only lead him astray and prevent him from ever recovering. Lee would have to take his chances. He couldn't imagine getting worse, and he didn't get worse. He would finally find hope and help. He would find others to save his life and help him back to health.

Even though Lee had been all but stripped of hope by those in whom he had initially placed his trust, he did find plenty of hope. As he now reflected on the part of the journey that had started the day after he took his last drink nearly five years ago, he realized that all the hope he had been given was the result of that one quick prayer of desperation he had made driving home from the visit with his sisters, "God help me!" He shouted it at the top of his lungs three times. It had not been just a mindless exclamation born of terror. It was the plea of a man who knew he would soon be dead if someone didn't intervene and rescue him. He now knew that "someone" must be the Creator. No one else could have done it. He had been in huge trouble. He had failed himself time and time again. The Creator would not fail him.

Of course, at the time, as days had gone by and Lee's anxiety only worsened, it had seemed like his prayer was for naught. He wanted immediate results or at least some sense of relief. Looking back now, Lee was certain that, if he had gotten well quickly, he would have been drinking again in a matter of days or weeks. Ruth and he had discussed it many times. The Creator's seemingly nebulous plan at the time was crystal clear now. Lee would have to go through some major suffering to ensure he never picked up another drink. Lee had a deep appreciation for the compassion and wisdom of that plan now. At the outset, the plan had been to "lead" Lee from one source of hope to the next until he had reached the end of the journey. There would be "decoys" along the way which Lee would have to either avoid or struggle through on his quest for hope and ultimately healing and wellness. Even now, Lee wasn't sure if he found the hope on his own or if he was simply guided to it in some supernatural way.

Chapter Fourteen

One of the first "nuggets" of hope had come from a website Lee found online. He had been pretty sure that his sudden drop into the pit of anxiety, panic and depression had something to do with alcohol. Although he had never experienced acute withdrawal from alcohol with the delirium tremens, he knew that it only lasted for a week or two. What he had been experiencing was similar and yet different. It was not going away. He had soon learned that what he had was post-acute withdrawal syndrome (PAWS). He read all the information on the website and was certain he was suffering from PAWS. He even purchased a book which explained PAWS in greater detail. The website itself had given him his first noticeable bit of hope. He realized he was not going crazy and that he might not die. There was hope. PAWS didn't last forever.

Neither the website nor the book had many personal stories of individuals navigating through PAWS, so he went to the one source he knew about that had many stories about alcoholics who had suffered and recovered – the fourth edition of *Alcoholics Anonymous*. Lee found enormous help there.

In the first few months of his journey through withdrawal, Lee had written many notes in his copy of *Alcoholics Anonymous*. On the inside cover he had scribbled word after word of hope intermingled with words of severe anguish. As he pulled it from the shelf, Lee now remembered his desperation. It brought tears to his eyes. Nearly five years ago he had written: "I miss the Lee who felt normal. My family misses him too. This is a complete overhaul (no alcohol and no benzos) spiritually and emotionally. It's the hardest thing I've ever done. I am trusting (trying to) the Creator to make me a new man as the Creator helps me through this." He even signed it, "Lee." He was now glad he had not known at the time that it would be another two years of torture until he even began to feel somewhat well again. It gave literal meaning to the adage, "One day at a time."

He had also written something that he had forgotten but now recalled as he scanned his notes. Over the last two years, he had focused primarily on withdrawal from benzodiazepines and had read a great deal about it from online sources and recovery groups. It was often considered "common knowledge" that withdrawal typically lasts twelve to eighteen months. That timeframe came from pioneering work done by Dr. Heather Ashton in the United Kingdom. Lee could not recall the exact number of patients in her studies who were withdrawing from benzodiazepines, but he knew they numbered in the hundreds. Lee had read that PAWS from alcohol withdrawal lasted generally from eighteen to twenty-four months. That was the range that he had written on the inside cover of his copy of *Alcoholics Anonymous*. It was based on observations of thousands of alcoholics. The much larger dataset meant these results were based on greater statistical power, so, Lee reasoned, it was a more realistic range to expect recovery from the withdrawal of both alcohol and benzodiazepines (since they were known to affect the same neuro-receptors). He had focused more on the twelve to eighteen months for his own recovery probably out of wishful thinking. Now that he was well and had read and heard many withdrawal stories, Lee could see the higher range was more realistic for most people.

As Lee leafed through his copy of *Alcoholics Anonymous*, he was amazed at the amount of text he had highlighted and the penciled remarks in the margins. It was obvious that it had been scoured by someone who was searching for every tiny morsel of hope he could find. His favorite quote from the book had always been "Yes, I am one of them [alcoholics] too; I must have this thing." In his copy, it was on page 29. To Lee, "this thing" was the joy and freedom of being well and sober and truly never wanting another drink. Now that he was well, it had even greater meaning, and he understood it with a profound appreciation.

He wished there would have been a book similar to *Alcoholics Anonymous* for those going through benzodiazepine withdrawal when he was ill. It would have been a compilation of success stories of people who had weathered and survived the terrible withdrawal process. It would have been overflowing with the hope that is so critical in surviving withdrawal. In a way, Lee possessed a "prototype" of such a book. He had printed out dozens of success stories and positive posts from online benzodiazepine withdrawal forums which he read every day for well over a year when he was in withdrawal. His daily ritual had been to take his rather thick wad of stories downstairs and start reading through them while trying to relax on his big, cushy easy chair. After ten minutes or so, Ruth would bring him a plate with two slices of toast with jam and a glass of herbal iced tea. Peach mango had been his favorite. He had memorized many of the stories from reading them so much. They provided enormous hope, but there had always been that lying voice from his ailing brain taunting him and telling him all the authors of the stories had conspired to give him false hope. None of them had ever really gotten well, and they were all laughing at him. Lee was so thankful that now the paranoia and fear of withdrawal were only memories.

As Lee looked back now on his experience with Alcoholics Anonymous, he realized one very important truth that he had never known from attending any of the hundreds of meetings or from reading *Alcoholics Anonymous*. That truth was simply that there was something known as PAWS which usually included a multitude of symptoms and behaviors that were nearly always attributed to the character flaws of alcoholics. Things like resentment, bitterness, selfishness, anxiety, fear, and depression were typically chalked up as part of the moral and behavioral deficiencies of the alcoholic. The alcoholic was viewed as one who was unable to "live life on life's terms." Lee had never heard anyone mention anything about an alcohol-damaged central nervous system being the culprit that induced such difficulties. The assumption had always been that these characteristics were solely personal moral issues that the alcoholic must conquer by working the twelve steps of the program. No one had ever mentioned that many of these problems could and would improve merely by the brain healing through time and that such healing could literally take years to occur. Certainly, the Creator (as Lee viewed the Higher Power of the program) could take away the desire to drink as one followed the twelve steps, and the Creator could also produce the literal physical healing of the brain. Of course, each alcoholic drank for a reason or reasons that needed to be addressed, but too often it seemed like many of the symptoms of PAWS were being judged as the cause for the alcohol abuse when they were actually the result of the abuse.

Lee would often marvel at one "class" of individuals at Alcoholics Anonymous meetings. These were the ones who had not only quit drinking but were now "happy, joyous and free." They loved life – for real. There was no pretense or faking it. They had no desire to ever pick up another drink. None. They were high on life. During his first year in the program, Lee could not understand them. He wondered how they had gotten that way. He could not imagine never wanting a drink again. He had stayed sober for six months at one time, but he always knew he would drink again. After he had gotten through PAWS and withdrawal from benzodiazepines, he finally began to understand them. They must have each gone through a similar sort of torment and survived without drinking or taking drugs – prescription or otherwise. Compared to the immense struggle of PAWS, "normal life" was a breeze and infinitely enjoyable. It was, indeed, something to be joyous about. He finally understood how to be high on life.

He had also met many individuals at meetings who had not taken a drink for many months or even years, but they did not exude that same joy. He wondered how many of them had actually gone to the doctor during the initial stages of PAWS and succumbed to the medical opinion that they were naturally depressed, anxious, or even manic and submitted themselves to psychotropic drugging. Lee understood how the drugs could keep them from sharing the joyous life with their comrades in the rooms of Alcoholics Anonymous. Maybe they had not allowed their brains sufficient time to heal from PAWS and re-imprisoned themselves with psychiatric drugs. It had unknowingly happened to Lee seventeen years ago, and it had thwarted his attempts to cease drinking over and over. Lee wondered how many others had been similarly deceived. He sensed that there were probably thousands who had fallen into the same trap but could not find their way out.

This had become a day of reminiscing, so Lee searched through some of the books on the top shelf in one of the bedroom closets. He found a three-book series by a guy named "Guy" – Guy Kettelhack. Each one was about sobriety – one for each of the first three years. Lee had underlined and written all sorts of comments and notations in the first two books. It was very clear from the content of those two books that, for many alcoholics, PAWS often lasted two years. It was not until the third year that many alcoholics felt human again. They finally regained control of their mental capacity and emotions. In fact, it mirrored his favorite benzodiazepine withdrawal success story written by a woman who chronicled her first three years of freedom from benzodiazepines. In hindsight, Lee could see that the timeframes for recovery from PAWS were strikingly similar to the timeframes for healing from benzodiazepine withdrawal. Some healed quickly. Some healed slowly. The mental and emotional symptoms of both were very similar as well, but benzodiazepine withdrawal seemed to have more lingering physical symptoms than PAWS from alcohol withdrawal. It was something Lee had observed in himself and others, but he didn't know the reason for it.

As Lee looked through the books now, he noticed little tidbits of hope that he had written in margins and on inside covers. "This too shall pass." "Wait for the miracle." "It does get better." "Trust the Father." "There is no quick fix." "Clean time is the only way." There were many others. He noticed a Dove almond dark chocolate aluminum wrapper he had flattened and placed in the first book. It read: "You are exactly where you are supposed to be." Bill had told him that same thing many times when he was desperate. Now Lee could finally believe those words. In the second book, he had placed two strands of two different shades of purple yarn that he had used to latch hook a wall hanging for his friend, Harold. Latch hooking had been one of his huge distractions from the agony he had endured at the time. He had still been very ill and had felt like he was out of his mind when he made Harold's wall hanging. He had placed the strands in the book in hopes that one day, when he was well, he would rediscover them. Today was that day. Today was the payback for that small act. Now it seemed huge.

In the bottom drawer of the nightstand beside his bed were nearly three dozen copies of a daily devotional Lee had saved from his withdrawal experience. Every morning, without fail, he would fearfully get out of bed, put on his sweats, and make his way to his chair in the living room to read that day's message in *Our Daily Bread*. He had done it day after day during his many months of illness, and it was still an important part of each day's beginning. In withdrawal it had been one familiar part of his daily routine that was a partial answer to the same terrifying question he would ask himself every morning before going downstairs to meet the day, "How am I going to get through another day? What will I do?" The day had always started with the devotional. It gave him time to try to determine what he could do to get to three o'clock in the afternoon when he could sit with his success stories, toast, and herbal iced tea. From there the day followed an easier routine – "toxic" nap (if he could fall asleep) from which he always awoke numb with terror, a little latch hook before dinner, more latch hook after dinner, mental preparation for the next morning of likely dread, and bedtime.

The first monthly copy of the devotional that Lee had saved was from January 2011 when Lee was only five months off his last dose of clonazepam. As he now held the issue in his hand, he noticed the picture on the front cover. It was a peaceful scene of a snow-laden field with snow-covered trees and a fence. The sun was creating contrasting areas of shadow and light on the surface of the snow. It was a very serene scene. Over the years preceding his withdrawal, Lee had gotten into the habit of looking at the cover of the devotional before opening it. He could not recall doing that during his illness. He had seen no beauty during withdrawal – or at least none that he could recognize. Peace had been a stranger for what seemed like an eternity.

Lee opened the book to the first message. He had underlined many words and circled a few. In this particular entry, he had underlined and circled the words, "wilderness experience." That was something to which he could truly relate. On the second page he had written, "Sometimes it's dark under His wings, but we are still under His wings…protected." This was a quote he had heard from someone which he had modified. This was followed by a simple prayer he had written: "Father, You are here with me. Thank you." He had written and voiced thousands of similar, simple prayers during his withdrawal journey. He also noticed at the bottom of the second page five numbers he had scribbled. They had something to do with how many days he had taken different drugs or had been withdrawing from different drugs. At five months into his withdrawal, he had still been searching for the "magic pill" that would relieve his agony. He had been getting on and getting off drugs constantly until Ruth and he finally realized that no "magic pill" existed. Healing, and ultimately total relief, would come only with time. That was a realization that had been the hardest pill to swallow. This was purely a waiting game. It had been another two and a half months until he kept track of only how long he had been free from benzodiazepines.

In his constant quest to find hope and comfort, Lee had circled words that he knew should provide him with good feelings. He had felt none of them at the time, but something inside him urged him to circle those words. In a sense, the circled words had been "reminders" of the hope, peace, and comfort that he must have known at a previous time in his life. They had hopefully once been a part of his reality and could possibly be again. Something inside him had told him it would be so, but he doubted it in his mind. Lee looked at some of the circled words – faith, trust, wait, peace, love, gentleness, long-suffering, blessed, harmony, mercy, joy, glad, rejoice, goodness, and many more. They spoke to him now that he was well, but they had been silent when he circled them many months ago. Still, it had been an important exercise. It had kept Lee aware of the presence of hope even when he could barely tell it was there. He was now alive and well. Now he could see that hope had been all around him even in his darkest moments.

As Lee now perused the devotionals of 2011, he noticed that the underlining, word circling, and writing in margins had suddenly all but ceased at the end of October. He recalled that time very vividly. It had been when the cloud of anxiety, terror and depression began to lift noticeably. In fact, he remembered the exact day when he knew he was going to be well again. It just happened to coincide with his grandson's, Eli's, first birthday party. He had no longer needed to underline and circle words after that day. The truth, which the spirit inside him had known all along and had kept pushing him to believe and hope for, had finally become perceptible to his brain. His spirit and his brain were finally in agreement. It was the day for which he had been waiting and hoping. He had begun to feel human again and the process would continue to do so until he was completely well. It was a great day.

Now that Lee was well and was no longer seemingly selfishly focused on himself, his perception of the writings in *Our Daily Bread* emphasized a reality to which he had never given much thought. The writings were about hope, love, peace and comfort – all necessities for people to live a happy, fulfilling life. These messages had been written for "regular" people most of whom would never experience benzodiazepine withdrawal or any other type of withdrawal. Hope, love, and all such things were needed by every person. They helped to prevent and ward off the anxiety, depression, and other emotional and mental difficulties that arise from the regular struggles and stresses in life.

Whether or not one believed that love and hope came from the Creator, it was clear that they were meant to be shared with one another. Anxiety, depression and innumerable similar emotional symptoms were often rooted in a common malady that could be "cured" or ameliorated by simply sharing hope, love, joy and peace with one another. Often when these needs were not met in a person's life, he or she turned to drugs (prescription or otherwise) and ended up with additional problems that dwarfed the initial unmet emotional needs. If Lee had realized this need from the outset decades ago, he would never have had to endure benzodiazepine withdrawal or any withdrawal. Lee was certain that everyone needed hope – lots of it. One didn't have to be going through withdrawal for that to be true.

There was one other written source of hope and wisdom that Lee had relied upon early in his withdrawal experience. Looking back, the words that he had read in that book may have been responsible in large part for the way he now viewed life and his perspective on the human condition. It was a rather unique version of a book he had read many times in his fifty-some years of life. He had never really given his imagination permission to explore it in its fullness that he had overlooked for so long. There was much more to the message contained in that book than he had ever been taught or realized. Some of its content, as it had been taught to him, was now not credible causing Lee to question it and leaving him with the feeling of an unbelieving skeptic. In the past, to entertain such thoughts would have produced a self-imposed fear and dread. No more. He had weathered the terror and depression of both PAWS and benzodiazepine withdrawal. There could be no greater horror than that experience. His mind was now freed to look deeply into the truths of this book.

At an Alcoholics Anonymous meeting on December 30, 2009, two months after Lee's last drink, a friend named Don S. had given Lee a gift. It was a Bible. Over the years, Lee had owned at least thirty different Bibles of various versions and paraphrases. Some were study Bibles. Some had maps and pictures. Some were hardbound. Some were paperback. None of them were like this one. This one was a New International Version paperback, but it was more than that. This one seemed like it had been personalized for him and would help him to understand his life up to that point and beyond. This Bible had helped him to endure the extreme suffering of the next two years. It was a *Recovery Devotional Bible*. It was written for individuals "'recovering' from addictive, compulsive or co-dependent behavior patterns." Lee was one of them, and he knew it.

Lee had accepted it from Don S. that evening with no real sense of appreciation. Don had been the first person Lee had met at his very first Alcoholics Anonymous meeting nearly two years earlier. Don had had that "happy, joyous and free" attitude from their very first encounter. Lee had not been able to fathom such happiness at the time and truthfully still could not do so on December 30, 2009. Lee had been experiencing PAWS as well as tolerance withdrawal from clonazepam and, although he felt no gratitude, he had been able to verbally express thankfulness for the gift. What he had really wanted from Don was something to help him get rid of the extreme anxiety and depression. He didn't care if it was pills, words, or simply real advice to help him find relief from the mounting mental torture. All he had gotten was one more Bible to add to his collection.

When Lee had gone home after the meeting that evening, he removed the plastic wrapping and simply stared at the Bible with no desire to open the book. As each day passed, he had been unable to read much of the biblical text. His brain had felt like it was becoming paralyzed with fear. Still, he leafed through the book, more out of obligation than seeking hope that the words would help him. He had already read parts of one of his other Bibles since he had stopped drinking but found no comfort or help from the words. In fact, the only message he had received from those readings were thoughts and feelings of abandonment, accusation and condemnation. His depression had already supplied him with plenty of those. He certainly didn't need anymore.

Over the next few days, Lee paged through the *Recovery Bible* in search of anything that would provide the slightest bit of hope and comfort. He found quite a few readings that were evidence that what he had been experiencing was real and that it could end in something exquisitely good.

As he initially flipped through the pages of this Bible, he noticed a couple different things. Every so often in the text, there were "Life Connections." These were comments relating short portions of the text to addiction or codependency. Interesting. There were also "Meditations." These were longer sections of text that were designed to be read one per day. Lee had looked at a few of them and was able to relate his current experience of anxiety and depression to the ideas expressed by the printed words. He wondered if maybe this book could be useful. Maybe it could help him through whatever it was that he was going through.

Over the next fourteen months, Lee read through many of the Life Connections and all the Meditations attempting to glean any hope and comfort he could find in them. He underlined and circled words. He penciled ideas, prayers, and questions in the margins. He put bookmarks in a dozen or so of his favorite Meditations and read them over and over attempting to keep the tiny spark of hope alive. The strange thing was that he had read almost no text from the actual scripture itself. He found more value in the interpretations of parts of scripture. These interpretations had obviously been written from the perspective of others who had recovered from or were recovering from some sort of addiction or codependency. They spoke to him in a way that nothing else had because the authors of each one had been in a place very similar to where he now was. They were writing from that place. They understood as no one else could.

There were about four dozen Meditations that had spoken profoundly to Lee at a very deep level. The subjects were diverse but always had one commonality. They applied to addictive or compulsive behavior and the pain that such behavior created. His concern had nothing to do with the addiction that was causing his agony. His focus had been the agony itself and getting away from it. He concentrated on anything he could find in the Meditations that spoke to this torment. He had been terrified that he was losing his mind and needed to know that maybe another had experienced this same thing and did not lose his or her sanity. He needed to know that the misery would end and that he would not be like this forever. The twelve steps were not the answer to his current mental distress. He needed hope to believe he could survive. He had found hope in the Meditations.

There was a Meditation in the *Recovery Bible* about feeling abandoned by the Creator. Lee had been relieved to know someone else felt that way too. He bookmarked it. There was another one that spoke of the "dark night of the soul." Lee could relate. It also spoke of the "dark night" being a gift and that, at some point, the darkness would disappear and the Creator would reappear more real than ever. Whoever had written that had survived the "dark night." It was a huge dose of hope. Lee bookmarked it. Somewhere in the Psalms was "The new song of recovery." Lee liked the sound of those words, and its subject of the joy and laughter that awaited Lee when this was over almost made him sob with relief. Yes, people had gotten through this struggle and were actually joyous. Bookmarked. There was "The laughter of healing." Definitely bookmarked. Not only survival and healing awaited, but also laughter. Tears had come to Lee's eyes because the vision of him actually laughing again one day was too overwhelming for his brain to fathom without some sort of emotional release.

Lee had placed a Dove chocolate wrapper inside the *Recovery Bible* shortly after the book had been given to him. It was one of his many "hope markers." In his illness, he had often placed written notes and messages or other small items in drawers, closets, books or anywhere where he might find them in the future on a day when he was well – a day he could say, "Wow. That was bad, but now it's over." Written on this chocolate wrapper hope marker were the words, "Miracles aren't limited to the holidays." At the time, Lee had hoped it was true – and now he knew it was.

Chapter Fifteen

Today was a "free" day. In fact, it was the only day of the week that Lee and Ruth did not have some sort of planned activity. They kept Eli, their grandson, three days a week and stocked the food pantry at church one other day. Five days minus three minus one equaled one: and today was that day – Friday. Every free day started with coffee, and this morning was true to that routine. Lee followed the schedule perfectly. Favorite chair. Mug of coffee. Blinds open.

He watched a rabbit foraging for food under the birdfeeder in the front yard. In the past week, that one small rabbit had devoured all but one purple blossom from the petunias growing adjacent to the bird feeder until they no longer resembled flowers. Ruth had been ready to declare the petunias a lost cause and pull them from the ground. Lee had been a bit more reluctant to do so. He had found a bottle of nasty-smelling rabbit repellent in the garage that Ruth had purchased for such a crisis and sprayed the petunias with it. He could understand why it would repel rabbits because it had nauseated him with one breath. He had made a quick retreat after dousing the flowers.

This morning the flowers were beautiful. There were dozens of purple blooms. The rabbit was settling for bird seed. The crisis had been averted. Lee smiled as he watched the rabbit and a squirrel that had now joined in the search for food. It was simply a matter of perspective. The rabbit had done Lee a favor by dead-heading the petunias. That was a chore for which Lee had yet to find any appreciation.

His eyes looked over at the former combination bush-tree in the neighbors' yard. Less than a week ago, he had mused about his frequent thoughts over the years concerning that strange plant. This morning it was no longer an odd looking growth. It was simply a tree – a very nice tree in Bennett and Trudy's yard. It reminded Lee of the Keebler elf tree except that its trunk was not as thick and there were no elves working in it. It was a tree with a very unique appearance. There were no other trees in the neighborhood quite like it. Lee liked it.

Last Sunday afternoon Lee had noticed that the bush-tree had been trimmed from top to bottom. His first thought was one of wonderment. He had no idea how whoever did the trimming had reached the top. Later in the afternoon he noticed that several branches from the back of the bush-like part had been removed and were piled behind it. It was a hot, humid day, so he assumed the trimmer was taking a break. Later in the afternoon, he noticed Trudy cutting away more growth. There was a severe thunderstorm warning at the time, and the sky was getting dark, so Lee decided he would offer her some help. Besides, his curiosity was piqued.

There were still quite a few large stalks growing from the bush, so he cut them off with a razor saw. While he was working, he offered to cut down the tree that he knew was growing in the middle of the bush. He had wanted to do this for years. Lee was finally going to get the opportunity to do it. As they cut away the last vestiges of the bush, Lee stepped back to discover the easiest angle from which he could hew the tree. What he saw was a very attractive tree standing alone in full view. For years he had not been able to see the beauty of the tree because it was enshrouded by the huge bush. He commented to Trudy that he liked the tree and that, if it were his tree, he would keep it. He walked across the street to look at it from his daily vantage point and even asked Ruth for her opinion. Trudy said she would talk to Bennett about it. Since a storm was fast-approaching, Lee offered to dig the roots of the honeysuckle bush out during the upcoming week.

Early in that week, Lee walked the twenty yards across the street to the tree and removed the mass of honeysuckle roots from around it. He discovered that the tree was an Osage orange tree. The long thorns that he had bumped his head against were a dead giveaway. He also discovered that the tree had been planted on purpose quite some time ago. The original owner of the property had wedged some flat, black rocks into the soil at the base of the tree to prevent it from growing crooked. He noticed that the roots at the base of the former honeysuckle bush had intertwined themselves with the tree roots at the base of the tree so that they were virtually inseparable. Lee cut the lateral roots from the former bush's root ball. The root ball would eventually degrade. Lee suspected that the bush had been planted originally and was later replaced by the tree. Apparently, not all the roots of the bush were removed at that time, and they grew back with a vengeance until they all but concealed the tree from view.

The history of that tree was starkly analogous to Lee's life. Anxiety and fear had taken root early in Lee's childhood. His mother had apparently been depressed throughout the entire first eight years of his life at which time she died. The roots of the anxiety spread. A few months later, his grandmother died, and the roots continued to grow. Life got no better over the next several years, and he began drinking as a teenager. The roots put out shoots that continued to grow over the years below the surface creating more and more anxiety. Eventually this growing anxiety, combined with the use and abuse of alcohol and the stresses of life, caused panic and anxiety attacks. He had felt like he was slowly disappearing from sight. He had sought medical attention and had been given psychiatric drugs for the next thirteen years. Those drugs and the increasing use of alcohol they had caused accelerated his pace toward complete disintegration until he had all but vanished from others and even himself. There had been a point at which he had no idea who he was, and he was absolutely terrified. All he had received at every turn from those who were supposed to be helping him find himself had been a declaration that he was and always would be a mentally ill addict married to his drugs. He had been told he would always need to be medicated to function in society. It was a repulsive thought and a shameless way to treat any human being.

But now Lee was well. He suspected that he might be more mentally healthy than most, if not all, of those dozens of mental health professionals whose responsibility it had been to help him. The honeysuckle bush and all the roots were now gone. He was a tree standing strong and free unfettered by any of those psychotropic drugs he had been told he would need for the rest of his life. The roots of the symptoms of withdrawal from those drugs were all but gone as well. He was now an Osage orange tree in full view who finally knew exactly who he was and his purpose and place on earth. He was now thriving just as the beautiful tree across the street was thriving.

Lee looked toward the tree and nodded. This would be his personal Tree of Strength and Truth. Lee noticed that, remarkably, his Tree of Hope, that special tree on the mountainside, was in the same line of sight as his Tree of Strength and Truth. He sipped his coffee as he admired his trees. Hope. Strength. Truth. Everyone should have a tree – or two.

Friday afternoon Lee received a message from his friend, Brad, who was in the throes of withdrawal from benzodiazepines. Brad had moved to the area from up north where he had been living in a small room in a house with four or five other individuals nearly ten months earlier. The conditions had been woefully inadequate for someone suffering through the torment of withdrawal. Brad had taken his last bit of diazepam over fifteen months ago and was still struggling immensely.

When Brad had moved to the area, he was able to function enough to shop for his food and take care of his most basic needs. Lee had offered at that time to help in whatever way he could, but Brad was determined to do as much as he could for himself. As time went on, Brad seemed to slowly improve. He and Lee had taken several long walks around Wildwood Lake and shot hoops many times at the church Lee attended.

Brad had many different symptoms of withdrawal, but he struggled most with intense physical pain that seemed to constantly move from place to place inside his body. He often complained of extreme pain in his head and spine frequently describing it as a spear going through the top of his head and down his spine. Although Lee had never had that type of pain, he had talked with and messaged many others in benzodiazepine withdrawal who were familiar with it. In the last month, Lee had seen Brad writhe in anguish on the floor screaming as if he was being tortured. All Lee could do during those times was to sit silently and simply "be there." While it was agonizing to watch, Lee was certain it was far more brutal to experience.

That appeared to be the biggest problem others had with friends and loved ones in benzodiazepine withdrawal. It seemed to be human nature to want to do something to help. This natural desire to help often translated into advice to go to the emergency room or the psych unit. The society, at large, seemed to be under the impression that the health care system was more than adequate to address all issues that appeared to be related to mental health. Lee had once believed this too, but his experiences had taught him otherwise. Unless one had been in the grip of withdrawal at some point or was an extraordinarily discerning and compassionate individual, he or she simply did not have a true understanding of the agony. The opinion of such individuals, while well-meaning, lacked credibility and usually only served to frustrate the one in withdrawal and heighten the suffering. This included the majority of professionals in the current system. They had proven that to Lee time after time. They simply did not understand. It had taken a long time, but Lee now realized there was no pill and no therapy that could heal a central nervous system that had been damaged by anthropogenic psychotropic chemical agents – prescription or otherwise. It was time for the mental health care system to catch up.

This was in no way a condemnation of the many caring individuals in the health care system. It was a statement of fact. Lee had been through benzodiazepine withdrawal and suffered the indescribable misery, and he still had trouble believing such intense and persistent agony could be the result of those little pills. But the pills were the culprits. Lee knew that. He had experienced it. Sadly, he had seen countless others experience it. He could understand why others who had never experienced withdrawal could mistakenly believe that a person in withdrawal was mentally ill and in need of medication. After all, withdrawal from psychotropic drugs (and the use of the drugs themselves) often made one appear to have a mental disorder. This simple truth was counterintuitive to the medical culture that society had been deftly led to accept and put its trust in.

In the last two months, Brad's symptoms of withdrawal had intensified greatly until he was in such mental and physical pain that he could not function or provide for his most fundamental needs. He was in what those familiar with benzodiazepine withdrawal termed a "wave." A wave was a period of time in withdrawal when existing symptoms increased in intensity or symptoms that had disappeared now reappeared. Sometimes symptoms that had never been experienced emerged for the first time. Waves could be brutal and render one a completely non-functional blithering mass of sobbing, screaming, terrified humanity for days. Waves could also be much less intense and short in duration. Lee had not healed in this way, but he had communicated with hundreds of others whose healing included waves.

It was heart-rending for Lee to see, hear and read about such suffering. The symptoms of waves were extremely punishing, but their cruelest effect was psychological in nature. During periods when symptoms were kept at bay or even temporarily gone (termed windows), one in withdrawal could see and "feel" the healing. There was evidence of it. When a wave hit, the memory of the window often faded within seconds and the person's hope quickly evaporated. The sufferer would begin to believe that he or she was truly mentally ill or was permanently damaged and would never be well. That was exactly the time when that person simply needed someone to "be there." Someone to listen to the constant words of misery and fear. Someone to repeat over and over that it was withdrawal and it would end. The sufferer needed continuous positive reinforcement. He or she needed to be soothed in any way possible.

It was a very daunting task for caregivers and friends. Watching someone self-implode from withdrawal symptoms looked very much like mental illness especially when one could discern no visible cause for those symptoms. The knee-jerk reaction was always to get drugs to ease the symptoms or therapy to discuss and resolve issues, but those things didn't help and often created more anguish. Lee had been down both roads. He had needed TLC when he was in benzodiazepine withdrawal just as others now in withdrawal needed TLC. It was hard for caregivers to give TLC when the one they were trying to help was accusatory, angry and often in a rage. It was not a job for the faint of heart.

In this wave, Brad had become agoraphobic and was afraid to leave his house. He was not afraid of anything in particular. He was just afraid. Lee remembered it well from his own withdrawal. Lee had spent many months in irrational fear. It had not been a fear of anything specific but of everything in general. It was just fear and dread. Going outside had been brutally painful and nearly impossible. There had been no "trying harder" and there were no "bootstraps" to pull himself up by. He had pulled his bootstraps completely off early in withdrawal. There had been none left. Brad's bootstraps were long gone as well.

Brad needed food and something to drink, so Lee did a little grocery shopping and dropped the purchases off at Brad's place earlier in the day. Lee returned later in the evening and decided that he would spend the evening there and that he should continue to do so until this wave was done tormenting Brad. At this point, Brad had no one else. His family had declared him to be mentally ill, and they would not believe that Brad's condition was caused by benzodiazepine withdrawal despite his insistence to the contrary. It was a story Lee had seen and heard time after time. It was very sad. In withdrawal from psychotropic drugs, blood was often not thicker than water.

As Lee lay on the air mattress on the floor in Brad's living room, he spoke out loud, "It is what it is." Ruth and he had decided they would do everything they could to help Brad back to health and wellness. They knew Brad would eventually make it to shore, and they would hopefully be there to see it.

Lee had learned some very simple yet profound life truths from his addiction and withdrawal experience. Lee had once been told by a woman who counseled other women with sexual addictions that everyone had at least one addiction. That addiction could be anything. Lee had to admit that, in his sixty years of life, he had come to the same conclusion. He obviously could use himself as an example, but he was certain that everyone had their own addiction or addictions. The difference seemed to be that some people openly acknowledged their addiction and even sought help for it while others tried to hide it. Lee found it sadly amusing in several ways.

From his own experience, he had known what his addiction to alcohol was doing to him. It was sapping the enjoyment from his life and turning him into a slave. It was creating guilt, shame, anxiety, and a sense of hopelessness and helplessness. It had been the reason he was prescribed clonazepam for thirteen years. Although he didn't know it for several months after he had quit drinking, the clonazepam had only added to the problem. He had tried to battle it on his own, but it had gotten to be far too big. The booze and clonazepam had been destroying him from the inside out. When he had finally admitted that he could not conquer the monster of alcoholism quietly, he sought the help of others who had found victory. He had not been shy about seeking help in any place he could find it. Once the truth had been exposed, it had a freeing effect on him. He no longer had to pretend or hide.

Now he marveled at the many people he knew who each had their own addiction and the misery it created in their lives, but who would not seek help of any sort from others. Many were believers who would pray for the Creator to heal them, yet they could not admit that, perhaps, the Creator had placed another person or persons in their life to help them – to be an answer to their prayer. He had done the same thing for years. Lee chalked it up to the statement he had heard in the rooms of Alcoholics Anonymous many times: "Everyone has a different bottom." At first he didn't understand that phrase, but now he did. He had not gotten serious about seeking help until he hit his own bottom. By the grace of the Creator, his bottom was not six feet underground, although he acknowledged he had come quite close to it. He had known some who ended up there.

Another thing that Lee found strangely contradictory had to do with meetings of alcoholics in churches. Lee had gone to churches all his life, and he had attended hundreds of Alcoholics Anonymous meetings in some of those same churches. Often, despite the frequent salty language, the Alcoholics Anonymous meetings "felt" more like a church service. Group members were "real," and they spoke of serious and often heart-rending problems. Many were broken, and they were not shy about sharing that brokenness with others in hopes that their brokenness could begin to be healed. Those meetings often seemed much more spiritual than the church services held in the same building. The subjects discussed in those meetings mirrored the subjects of the Meditations that Lee read in the *Recovery Bible* for hope during his own personal struggle: prayer, pain, resentment, faith and trust, forgiveness, abandonment, depression, joy, gratitude, loving others, and loving oneself.

Now that Lee was well, he was aware of another truth that he had never known prior to his withdrawal experience. He had discovered that there was a divide, something like a chasm, between what we see, hear and feel and "that which is us" – our spiritual selves which don't "feel" or sense in a physical, mental or emotional way. It had something to do with eternal purpose and meaning and the one who created us. It had something to do with our position to and relationship with not only the Creator but also with our position to and relationship with each other. Lee had been in a place of absolute agony and indescribable horror caused by a central nervous system that had been severely compromised by psychotropic chemical agents. All sorts of bizarre thoughts, ideas, and perceptions emanated from that state of mind. Yet, there had been something inside him that did not falter, did not change, and had been unaffected by the mental and physical anguish. It was something eternal and immutable, something that would not bow to the suffering. It just "was" and maybe always had been and always would be. He was certain the mysterious "something" was actually a "someone" – the owner of the voice of hope who had spoken to him throughout his withdrawal ordeal. He was equally sure that this same voice of hope spoke to every living being on the planet – sometimes directly but most often through other individuals. That was why it was now so important for him to try to help others through withdrawal – so they would also hear the voice.

It had taken Lee fifty-eight years to learn another deep reality. Human life on earth is an experience in bipolarity. It must necessarily be so. Everyone will experience difficulty and suffering simply as a result of living life. Similarly, everyone will experience happiness and peace. Life is not static; it is changing constantly. Our perceptions and perspectives must also change continually. Otherwise, we only exist on a flat line without purpose or meaning. We don't experience and "feel" life. We wait only to die. It is like viewing birth as the beginning of death rather than the beginning of an ongoing adventure fraught with the ups and downs of a continually changing existence. Lee had come to believe that the sense of an ongoing, never-ending adventure is fueled by a hope that has been forged from somewhere in eternity past. It was hope that he had sought, that he had craved moment-to-moment in his journey through his suffering. It would be that hope that would help him to always look forward and anticipate what awaited him as he traveled through his earthly existence.

For now, Lee would set his sights on the near future. He would look forward to sharing at least part of his story and some of the perceptions he had gained from his experiences as a player in that story. If, for some reason, that opportunity did not arrive or if he would get distracted chasing some rabbit down another trail and into its hole, that was fine with him. There were always more rabbits. He had learned to enjoy the adventure.

There were many things to share about his experience, but by far the most important one would be addressed to those going through benzodiazepine withdrawal and those imprisoned by alcoholism or any other life-threatening addiction.

The most important message was simply that there is hope – much more than one will recognize with only five senses. Just as importantly, one doesn't need a huge amount of hope. A small portion will do. Just enough to get one through the next minute until the minutes turned into hours, days, weeks and months.

For Lee, hope had been the ever-present miracle that led him to sobriety after forty years of alcoholism and held his hand through more than two years of the gruesome suffering of post-acute withdrawal from both alcohol and clonazepam. Because hope had not abandoned him, he was now alive and living a life he never would have thought possible.

If he could do it, anyone could do it. It was a promise.

Made in the USA
Lexington, KY
15 March 2017